STROKE OF MIDNIGHT

Carly Phillips
Janelle Denison,
and
Jacquie D'Alessandro

AN ONYX BOOK

ONYX
Published by New American Library, a division of
Penguin Group (USA) Inc., 375 Hudson Street,
New York, New York 10014, USA
Penguin Group (Canada), 10 Alcorn Avenue, Toronto,
Ontario M4V 3B2, Canada (a division of Pearson Penguin Canada Inc.)
Penguin Books Ltd., 80 Strand, London WC2R 0RL, England
Penguin Ireland, 25 St. Stephen's Green, Dublin 2,
Ireland (a division of Penguin Books Ltd.)
Penguin Group (Australia), 250 Camberwell Road, Camberwell, Victoria 3124,
Australia (a division of Pearson Australia Group Pty. Ltd.)
Penguin Books India Pvt. Ltd., 11 Community Centre, Panchsheel Park,
New Delhi - 110 017, India
Penguin Group (NZ), Cnr Airborne and Rosedale Roads, Albany,
Auckland 1310, New Zealand (a division of Pearson New Zealand Ltd.)
Penguin Books (South Africa) (Pty.) Ltd., 24 Sturdee Avenue,
Rosebank, Johannesburg 2196, South Africa

Penguin Books Ltd., Registered Offices:
80 Strand, London WC2R 0RL, England

First published by Onyx, an imprint of New American Library,
a division of Penguin Group (USA) Inc.

ISBN 0-7394-4622-3

Midnight Angel copyright © Karen Drogin, 2004
Meet Me at Midnight copyright © Janelle Denison, 2004
Mine at Midnight copyright © Jacquie D'Alessandro, 2004
All rights reserved

 REGISTERED TRADEMARK—MARCA REGISTRADA

Printed in the United States of America

Midnight Angel

Carly Phillips

To Phil—for giving me my girls and such a great life. And to Jackie and Jen—I'm so glad I have two girls so we can go see the movies Dad would never want to see. Win a Date with Tad Hamilton *led to the idea for this story. I'm so glad we all love Leo on AMC. I love you!!!!!!!!!!! Love, Mom*

Last but not least, to Janelle—for everything!

New England Express
Daily Dirt Column

The pride of Acton, Massachusetts, returns! Welcome banners drape the streets of the small New England town when favorite son and Hollywood action hero comes home for Christmas. But are all residents really as thrilled as appearances imply?

Stay tuned as events unfold.

Chapter One

Dylan North walked down the streets of Acton, savoring the familiar sights. Old man Roscoe still sat outside the diner, refusing to give up his spot on the bench for people who were waiting to be seated. In his hometown, the cars ran at a slow pace, the people even slower. As a kid, Dylan couldn't wait to get the hell out and never look back. As an adult, he appreciated everything he'd once hated because this place possessed the peace and tranquility that were nowhere to be found in L.A.

As he strode down the street, destination in mind, one more important thought struck him, cementing his reason for coming back now. Everywhere he went reminded him of Holly Evans.

Dr. Holly Evans, he thought, shaking his head. Damn, but he was proud of her. She may not know his feelings, but by the time his short trip home was over, she'd know that and a whole lot more. But first he needed to find firm footing. To see where he stood with Holly now. They hadn't spoken in over ten years, and Dylan understood that the girl he'd left behind might want nothing to do with him. He also realized that his own feelings might have changed too. He doubted it, but he needed to keep an open mind.

He understood these things deep in his gut, in a way he couldn't have managed in his youth—and not just because his manager, his publicist and his personal assistant all told him he was an ass to turn his back on the beautiful actresses at his beck and call. Specifically Melanie Masterson, his latest and longest-lasting relationship. Melanie desperately wanted a reconciliation, but only, he thought, because being on his arm benefited her career. But he was finished hanging on to Melanie or any other woman in a futile search for the normalcy he'd experienced only once before. With Holly.

He wasn't a man prone to believing in omens, but a month ago he'd dreamed of Holly—which wasn't unusual since he dreamed of her often. But this time had been more vivid. In the dream, it was Christmas Eve and they sat in his house, opening gifts they'd bought for each other with their hard-earned money. Feeling warmer and more content than he could ever remember, he'd drowsily reached for Holly only to find Melanie in bed beside him.

The shock to his system had been greater than if he'd crawled into a cold bed all alone. It was a wake-up call he'd taken seriously.

So now he entered the office that had once belonged to Holly's father and glanced around, noting that although much was the same, such as the old doctor's diplomas and the black-and-white photos, Holly had added her own touches too. Aside from the Christmas tree in one corner, tinsel draping the walls and decals on the windows, there were more permanent fixes. She'd painted the place a cheery yellow color, a corner of the waiting room held a large toy box and a shelf filled with children's books, and an array of magazines lay on the center table.

Doc Evans had a great bedside manner, but he'd never updated the decor. His daughter had. Dylan wondered if the old man had lived to see it. Today Dylan had learned that the dad Holly adored had passed away last year, and right now her mom was out of town visiting her sick sister. Dylan hadn't been here to cushion the loss of her father. Had anyone? he wondered. The thought caused a cramping in his gut.

How many other major events had he missed in

her life? And was it too late to even approach her now? So many questions.

"Can I help you?" a red-haired woman he didn't recognize asked, interrupting his thoughts as she grabbed her coat from one of the hooks in the hall.

"I'm looking for Holly—I mean Dr. Evans."

Without looking up, the other woman shrugged her coat over her shoulders. "Dr. Evans is in the back, but we've seen our last patient for the day unless it's an emergency. Is it an emergency?" As she spoke, she finally glanced into his face for the first time. "Oh my *God*! You're him! I mean, you're Dylan North. The actor."

Used to this reaction, Dylan merely treated her to his stock fan smile and reached out a hand in greeting. "Pleased to meet you."

She pumped his hand with enthusiasm until he thought his arm might fall off.

He eased his hand out of her grip. "And you are? Your name, I mean?"

"Oh, sorry," she said, her cheeks turning as red as her hair. "Nicole. Nicole Barnett. Oh my goodness, I can't believe you're standing here."

She gushed like every other fan he met, and though Dylan understood the reaction, he hoped that the more time he spent here, the more people would get used to him and treat him no differently than anyone else. Funny how after craving the spotlight, he now wanted the ordinary.

But Nicole continued to ramble in the face of idol worship. "I'd heard you were in town, and of course Holly's been talking about you, but I didn't think I'd meet you in person. Oh my gosh, this is so exciting."

"Holly's been talking about me?" His heart rate kicked up a notch. That his return was on her radar had to be a good sign.

"Your return is all anyone can talk about. Our patients keep reminding her that you two used to be an item, not that she *wants* to remember. . . ." Nicole's voice trailed off as she realized that in her excitement, she'd slipped big-time. "I'm sorry. I really do need to get going. Should I tell Holly you're here first?"

He shook his head. "I'd rather surprise her."

Nicole grinned. "Good idea. And if you don't mind a suggestion, if she gives you a hard time, just say you're here for a flu shot. Holly can never turn down a patient in need. Unless you've already had one?" She raised an eyebrow in question.

"No, haven't had one." Nor did he desire a shot, but he supposed the cause was worthwhile. "I'll keep your idea in mind."

Nicole smiled. "It was really nice to meet you,

and good luck," she told him, and eyes still impressionably wide, she slipped out the door.

Dylan exhaled hard. He hung his coat on a hook in the hall, then turned the lock, ensuring his reunion with Holly wouldn't be interrupted. In silence, he headed for the back room.

Holly stood with her back to him. Her silky blond hair had been clipped back into a ponytail that hung to her shoulders, a huge difference from the long cascading hair she had favored in high school. He couldn't wait to see it framing her beautiful face.

Since she hadn't heard his approach, he took a minute to watch. To cement his certainty that the emotions and feelings in his heart weren't shadows of the past. And doing so, he was more certain than ever that they were just as intact today as they once had been.

She scribbled in a chart and then glanced at the calendar on the wall. For a brief second, he caught a glimpse of the profile he remembered, her features more defined and grown up but still the same. Her makeup had faded from a day of hard work, something the women he knew would rarely let happen, hence the entourage of traveling makeup artists to handle touch-ups and constant trips to the restroom to powder their noses.

The woman before him was real, and he wanted her to be his again. This time forever. Steeling himself, he cleared his throat and knocked twice on the doorframe.

"I thought I told you it's okay to go home, Nicole," Holly called without glancing up from replacing the paper on the examining table. "I can clean up the last few things and get the office ready for tomorrow. Go get ready for the Christmas party at Whipporwill's tonight."

Her voice hadn't changed either. The light sound was still capable of sending rippling waves of desire through him, especially when she laughed. If he accomplished nothing else on this first encounter, he wanted to make her laugh.

"It's not Nicole," Dylan said, drawing attention to himself at last.

She inhaled sharply and turned around fast. Shock, pleasure and anger all flashed across her features until finally she folded her arms across her chest, schooling her face into a blank mask. Just not soon enough to prevent him from discovering she still had a variety of feelings for him, and he hoped to tap into the more pleasant ones.

"Dylan," she said, having regained her composure.

He inclined his head. "Holly. How've you been?"

She narrowed her gaze, obviously assessing him. "Is that really the best opening line you could come up with?" she asked, then chuckled, a sound he knew was forced because it lacked the warmth and genuineness he remembered.

It didn't count as the laugh he'd promised himself. He shrugged. "I didn't think you'd appreciate it if I tossed some old line your way."

Holly nodded slowly, still unable to believe Dylan had come to see her here. She knew all about his return; how could she not when it was all her patients could talk about? But she didn't think he'd bother to look her up.

She tried to breathe steadily, a nearly impossible feat when he was still so good-looking, sexy and, damn him, charming in person. His raven hair had barely any gray and those blue eyes were just as bright.

"You're right. I wouldn't have appreciated a flip line," she said, surprised that he remembered how important honesty was to her, when he'd forgotten all about truthfulness in his rush to leave all those years ago.

She and Dylan had a history she'd never been able to forget. They'd met at thirteen when Dylan's family had moved to town, started dating at sixteen, begun sleeping together at seventeen and by eighteen and their high-school graduation, Holly had been planning their happily ever after.

She'd go to Yale University and then to medical

school like her father and his father before him, and though Dylan hadn't chosen his college yet, he'd go close by, major in theater arts or drama, and they'd stick together as he tried for a career on Broadway. They'd have a house, kids and a happy life. That had been their plan, or so she'd thought until she woke up the day after graduation with a good-bye letter in her mailbox. A note on a flimsy sheet of paper, hastily written as if she'd meant nothing to him at all.

He'd been her first love, and he'd unceremoniously dumped her with the printed words *A high-school crush was never meant to last. It's time we both move on. Dylan.* Not even *Love, Dylan.*

Then he'd gone on to change his name from Dylan Northwood to Dylan North and quickly became America's heartthrob, staring at her from the cover of every magazine in the supermarket and drugstore.

Now he stood before her. Holly exhaled slowly, trying not to let Dylan see that his return had her trembling.

He stared with the half smile and the dimple America adored on his face. "How about a hello hug for an old friend?" he asked with more than a hint of challenge in his voice.

Touching him would be like looking for an electric shock, but if she turned him down, he'd assume she still had feelings for him. Which she didn't, she assured herself. None at all.

Liar. "Yeah, I think I could manage a hug. For a friend," she added, more for her benefit than his.

She stepped forward and was immediately surrounded by his heady masculine scent and engulfed by his strong arms and a wealth of emotion she'd tried hard to bury. Her cheek nestled into the nubby wool of his sweater, and his jean-clad thighs brushed against her light slacks.

Shaking, she stepped back before she embarrassed herself, the practiced smile she reserved for her most trying patients on her face. "So what brings you by?"

His steady gaze met hers. "I couldn't come home without seeing my Midnight Angel . . . I mean, without seeing you again."

She swallowed hard, his use of the endearment taking her off guard. Dylan's father had walked out when he and his sister were young, only to return again for another try. When that second chance failed a few weeks before Christmas their junior year in high school, his mother had broken the star on their Christmas tree in frustration. Holly had bought the family an angel to put on top instead. New memories to replace the old, she'd explained when she'd given it to him at midnight on Christmas Eve.

He'd called her his Midnight Angel.

She'd believed they would last forever.

She shivered and forced herself back to the present. "Well, I'm glad you came by. It was good to see you again." And it would be just as good to have him gone. "As you can see, I was just finishing up here. I've had a long day."

She was sure she looked as exhausted as she felt, yet somehow she resisted the urge to fix her hair or excuse herself and run to her office to touch up her makeup. This was who she was. No sense hiding it. Though she considered herself attractive on a good day, today wasn't one of those.

The Hollywood hunk might have dated her once, but the gorgeous women he saw daily and at award shows and premieres made her look like roadkill in comparison. Especially in contrast with Melanie Masterson, the actress the magazines constantly paired him with.

He glanced at his watch. "Actually, I was hoping you had time for one more patient today."

"You?" she asked, surprised. He didn't look sick.

"Flu shot. I never managed to get one before I left L.A." He shoved his hands into his back pockets and grinned at her like an adorable little boy who'd forgotten his lunch money and was begging for a loan.

The effect was potent, more than any other good-looking man had had on her ever. Guiltily, thoughts of John, her on-again, off-again boyfriend, arose. She and John had started dating when she'd returned home to take over her sick father's practice a little over a year ago. But while John was ready to settle down and had begun pressuring her for more of a commitment, she wasn't ready, and lately she'd been wondering if she ever would be.

She'd been putting him off with flimsy excuses, but *I need more time* and *Let's get to know each other better* didn't hold much weight when they'd known one another since grade school. John provided comfort and ease but not this overwhelming sexual desire she felt just looking at Dylan again.

"Hello?" Dylan waved a hand in front of her face. "I asked if you'd give me a flu shot." He studied her with concern.

She shook her head to clear her thoughts and focus on keeping Dylan in the past where he belonged. Forcing a smile, she said, "Sure. I can manage one more shot."

She gave him a quick exam, not wanting to spend too much time examining his broad, tanned, muscular chest or any other part of his body that created that longing feeling swirling inside her. After a quick escape to gather her equipment, she walked back into the exam room.

"So are you going to Whipporwill's tonight?" he asked about the town's annual Christmas party. He pushed up his sweater sleeve in preparation for his shot.

She shook her head. "I haven't had any downtime lately. I thought I'd head home and relax." In fact, she'd already called John and cancelled, claiming exhaustion. Her bed beckoned.

Once she'd slept, she would wake up refreshed and full of holiday spirit, ready to shop for the gifts she normally purchased way ahead of time. But since her father died, she'd been so busy keeping his practice alive that she'd had no time for anything that resembled fun.

"That's too bad. I was hoping I could steal a dance."

She shot him a disbelieving glance. A dance? Was that something like their hug? Did he really find being around her that easy, making conversation that simple, as if they'd never meant anything to each other beyond friends? Was the attraction that swirled inside her even now nonexistent for him when he looked at her? She clenched her jaw in pain and frustration.

"I thought we could hang out and catch up. You know, like old times. Come on, Holly. Please?"

She closed her eyes and counted to ten, seeing her relaxing night evaporate. If she didn't show up at the party, Dylan would think she was avoiding him, or worse, running from her feelings.

"Fine," she said with forced cheer. "I'd love to hang out with an old *friend*." As long as he didn't call her his Midnight Angel again.

And since he found it so easy to be her *friend*, she decided there was a nice, fleshier place than his arm for her to insert the needle for his shot. One where he wouldn't forget her quite so easily this time.

"Oh, Dylan? I need you to do me a favor first."

He grinned, obviously pleased she'd agreed. "What's that?"

"Drop your pants."

He groaned, and she laughed, her first free and easy laugh since he'd walked into her office unannounced.

Chapter Two

Whipporwill's was the fanciest restaurant in Acton and often doubled as a catering hall for weddings and other assorted affairs. By L.A. standards, it fell short of chic, and by Boston standards it was a family-style restaurant at best. Still, it was the best Acton had to offer, and tradition dictated the whole town show up for an annual bash the week before Christmas.

Dylan leaned against a scarred, wood-paneled wall, smiling and greeting friends, both old and new. His mother, Kate, stood on the opposite side of the room, holding court, gesturing proudly to her famous son. He'd flown his mother to L.A. a few times a year and he'd come home to visit and left just as quietly. Having him here to show off was a first, and she reveled in the attention. Meanwhile, he was looking around for Holly, who was nowhere to be found.

Dylan had all but dared her to show up tonight. In his arrogance, he'd thought that just because he'd once been able to anticipate her actions, he could still do the same. But as the minutes passed, he was forced to admit he'd miscalculated. Badly enough for him to admit defeat.

Before he could come up with an excuse that his mother and everyone else would accept so that he could leave gracefully, a guy he recognized from high school walked over and joined him.

"Dylan, I heard you were in town. It's good to see you." The other man held out his hand.

Dylan grinned. "John Whittaker? Damn, it's been a long time." He pumped his old friend's hand.

"Last time I saw you, we were cleaning toilet paper off the football field to keep Coach from calling the cops and reporting the school had been vandalized."

Dylan laughed. "I remember." It had been their high-school graduation farewell prank. Dylan had left for L.A. a few days later.

"I can't tell you how many times I've thought of that night over the years. Every time I see your ugly mug on the cover of a magazine, in fact." John shoved his hand into the back pocket of his chinos.

He still favored the preppy look while Dylan had always liked jeans and T-shirts best. Unlike many of the guys Dylan had greeted tonight who sported bald spots or comb-overs, John still had a full head of sandy-brown hair.

"Tonight must feel like a high-school reunion for you," John said, understanding in a way that surprised Dylan.

He grimaced. "Worse. I think you're one of the first people who's happy to see me for the right reasons." *Friendship, not awe,* he thought.

"As soon as they all realize you're still the same, the fame thing'll pass."

Dylan shrugged. "I hope you're right. So what've you been up to?"

"I work at an investment firm in downtown Boston," John said, propping one shoulder against the wall.

"That suits you. Married?"

"Not yet, but I'm trying to get the woman I've been seeing to settle down."

"Anyone I know?" Dylan asked.

John studied Dylan in pointed silence. "Actually—" John's cell phone rang, cutting him off. He glanced at the incoming number. "Hang on, and we'll pick this up in a few minutes," he said to Dylan. He answered the call, walking off to talk in private, leaving Dylan to watch the door some more and hope Holly would show up after all.

*   *   *

After heading home for a nap, a shower and some serious primping, Holly met up with Nicole on the steps outside Whipporwill's. The chill in the air and impending snow signaled Christmas was coming soon. Holly loved the holiday season. She was suddenly glad she'd come tonight, and the festivities weren't the only reason. Neither was the challenge Dylan had issued earlier. Dylan himself was the man motivating her actions.

"I still think you should have surprised John instead of calling him and telling him you'd decided to come tonight," Nicole said, interrupting Holly's thoughts. "Spontaneity is good for relationships, and from what you've told me, John could use some good old-fashioned surprises in his life."

Holly couldn't deny that comment. "I just thought he deserved to know I'd changed my mind." She'd show up at the party, spend time with both the past and present men in her life and hopefully leave Whipporwill's with a clear mind, ready to move on.

"I bet you were afraid he'd think you came just to see Dylan," Nicole said knowingly.

With a groan, Holly pulled open the door and entered the festive party. Red and silver velvet bows adorned the walls, and tinsel fell enticingly from each potted plant and fern, while poinsettias were strategically placed around the room, their beauty enhancing the holiday atmosphere.

"Do you want to stick with me?" she asked Nicole, knowing her friend was still fairly new to town and didn't know everyone yet.

Nicole shook her head. "Actually, I see someone I want to talk to," she said and, with a brief wave, disappeared into the crowd.

So much for needing a guiding hand, Holly thought wryly. She paused to hand her jacket to the coat-check girl before heading inside.

No sooner had she glanced around than her first challenge came to greet her. "Holly, I'm so glad you changed your mind and decided to come," John said, grasping her hand in his. "You look beautiful."

"Thank you." She took in his polished look, the pressed chinos and collared shirt paired with a polo sweater, and smiled. "You look pretty good yourself." She kissed his clean-shaven cheek, his familiar aftershave surrounding her.

"Well, well, look who decided to show up after all."

Dylan's deep voice sent sizzling awareness shooting through her veins, leaving no part of her body unaffected. While John's scent had been warm, *Dylan's* cologne caused a distinct path of heat to travel along her nerve endings and settle in the pit of her stomach.

"I thought you said you'd be missing this shindig." He cocked his head and pinned her with a knowing grin.

"You two have seen each other already?" John asked, obviously surprised.

Dylan was the one subject John never broached with Holly. He knew the history. He'd been through school along with them, but John and Holly had begun dating once they'd returned home as adults. As if by mutual agreement, they'd left Dylan behind and started fresh. But Holly realized that Dylan had always been with her even when she wasn't aware of it.

She wondered if Dylan had heard she and John were an item. She wondered if he'd even care. After clearing her throat, she tackled John's comment. "Dylan stopped by the office this afternoon."

"I wanted her to promise me a dance tonight," Dylan said with that sexy look back in his gaze.

Obviously he hadn't heard anything about her and John being a couple. She winced and jumped to explain his comment to John. "Actually, Dylan came by for a flu shot."

She didn't want John to get the wrong idea. *Or was it the right one?* Holly wondered, her traitorous heart beating hard in her chest because Dylan was near. Obviously the old feelings weren't gone. Not even the anger or sense of betrayal, which still lay in her heart like lead, could dilute the spike of desire he caused.

"The good doctor didn't mind giving me one, either." Dylan grinned and rubbed the affected spot just below his hip. He laughed until his gaze fell to Holly's hand, still enclosed in John's grasp.

His eyes opened wide, and an uncomfortable silence fell until finally Dylan spoke. "This is the woman you've been seeing? The one you've been trying to get to settle down?" His voice sounded hoarse to Holly's ears as he cocked his head to one side, understanding dawning.

Instinct had her pulling her hand back from John's.

"And you're the reason she's been avoiding commitment. I don't know why I didn't realize it before," John said, sounding certain of his conclusion.

"Excuse me." Holly interrupted the two men. "But could you both stop speaking about me like I'm not here?" She turned to John first. "Dylan has nothing to do with my feelings about commitment," she assured him. But her queasy stomach and sweaty palms made her wonder if her words were a lie.

"I know you want to believe that, but I'm ready to move forward with you or without you." John turned to Dylan. "How long are you in town for?"

Dylan looked as stunned as she felt as he replied, "Through Christmas, but—"

"That's decided, then."

"What is?" Holly asked, nothing around her making sense.

John stood up straight and pulled his coat check ticket from his pocket. "Spend the next few days with Dylan or alone with your own thoughts—I don't care which. But deal with the past and decide what you want for your future."

Holly blinked. "Can someone please tell me when I lost control of my life?"

"Oh, about the time this guy took off for Hollywood." John reached out and squeezed her hand tight. "I care about you, and I want what makes you happy. But I want to be happy too, so let's both agree to use these few days wisely, okay?"

She had thought she would walk in here tonight, take one look at John, who was ready to give her a future, take one look at Dylan, who'd caused her nothing but pain, and be ready to ride off into the sunset with John. Well, her thinking had been naive in the extreme, because Dylan wreaked a kind of havoc on her body and soul that she couldn't explain or understand. He promised nothing, and yet she couldn't give herself completely to any other man.

She had to take this time with him now. Knowing John had understood that even before she had, she nodded. "Okay."

To her shock, John turned and shook Dylan's hand, then kissed Holly on the cheek, not on the lips. Not, she noticed, like a man staking his claim or giving her something to remember him by as she weighed her options. But, then, she and John had always been about companionship and caring, not all-consuming love and desire. Wasn't that what made him the perfect choice for her future?

Dylan's return was temporary, and he certainly wasn't offering forever. They barely knew each other anymore. Yet she felt like she still did know him. So even if the likelihood was that he'd leave for L.A. and her heart would be broken once more, she needed closure. Once again something John had understood before she had.

"Well, well, that certainly was interesting." Dylan watched John's retreating back. "I had no idea you two were involved."

His voice brought Holly back to the present. To the man who'd caused more upheaval in her life than anyone she'd ever known. "How would you know anything about me? It's not like you kept in touch over the past decade."

"True." He inclined his head. "And I'm sorry for that. I'm sorry for a lot of things we've yet to hash out. But I'm back now and plan to make up for lost time." His eyes glittered with determined fire.

The same fire she'd bet kept him stoked and primed as he'd quickly climbed through the ranks in Hollywood. Holly shivered. "What makes you think I want the same thing?"

He shook his head and let out a low, chiding sound, but his lips were turned upward in a grin. "Don't make me kiss you senseless in front of this crowd just to prove a point." He leaned in closer, his roughened cheek against hers, making her skin tingle. "Because when I kiss you again, and you can be sure I will, we're going to be alone, where I can take my time and go oh so slow and deep." His husky voice rumbled over the last two words.

Her breath caught in her throat, and her own vivid imagination took over. She envisioned his lips covering hers, his tongue thrusting inside her open mouth while his body made love to hers just as he'd described.

A low moan escaped her throat, but thank goodness the music was loud and their audience, though rapt, couldn't possibly capture the subtle undercurrents running between them.

"Don't you have a beautiful girlfriend waiting for

you in L.A.?" she asked, wondering why he was bothering with seductive come-ons with *her*.

"Nope." His serious blue-eyed gaze met hers.

"The papers said—"

"The first thing you're going to need to learn is that you should never ever believe anything you read in the papers, respectable publication or otherwise. Always confirm the story with me first, or better yet, trust your gut."

"You talk like you're going to be around long enough for it to matter. It doesn't. I'm sorry I even brought up the subject."

"No you aren't, and neither am I. I want you to know everything about me now, just like I intend to learn everything about you. But first, I want that dance you promised me."

"I never—"

His finger halted her moving lips, the touch both firm and gentle. "Are you going to deny us something we both want?"

She sighed, then placed her hand in his and let him wind their way to the dance floor. His hand came to rest at her waist, intimately pulling her against him until their lower bodies swayed in unison to the sultry beat of the music.

She shut her eyes and gave herself over to feeling, suddenly understanding why John had never been enough. Why no man had ever come close. No one could ever live up to the memory of her first love, and now he was back, wreaking havoc with her life again.

Though she was older and wiser this time, the thought gave her no sense of comfort because she was no more in control of her emotions and desires than she was over the inevitable outcome of this brief reunion.

The snow had started falling sometime during the party. White flakes drifted down and stuck to the ground and, combined with the weather forecast over the next few days, brought with them the certainty of a white Christmas. It'd been years since Dylan had enjoyed snow and even longer since the promise of tomorrow looked so damn good.

He waited as Holly pulled her wool coat tight around her and cinched the belt at her waist. Dancing with her, holding her in his arms again, had convinced him this return home had been exactly what he needed. And if the byplay between Holly and John was any indication, Dylan was exactly what she needed too. He hated like hell that his old friend John would be a casualty, but obviously things between him and Holly hadn't been all that good before Dylan returned to the picture.

Dylan knew Holly was wary and had good reason to mistrust both him and his motives, but he'd made progress already. He had but one crucial week to cement her trust.

"Ready?" he asked her.

She nodded.

"Where do you live now?"

She pulled on a pair of black gloves. "I took over the apartment above the office that Dad used to rent out to students."

"Smart move. So you walked here?"

"Yes." She inclined her head. "What about you? Are you staying with your mother?"

"Would she let me live if I didn't?" He chuckled. "She's so happy to have me back home that she's already cooked me breakfast, lunch and dinner."

They started down the street.

"Careful or she'll spoil you. Do you cook for yourself back home?"

He took the fact that she was asking questions about his life as a positive sign. "If it can be de-frosted in a microwave and zapped, I can cook it," he said proudly.

She laughed, and the sound carried on the wind, churning in his gut. "That sounds pretty close to my life lately. But I hired a partner who's supposed to start working after the first of the year, and I really hope it'll take some of the burden off me."

"Assuming the old folks take to her?" Dylan asked knowingly.

"It's a him," Holly said. "Lance Tollgate. I think the patients will like him," she said, her voice warming. "He's young and friendly, and he's got kids, so he can relate to the grandparents and parents. It should be a good fit."

"Your father would be really proud of you."

"Yeah, he was." Her voice cracked with emotion. "Sorry. It just hasn't been that long."

Dylan swallowed hard. "I'm sorry I wasn't here." He reached for her hand and held on tight.

"I got through it. There was a lot you weren't here for," she reminded him.

He knew they'd have to discuss and deal with his abrupt departure if he had any hope of her believing he wouldn't abandon her again. But he wanted her to get to know him again first.

They approached the office, and she led him around back to the private entrance. He followed her up the few steps to the front door and paused.

"Do you want to come in for a cup of coffee or a drink?" she asked while fishing for her keys.

He did, but he had other plans. "Thanks anyway, but I need to get up early."

She shrugged, a "suit yourself" gesture, but he saw the hurt and lack of understanding in her gaze.

He reached out and cupped her cheek, his thumb

caressing the soft skin in broad strokes. "Do you have plans tomorrow?"

"I'm off. I'm forwarding patients to a covering doctor in the next town. If I don't get some time to myself, I won't be good for anyone." She spoke quickly, obviously in a rush to get inside and away from him.

"How about I pick you up early and we head into Boston for some holiday shopping?" he asked.

She turned to face him. The glow from the outside light illuminated her blond hair and exquisitely made-up features. He hadn't thought about it before, but not only had she shown up at the party, she'd gone all out for it too.

Pleasure took hold inside him. "You're beautiful, you know. Not in the young-girl way I remembered, but in a womanly way I appreciate so much more."

She narrowed her gaze. "What kind of game are you playing, Dylan? You can't come in for a drink because you have plans; then you offer to pick me up early tomorrow. What's going on with you?" Thoroughly annoyed, she perched her hands on her hips while her lips puckered into a pretty pout.

He shook his head. "Sorry about the mixed signals. I want nothing more than to come in, but we both know where that'll lead, and I can't believe I'm saying this, but I want to take it slow."

"Slow?" Her lips mouthed the word. "Ten years isn't slow enough? You'd rather just torture me, is that it?"

"I want you to go to sleep and dream of nothing but me." He let his fingers trace the outline of her glossed lips. "So when I pick you up tomorrow, you're ready to focus solely and completely on getting to know me again, and me getting to know you."

"You want to discover what makes me tick now?" she asked, a sparkle and teasing glint in her eyes.

"In a word, yes."

Unexpectedly, her tongue darted out and licked the pad of his thumb, being deliberately seductive. He felt the sensation straight through to his already hard groin.

Before he could think it through, he slipped his hand around the back of her neck and pulled her towards him, capturing her mouth with his. Her lips softened but didn't part. Obviously she intended to make him work for what he wanted, and that was okay with him.

He slid his lips back and forth over hers, floored by the gratification he found in tasting her at last. The longer they kissed, the more he realized that his memories had grown fuzzy and reality was so much better and definitely hotter. He braced her face in his hands, tilted her head and continued to tease and taste, just as he'd promised, kissing her slowly, intent on branding her and making sure that if she slept, her dreams would be of him.

His tongue glided over the seam of her lips, and he was rewarded with a low moan from the back of her throat as she opened her mouth and let him inside. He savored the absolute sweetness and desire flooding him. His groin pushed hard against his jeans, the urge to possess her with his body strong.

Before he could go back on his word and join her inside, he stepped back, reminding himself that he wanted to win her trust for the long haul. Not just for one night in bed.

She met his gaze with heavy-lidded eyes, her mouth reddened from his kiss. "You've perfected your technique," she murmured.

He grinned. "I'll take that as a compliment, babe, and you should know, your technique's gotten pretty good too. Still, I don't think technique has anything to do with it."

"No? Then what explains two people who don't learn from their mistakes?"

"Speak for yourself. I've learned a lot from the past. And I think it's *us* that's so potent."

She raised an eyebrow. "This from the man who said we were nothing more than a high-school crush?"

He accepted the blow. "An immature boy said that, not the man I am now."

She swallowed hard. "Who is that man, and what does he want from me?" she asked.

"Time will tell." He didn't mean to be cryptic, but he could hardly say, *I've come back for you,* and expect her to believe his words when his promise had failed her before. "Just give me some time."

Her fingers touched her moist, red lips. "Sex wasn't enough before."

"We're older and wiser now."

She grinned. "We can always hope." She let herself into the apartment and shut the door behind her.

He expelled a breath and tried to pull himself together. He'd been her first, Dylan remembered, and though she'd been an eager learner, she'd rarely initiated sex. This teasing side of her was new, and he liked it a whole lot.

He couldn't wait to explore more.

Chapter Three

Holly knew she'd either lost her mind or she was experiencing an early midlife crisis. There was no other explanation for kissing Dylan and then agreeing to spend more time with him. Then again, what choice did she have? The clean break they'd taken—make that the clean break he'd forced on her—hadn't accomplished anything. Their chemistry and connection was still as strong as ever. She had no choice but to play this through to whatever conclusion awaited her, or she couldn't move on with her life. She'd be in the same limbo hell she'd been in for the last ten years.

So by the time he rang her doorbell the following morning, she was dressed in her favorite jeans and baseball cap and she was ready to shop in Boston with Dylan by her side.

She opened the door, and he greeted her with a

cup of Starbucks in each hand. "You come bearing gifts?" she asked, laughing.

"Straight up for me and a froufrou drink for you. I can't think of a better way to take the T to Copley," he said, speaking of Boston's version of public transportation.

"I must've heard you wrong. America's heart-throb is going to take the train? Do you want to get mobbed?" She shook her head, realizing she really hadn't thought about his ego or what his lifestyle must be like now. "Never mind. To be so success-ful, you must like the spotlight."

He shrugged, looking uncomfortable. "*Like* isn't the right word. It comes with the territory of being successful. You get used to it, but you don't ever enjoy not having a personal life or having to work for a solitary moment."

She studied his serious face. "You don't enjoy the fame?" she asked, surprised.

"I did in the beginning. But it got old fast, and I realized that no matter how many people sur-rounded me, I was always alone. And lonely."

The wistful sound in his voice caught her off guard and she narrowed her gaze. "Should I pull out the violin?"

He laughed at that. "I'm not looking for your pity. I'm just answering your question and telling it like it is. I want you to know me. Who I was and who I've become. Yes, I love my career, but I've given up a lot for it." Again he sobered as he spoke.

She met his serious stare and suddenly wondered if his return could have more to do with his emotional state than a brief visit to see his mother. He seemed so reflective. But she couldn't imagine that Dylan had suddenly decided that he missed home and Holly. Not after a silent ten years. Which brought up the question, just where did she fit into the equation of his life?

"We all make choices," she said of his decision to pursue a Hollywood career.

"And sometimes we live to regret them." He squeezed her hand, and she felt as if her heart were being clenched tight as well.

"Are you saying you're sorry you went to L.A.?"

He shook his head. "I'm sorry for how I went about it."

She swallowed hard and nodded, not certain she was ready for any further discussion on their past, yet she wasn't ready to end the talk just yet. "And now?"

He grinned. "Now we go about taking things one step at a time. We're going shopping, and we're going to take the train like regular people. Nobody's going to expect to see me on the T, so they'll think maybe I share a resemblance with the famous Dylan North, but they'll be so sure they're wrong they'll leave us alone." He wagged his eyebrows like a kid. "That's what I want. How about you?"

"That's what I want too." That's what scared her so much, she thought as she picked up her ski jacket and her bag. "So who are you shopping for today?"

"I'm a big brother," he explained. And during their trip to the city, he told her about Darrell, the kid he mentored, and the program he'd been funding with a percentage of his earnings for the last two years.

In Sports Authority he purchased a pair of Reebok basketball sneakers, a Spalding official NBA basketball, and some gym clothes for Darrell. Then he ordered basketballs in bulk for a youth program and arranged to have everything shipped to a community center in South Central L.A. Watching the care he took in choosing the gifts, Holly learned that the man wasn't just rich and famous, but he gave back to the community in which he lived, and it became even harder to rein in her heart.

Over lunch he changed the subject. He wanted to hear about her years in college and medical school, which she managed to condense into a short story since she wanted to hear more about him.

He told her about his trip and all his firsts in L.A. She learned about his initial glimpse of the Hollywood sign, his search for an agent and his first job waiting tables, a job from which he was fired for spilling iced tea down Dolly Parton's dress. Laughing, he insisted on paying the check.

While she shopped for family and friends, he revisited his excitement over his first acting job, when he learned which actors would take him under their wing and which were too afraid of losing their own success to help someone else. For the first time she was able to put her hurt aside and see what he'd been searching for as an actor.

She understood they still needed to talk about how he'd handled his decision to leave her, but for now she was content to enjoy his company in an adult way they'd never experienced before. They parted for half an hour, during which she bought *his* gift. By the time they'd gotten back home, he'd managed to avoid crowds and had signed only two autographs the entire day. Each time someone recognized him, they made a quick escape and found an entirely new place to shop. He was as adept at acting pleased to meet his fans as he was at ducking them at first opportunity.

Holly couldn't remember a more fun or sexually charged day. His cologne turned her on and kept her aroused with each breath she took, and he never stopped touching her. Either he held her hand as they walked, his palm tucked against hers, or he cupped the small of her back, steering her this way and that. Whatever they did, he made certain they were connected the entire afternoon, and as a result, her body tingled with awareness.

At the train station in Acton, they slid into the car and Dylan turned towards her, one hand over her headrest. "So what next?"

Holly's heart pounded hard in her chest. She'd wrestled with this all afternoon, wondering if she could really have Dylan in her apartment and still be the same when he returned to L.A. Probably not, but it didn't matter. Given the chance to be with him, how could she turn him away?

Her gaze met his. "I still have to finish decorating my tree. I could make you dinner in exchange for your help," she offered.

If he turned down this not-so-subtle invitation as he had turned her down last night, she was finished playing his getting-to-know-each-other-again game.

He reached a hand out and caressed her cheek. "I'd love that," he said, the smile on his face evident in his voice.

Tremors of excitement shot through her, and as he turned the engine over, her stomach rolled with anticipation at the night to come.

Whoever said you couldn't come home again didn't know Holly Evans, Dylan thought. Her apartment was cozy and made him feel welcome and at ease. While she put something together for dinner, Dylan kept himself busy stringing the lights on her tree. He couldn't believe the Holly he knew, who loved Christmas, hadn't decorated her apartment before now, but her hectic schedule was his gain. He put his own touches on her tree, and in doing so he hoped he was making a definite mark in her life.

He heard her footsteps as she walked in to join him. His gaze was immediately drawn to the way the tight denim jeans molded to her hips and thighs. Still slender, she'd filled out in a womanly way that made him hard just looking at her. It wasn't desire alone that beckoned to him but the sense of fulfillment and belonging he found only with her.

Today had shown him that his memories were but shadows of reality. Together they could share so much, if he could convince her to open her heart to him again.

"Hi there," he said.

"Hi. Dinner should be ready in about forty-five minutes. I hope you like frozen lasagne because when I offered to cook, I forgot I hadn't been shopping in a while. We're lucky I was able to find something to defrost so we could eat at all." She knelt down and sat on the hardwood floor.

"I'd have been happy to take you out, but I'm happier to have more time alone." He patted the empty space beside him, but she kept her distance.

She smiled, but after a day of laughter and relaxed fun, he recognized forced cheer when he saw it. "What's wrong?"

She glanced down, rubbing her palms against her jeans. "I just had some time to think, and I can't help but have questions. A lot of them, actually."

"Like?" he asked, prepared to deal with whatever was on her mind.

She lifted her gaze to meet his. "Like why you left so suddenly and why you came back into my life the same way."

He nodded slowly, glancing up at the empty tree top, wondering where to begin. Hoping he wouldn't push her further away.

Though she sat cross-legged on the floor next to him, their easy camaraderie was gone, and she went out of her way to make sure her bent knee didn't touch his. She was waiting for an explanation, and he wondered if anything he said would make sense—or make a difference to her now.

"You know how badly I wanted to act."

She nodded. "You said Broadway. We had plans. Dreams. At least I thought we did, but after you took off, I convinced myself they'd been *my* dreams and you'd humored me through high school before moving on." At times she even thought that he'd used her, Holly thought.

She bit down on her lower lip, not wanting Dylan to see the extent to which he'd hurt her. Certainly she didn't want him to know his betrayal had probably ruined any chance she had at trusting any other guy. Now that she was beginning to understand how deeply he still affected her, in a way she resented him even more.

He gazed at the needles on the tree as if they could offer clarity until finally he spoke. "The closer we got to graduation, the more trying for Broadway and acting in New York seemed like a sacrifice," he admitted. "Like I'd be accepting second choice without even trying for the big-time."

"So why didn't you just tell me? Or was I that much of a burden?" she asked, admitting her fears out loud for the first time. "Were you afraid I'd hold you back?"

He jerked backward and stared. "Are you serious? It was just the opposite. I didn't want to hold *you* back. Your family had dreams and goals for you. *You* had those same dreams."

Then, at the same time, they both said, "Yale, like your father and his father before him," laughing despite the serious conversation.

"You see? I knew if I told you I wanted to go to L.A., you'd probably have insisted on going with me. Yes, there was Stanford or other schools, but none of them were Yale, and none would uphold your family tradition."

"Wasn't that my choice to make? Unless it was an excuse and you really didn't want me—"

He grasped her hand hard. "I didn't want you to end up resenting me. And in case you need a reminder or proof of how much I did and still do care, here it is." Taking her by surprise, he leaned over and met her lips in a searing, demanding kiss.

A kiss she both wanted and needed, and this time she didn't hesitate. She parted her lips and allowed him inside. His tongue swirled in her mouth, teasing, tasting and demanding she understand. And though she still held the pain in her heart, a part of her accepted the explanation. His kiss and gentle touch went a long way towards helping her heal.

She placed her hands on his shoulders and pushed backward. He toppled to the floor, pulling her on top of him until they lay sprawled beneath her Christmas tree, her legs tangled with his. Their bodies fit tightly yet perfectly together, the hard ridge of his erection thrusting upward against her, making her very aware of his desire, which found a feminine answer inside her.

She couldn't deny the aching emptiness only he could fill or the trickle of desire dampening her panties. She wanted him. Scarier yet, she needed him.

He stared up at her, his sexy gaze smoldering with raw passion and emotion she couldn't mistake. "I missed you, Holly."

"I missed you too," she admitted, and then, to keep things light, she nipped at his lips with soft kisses and teasing strokes of her tongue.

His hands came to rest at her waist. "I told you why I left. Don't you want to know why I came back?"

She trembled, and desire wasn't the reason. "I'm really not sure I want to know. I can't imagine with all that's happened in your life that you just couldn't stop thinking of me," she said, forcing a laugh.

"I couldn't stop thinking of you."

Her heart filled with warmth. "You always knew how to make me feel special, Dylan." But common sense told her not to read too much into his comment.

He'd come home to visit, the first time since she'd been back home, and he came to see her in order to make amends. The chemistry was just a bonus he'd opted to act on, and she certainly hadn't said no. She didn't fault him for that, and she didn't fault herself for letting him back into her life. She needed closure in order to move on. Being with Dylan was giving her that now.

"I can charm anyone. That's a fact." He winked, and she saw the movie star America adored. "But not you. I never could bullshit you, and I don't intend to try and start now."

"Well, good. Then we both understand you came back to set things right between us."

He nodded. "That's one way of putting it."

And there was the probability that he meant his words at face value. That he was home for a short time only. Long enough to make things right and leave his mark, but short enough that he wouldn't get bored. For certain he'd be gone before the itch to move on set in.

Knowing that, she wouldn't mind getting all of Dylan North that she could. "I think we've done enough talking, don't you?" she asked, feeling a wicked grin take hold as she lowered her face to his.

"For now," he agreed.

She nuzzled his neck, her cheek rubbing against his and her lower body beginning to shift from side to side, seeking to increase the building desire and friction between them.

No sooner had she let out a low groan than he flipped her onto her back, switching positions. When they'd been together before, he'd always taken the lead. She was content to let him do so now, certain her time would come to show him how she'd changed and how she'd become more certain of herself and her sexuality.

He pulled her shirt upward, exposing her midriff, his eager hands branding her with their heat as he worked his way upward to her lace bra. His fingertips teased beneath the elastic, his palms finally coming to rest where they belonged, cupping her breasts in his hands.

"You've filled out," he said, approval and gruff desire in his tone.

"Like you'd remember."

His expression changed, his features taking on a wounded look. "You think I don't?"

Unwilling to kill the moment with talk of the women who'd come in between, she shook her head. "I was joking. I remember everything between us, and I'm sure you do too."

His gaze softened. He pulled her top up and over her head, then slipped her bra straps down her shoulders so that he revealed her bare breasts to his hungry gaze.

Shockingly, she felt no embarrassment, only a sense of rightness as he devoured her with one look. His thumbs brushed insistently over her nipples, back and forth, until they hardened into tight peaks and she felt the languorous pull straight to her core. He dipped his head and began a steady suckling with his mouth, his teeth lightly grazing, his tongue gently soothing, but every motion carefully orchestrated to bring her higher and higher, closer to the brink of orgasm.

She wanted his dark head bent at her chest and his warm breath and heat on her breasts as she came apart in his arms. And then she wanted him to fill her completely, so when he left this time she had adult memories to tuck away with the teenage ones she remembered.

"You always knew exactly how to make me come," she murmured, whispering into his hair as his mouth continued to work ultimate magic.

He chuckled and she felt the vibration throughout her body. "That's because you're so damn responsive." And as if to prove his point, he blew a wisp of air across her breasts, the cool breeze puckering her nipples and causing her hips to shift restlessly beneath his.

"See?" He splayed his hand across her belly. "And if I do this, you'll be moaning in no time." His fingertips teased beneath the waistband of her jeans, lightly brushing the triangle of hair just waiting for his touch.

"Dylan," she whispered, her body his for the taking.

"I hear you, babe." He reached for the snap on

her jeans at the same time she sought to release his confined erection.

But the jarring ring of his cell phone interrupted them. "I don't want to answer it," he muttered.

The doctor in her disagreed. "Just make sure it's not an emergency."

He rolled off her and groaned, grabbing for his phone. "Hello," he barked into his cell. "Mmm-hmm," he said, then listened some more. "Exactly what I'm looking for." More listening and then, "I'll be there."

His voice rose in definite pleasure, and she wondered if it was a role or a part in a movie he was talking about. She wondered too how preoccupied he'd be now that something big had obviously come up.

"Anything important?" she asked after he'd snapped his phone shut and rolled over to face her, head propped against his hand.

"Just some things I have in the works," he said vaguely, his eyes twinkling.

"Sounds exciting."

He reached over and rubbed his finger across her bottom lip. "Not as exciting as what I want to do with you," he said and pulled her beneath him again.

Chapter Four

Before Dylan could pick up where they'd left off, Holly jumped up and headed for the kitchen to pull the lasagne from the oven to let it cool a bit before dinner. He took the few minutes alone to evaluate things between them so far.

He knew he'd made progress with Holly, but not enough for her to believe in a future. Certainly not enough to tell her that the phone call had been from a real estate agent who'd found him five acres of wooded land and the perfect setting to build a house not far from Acton. Dylan had reached a point where he was ready to settle down away from the insanity that was Hollywood. With or without Holly in his life, he planned to purchase property and make it his permanent home between movie shoots.

They'd already talked about his reasons for leaving and coming back now, but she was still skittish and unwilling to trust emotionally. He didn't mind starting by winning over her body in the hopes that her heart and mind would soon follow.

He paused in her bedroom and returned with a blanket, spreading it out over the floor in the family room and waiting until Holly came out of the kitchen.

"Did we ever make love beneath the Christmas tree?" he asked her.

Instead of bolting or growing wary, a slow, sexy smile curved her lips. "Not that I recall. We'd have been too afraid of getting caught."

"There's no one to catch us now," he deliberately hinted.

"You don't say." She stepped towards him, an extra wiggle in her hips. He couldn't mistake the fact that she remained half-dressed in her jeans, bra and nothing else. She hadn't opted to dress or cover herself, another good sign.

He sat back and waited.

"So if I were to undress right here, no one would mind?" she asked, becoming a teasing seductress in front of his eyes.

Before he could reply, she tipped her head to one side, and as he watched, she reached for and released the front clasp of her bra.

His breath caught as she slowly shimmied the straps off her shoulders and pulled the cups away so her full breasts were bare, and he was drooling.

"I sure as hell don't mind," he said, awed by her rounded breasts, flat stomach and sense of confidence, all of which turned him on.

"Then this won't bother you either." She unsnapped the button on her jeans and lowered the zipper.

He swallowed hard.

Hands at her hips, she eased the waistband down. He didn't know where to focus first, the expanse of pale skin on her stomach or the blond triangle of hair she slowly revealed when she'd hooked her thumbs into her underwear and drawn them down too.

"You're gorgeous," he said, shocked he could formulate a coherent sentence.

She smiled.

Surely this physical trust had to mean he'd made more headway in breaching her barriers than he'd thought. If not, he was going to be one miserable son of a bitch in the morning.

But damn he'd enjoy tonight.

He reached for her, but she playfully smacked at his hand. "No touching until we're equally at risk of being caught naked," she said, laughing.

"If you're asking me to strip, no problem." He

grabbed for the fly on his jeans, which had grown way too tight, but she stopped him with one hand.

"I want you to put yourself in *my* hands."

Ironic. He wanted her trust. She was asking for his.

He raised his hands in the air and sucked in a deep breath as she popped the button on his jeans and, with some maneuvering on his part, removed his clothing.

Then she splayed her hands against his chest, her touch warm and inviting. "Did you mean it when you said you'd missed me?"

In her voice, he heard the uncertainty as the sassy seductress warred with the woman who still felt used and left behind.

He twined their fingers together and pulled her onto the blanket. "I missed you," he assured her. "Not a day went by that I didn't think of you."

She moistened her lips. "Me too," she admitted. "Even if it was just in my dreams."

His heart pounding hard in his chest, he leaned over her, his rock-hard erection poised at her moist entrance. He wanted to be inside her more than he wanted to breathe. But he also needed to know she felt and desired the same thing.

"Dylan?"

"Hmm?"

"Show me how much you missed me, because I

know I missed you," Holly whispered, telling him exactly what he needed to hear.

He reached down with one hand, teasing her dewy folds, easing first one finger and then another inside her. She arched her back and moaned, and with a shuddering breath, he thrust hard and deep, entering her at last.

He was immediately clasped in her moist heat, her inner walls squeezing him tight. Both the physical and emotional sensations were stronger than any he could ever remember, and his pulse beat hard in his throat as he lost any semblance of coherent thought.

As Dylan stilled inside her, Holly's breath caught and she lay motionless, adjusting to his size and length, to the exquisite feel of him hard and rigid inside her, where he belonged. She clenched him tighter, and the pulling sensation grew, spiraling and taking her to dizzying new heights.

He met her gaze and withdrew slowly, so she felt every hard ridge of his desire until suddenly she was empty and aching without him. "Dylan, please." She arched, trying to pull him back inside her again.

"Happy to, babe," he said and thrust with his hips, his hard erection filling her and making her whole once more.

She let out a sob of gratitude, unable to hide her emotions.

"Feels so right, doesn't it?" he asked, his voice gruff.

She could manage only a low moan from deep in her throat.

He chuckled, but his body trembled, his control obviously stretched to the breaking point. So was hers. She lifted her legs, pulling her knees backward and drawing him inexorably deeper inside her body, until they were so close, she couldn't imagine they were anything but one. And then with a groan, he released his tenuous control and began to grind against her, moving and pumping his hard body into hers.

Their connection was electric, their movements synchronized and perfect, as if they had an unspoken understanding of each other's bodies and needs. Her fingers gripped his back as she gasped for breath, shuddering and coming closer and closer to coming apart. She didn't think he could get any deeper, doubted she could *feel* any more emotion, when she instinctively hooked her ankles together behind his back. Locked in place, he rolled his hips against hers, grinding at the same time he found the perfect spot and her body shattered from inside out. Her orgasm hit hard, and she rode it out to its conclusion, her climax wringing everything out of her.

Just then he took her off guard and shifted positions. She caught on and helped until he lay flat on his back and she was astride him. She hadn't thought she could move or that another orgasm was possible, but when he shifted his hips beneath her, she changed her mind. The rhythmic rotation of his pelvis and the intimate contact of her feminine mound against his body had the contractions starting all over again.

"Do it," he told her. "Make me come," he said, his hands gripping her waist tight.

She did as he asked and took control, shifting her hips from side to side, lifting her body up and down over his, so he moved in and out at *her* whim. And it seemed that was what he'd been waiting for before he let himself go too.

His orgasm was explosive, his body practically slamming upward into hers and making her peak a second time. But now she forced her eyes open and watched him as he came, eyes shut tight, jaw clenched and lost in shared pleasure and ecstasy, and it was all she could do not to cry and let her overwhelming emotions betray her.

He fell back against the floor, his hands still on her waist, as sated and exhausted as she. She collapsed against him, their breathing coming together in rapid gulps. His heart pounded against her fore-head, and she swallowed hard, fighting back the feelings he'd inspired. The overwhelming love she felt for this man frightened her because she did still love him. Had probably never stopped.

He completed her, she realized now, and as he held her tight, she wondered if this moment to-gether would be one of their last. Because he'd never be satisfied in Acton, the small town with its slow pace and lack of excitement. The town he'd happily left behind once before.

A quick kiss, no explanation, and Dylan left first thing the next morning. Holly told herself she was glad, that things had played out as she'd expected. She told herself she could handle the brief fling he obviously wanted and intended. And she'd keep tell-ing herself that until she believed her own words.

She stopped at the office to do some insurance paperwork and see a few sick patients, before head-ing to the grocery store to fill her empty refrigerator and the department store for gifts. Christmas carols played over the speakers in the supermarket as she loaded her cart. As usual, the store was the central meeting place, and more than one friendly face commented on Dylan's return and how his car had been parked on her street late into the night.

Her face flushed hot with the first remark, and

she was certain her cheeks remained pink as she went up and down the aisles. By the time she reached the checkout line and pushed her cart behind Dylan's mother of all people, she was sure she had reached her maximum state of mortification.

"Holly, honey, how are you?" Kate asked, as she placed her items onto the belt.

"Just fine. And you?"

"Good. Good," she said, smiling. "About Dylan—"

"Yes?" Holly asked warily.

Because of her relationship with Dylan and all the time she'd spent with his family, she and his mother had remained close after he'd gone. By unspoken agreement though, they'd never discussed Dylan. Apparently that was about to change.

"I'm so happy you and my son have made your peace." Kate beamed, obviously unfazed that Dylan had been out all night at Holly's.

But Holly was even more humiliated than before. Not once last night had she given small-town gossip a thought, and since both she and Dylan were both adults, she certainly hadn't been thinking that his mother would notice his absence.

She gripped the cart handle tighter, her knuckles white as she tried to acknowledge Kate's comment without embarrassing herself further. "We've come to an understanding," she said diplomatically.

Better than admitting Dylan had spent the night

in her bed, his big body wrapped around hers, his hands doing all sorts of sinful, erotic things to her. And she had more than reciprocated, relearning his body, what he liked, what he loved and what really turned him on.

She shivered and forced a smile for his mother's sake.

Kate continued talking. "I told Dylan I expected you both for dinner tomorrow night. It is Christmas Eve, after all."

Before Dylan's return, Nicole had invited her over but she hadn't decided whether she'd rather be alone. "That's sweet but I'm not sure what my plans are yet," Holly hedged. She and Dylan hadn't made any more plans to see each other, and she didn't want his choices to be influenced by his mother's command.

But Kate waved a hand, dismissing Holly's words. "Your mother would never forgive me if I left you alone on the holiday when she was with her sister. Besides, look at all the food in the cart. I'll cook all day tomorrow. Dylan's already agreed, so it's settled."

Holly inhaled deeply and let the decision be made for her. "Then at least let me bring dessert."

"Nonsense, honey. You just spend time with Dylan and let me worry about dinner. Just bring yourself around four. Okay?"

"Okay," she said, knowing she'd bring *something* anyway. "I look forward to it." Which was true. She'd love to spend the holiday with Dylan and his family.

She just hoped Dylan felt the same way.

Dylan returned from his meeting with the real estate agent on an all-time high. He'd found the perfect parcel of land and had already made an offer. If he closed his eyes, he could envision exactly the kind of house he wanted to build there. He returned to Holly's, whistling as he rang the bell and waited for her to answer.

She opened the door, a smile on her face that widened when she saw him. She wore casual sweats and a pink sweatshirt she'd cut at the arms and across the middle. With her tousled curls and lightly made-up face, she looked delicious, good enough to eat and definitely good enough to come home to every single day.

He grinned and whistled louder.

"Someone's in a good mood," she said.

He stepped inside and swung her through the air before setting her bare feet down on the floor. But not before letting her slide down the length of his body and feel how much he'd missed her. "I'm just enjoying life."

She looked at him curiously, and her gaze narrowed as she studied him. "So just where were you that put you in such a good mood?"

"I was Christmas shopping. For you," he said, teasing her.

"You were out doing something for me?" Her blue eyes twinkled with delight.

"You bet." He debated whether to tell her about the land now or wait to give her her gift until Christmas Eve, like in his dream.

A chimelike ring sounded from the kitchen, drawing his attention. "I didn't realize I left my cell here." He thought he'd left it at his mother's place.

Holly nodded. "It's been ringing all afternoon. I'm guessing voice mail picked it up."

He could hear the withdrawal in her voice, and he rolled his suddenly stiff shoulders. The last thing he needed or wanted was his other life intruding on the headway he'd been making with Holly, but he couldn't afford to be out of touch for too long.

He glanced towards the kitchen. "Let me check the messages and then we can talk, okay?"

She nodded. "Sure. I've got some gifts of my own to wrap," she said with a wink and left him alone.

He grabbed a pen and a sheet of paper and retrieved his messages, jotting down notes of who'd called. Then he returned the most pressing messages.

Holly entered the kitchen to find Dylan on the

phone, pad and paper in front of him. She stepped inside, not wanting to bother him, but he gestured for her to come in, indicating she wasn't intruding on a private conversation.

Still, he was obviously absorbed in the discussion, and as she passed by the table, she saw he was noting figures and names on the paper, then tossing alternative numbers and people back at the person on the other end of the phone. He was animated and engaged, and it was obvious to Holly he loved what he did, down to what she assumed was negotiations on starring in a movie.

She was as much intrigued by his business as she was dismayed by the realization that she'd never truly have him. Not if it meant him settling in their small hometown and leaving the glitz, glamour and business of Hollywood behind. If she'd held any illusions or hopes, they were dispelled that instant.

Yet as much as the realization hurt, she'd never want to take something away from him that he loved so much. For the first time she understood what he meant when he said he'd left so she could pursue her dream and not resent him later on. She wouldn't want him to resent her either. She cared too much. So she would gladly take all he offered now and be grateful for this time they shared. A time she intended to make the most of as soon as he got off the phone.

While she waited for him to finish his call, she pulled a jar of Marshmallow Fluff out of the cabinet and a spoon from the drawer. She hopped up on the countertop the way she sometimes did when she was eating in a rush and feasted on her favorite snack.

"Yes, yes, I'll think it over and get back to you," Dylan said, his deep voice interrupting her thoughts. He paused before adding, "No, I'm not calling Melanie back. My decision about this has nothing to do with whether *she* takes the lead female role."

Holly's stomach jumped at the mention of the other woman's name. She scooped a heaping teaspoonful of Marshmallow Fluff and stuffed it into her mouth for good measure.

Meanwhile Dylan groaned. "Can you call Harry for me? I don't care how much he hates you, I pay you to run interference," he said and finally clicked off, ending the call.

"My agent," he said, turning her way. He shot her an apologetic look. "Sorry about that. It took longer than I thought."

She shrugged. "It's business. I understand."

He rose and strode over to where she sat. "Do you picture me as a superhero?" he asked.

"Would you have to wear tights?"

He laughed. "Why? Do you have a problem with my legs?"

"Nope." They were as strong and powerful as the rest of him. But something told her that despite their banter, this wasn't a lightly asked question. Rather, he was asking her opinion on his next role. "Wasn't your last film more serious?"

"You saw *Last Dawn*?"

She forced a nod. Hard as it was to admit, she'd seen all his movies. She made it a point to go alone to the theater in order to spare herself questions, comments and innuendo from her friends.

"My guess is that now you're worried if you go back to an action film or one based on a comic book character, you'll be taking a step backward when it comes to being taken more seriously as an actor."

"How'd you know?" he asked, surprise evident in his tone. Yet by the warm smile and gleam in his eyes, he was obviously pleased she understood his concerns without him having to explain.

"I watched the evolution of your work." She stated the truth for his benefit alone. Admitting she'd followed his career made her feel even more vulnerable to him than she already was.

"And what'd you think?" A muscle ticked in his jaw as he leaned against the counter beside her.

She wondered if the insecurity she sensed was a figment of her imagination or if he really cared about what she thought of his work.

She placed the jar down on the counter, pushing it out of the way. *"Last Dawn* was a real stretch," she said of his portrayal of a convict on death row. "You showed depth and range. Real growth."

"And?" he asked, correctly sensing she wasn't through critiquing him yet.

"And taking a commercial role now could damage the new reputation you're seeking to establish."

He leaned forward, his forehead close to hers. "You're suggesting I turn it down?"

She drew a deep breath, finding it hard to believe he'd need her opinion on something so important. "I'm saying you should think long and hard before agreeing. And—"

"And?" he asked, grinning.

"And the possibility of Melanie Masterson playing opposite you has nothing to do with that suggestion," she said, forcing the words out on a rush of air.

He tipped his head backward and let loose with a genuine laugh. "Nothing to do with it?"

She shoved his shoulder with one hand, hating that he'd caught her feeling any jealousy at all. "Almost nothing," she said.

"You need to know she was a fling," he told her.

"A long-lasting one though." She couldn't help but state facts and hope he'd fill her in some more.

He tipped his head to one side, studying her. "I was searching for something, trying to pretend she could fill a void. . . ." His voice trailed off.

His words reminded her of her own feelings about John and a distinct wave of guilt arose. She tamped it down. John had given her this time to figure things out, and from the look on his face, he already knew where her heart lay. She sighed and pushed thoughts of John out of her head, at least for a few more days. She'd promised herself this time and she needed to take it.

Meanwhile, Dylan sat waiting for her reply. "I get it more than you know," she murmured. "As for the movie, you have to know my opinion doesn't mean a thing. I don't know the business or the players. I don't even know how important commercial success is to you."

In short, Holly thought, she was on the outside of his life looking in. She felt like a complete fraud offering her opinion at all.

He stepped between her legs, his face inches from hers. "I beg to differ, babe."

His words caught her up short. "Why?"

"Because of all the people in this world, you know me. You get me. My agent was clicking his teeth at the money involved, and my publicist would kill to work on a project like this." He frowned, a testament to how few people in his inner circle had his own interests completely at heart.

"And it goes without saying that Melanie would like to lasso me and drag me kicking and screaming to the studio lot since it suits her needs. So I have no one to turn to except myself. And you. If I didn't want or trust your judgment, I wouldn't have asked."

"Oh." Her mouth had grown dry at his admission.

Her heart squeezed tight at the possibility that just maybe he was placing her in a position of importance in his life. She was too afraid to ask.

She'd rather reach out and enjoy *now* as she'd promised herself she'd do. And with him settled between her thighs, his lips inches from hers, he was in a prime position for her to do exactly that.

Chapter Five

Dylan had noticed the uncertainty in Holly's eyes from the moment she joined him in the kitchen. It wasn't him she mistrusted but the lure of his career. That's what had taken him away from her before. Damned if he knew how to convince her that she was exactly what he needed, not just in his life as a friend, but an integral part of it.

He didn't have time to think, let alone talk, any more, not when she was linking her ankles behind his back and pulling him deeper into the vee of her legs. Though the rational part of him knew she was using sex to escape serious discussion, desire flooded him, the need to be inside her again all-consuming.

"Holly," he said, trying to refocus her thoughts as well as his.

"Dylan," she mimicked, her hands sliding into the waistband of his jeans.

She pushed herself forward on the counter until she sat at the very edge and he was nestled between her thighs. He couldn't mistake her intent or her need. The warmth and heat emanating from her body called to him in a primitive way he couldn't mistake. His body throbbed, his erection thrusting against his jeans, and suddenly discussion could definitely wait.

Eyes glittering, she met his gaze. "You were saying?"

He shook his head. "It'll keep." His surprise would make a better gift given at the right time.

"I thought so. Now, how about letting me have my wicked way with you?" Her lips turned upward in a seductive grin.

He still wasn't used to this teasing side of her, but he sure liked it. "What'd you have in mind?"

She hopped down from the counter, and with deft hands, she opened his jeans. As he watched, his breath coming in shorter and shorter gasps, she pulled the denim over his hips and thighs. When they reached his ankles, he kicked the pants aside. His briefs quickly followed, and his freed erection sprang to life.

Pulse pounding, heart racing, he met her gaze. "What now?"

She patted the counter where she'd once sat. "Have a seat."

He complied, shivering when the Formica touched his bare skin. "Damn, that's cold."

"Don't worry. I have every intention of warming you," she said, her voice hot and thick. "Do you remember what my favorite ice cream topping is?"

He raised an eyebrow. "I'm guessing it's still that Marshmallow Fluff you were just eating."

She reached for the jar and brought it beside him. He glanced from the gooey white fluff to the wicked gleam in her eyes. "You wouldn't," he said, the blood rushing in his ears at the very thoughts soaring through his head.

"You don't think I would?" She dabbed her finger into the jar and slowly placed it into her mouth, sucking the creme from her finger with her tongue, grazing with her teeth, all her movements deliberately, seductively slow.

His erection throbbed harder and his mouth grew dry.

"Well?" she asked.

"I dare you," he said, using the words that had once provoked her into sneaking out of her house to meet him by the corner of her street so they could go make out in his car.

She met and held his stare for a brief moment before dipping her fingers into the jar. Drawing a deep breath, she coated the head of his erect penis with the Fluff. He'd wanted to watch, but as her fingers and the sticky substance touched his aching member, the sensation was too much. He leaned his head back against the cabinets and groaned aloud, knowing he was powerless and completely at her mercy.

Forcing his eyes open, he noticed that Holly was trembling, perhaps even more than Dylan, which told him a lot. Despite the playful teasing, she was deadly serious about him. He knew it in his gut.

Lowering her head, she bent and took him into her mouth, drawing him in deep. The moist warmth was nearly his undoing. He nearly came then, before she even began working him, but he managed to exercise control. He gripped the edge of the countertop hard with his fingertips, his head still resting against the cabinets, his body shaking with a restraint that lasted only until she began a steady, rhythmic sucking.

Her tongue licked the Fluff, licking at *him*, pulling, teasing up and down. She grazed the head of his penis with gentle teeth, then soothed long, luxurious laps of her tongue, never letting up. He was shaking even before his climax hit, and when it did, the sensation rocked him hard, wave after wave consuming him. Lost in the world she created, he came. And came. And came.

When he'd caught his breath, he opened his eyes to find her staring back at him. He cupped her head in his hands and looked into her warm, giving eyes.

"I love you, babe." He'd meant to kiss her. The words toppled out instead.

She straightened and took a step back. Dylan realized his mistake immediately. He'd spoken too soon, and he'd shaken her up badly. But before he could say a word to smooth things over, the telephone rang and she dove to answer it.

Cursing, he jumped down and pulled on his pants. He wanted to deal with her fully dressed and fix his mistake as quickly as possible before she withdrew even further.

Unfortunately, she returned from the phone call, reaching for her purse. "It's an emergency. I have to go."

She'd turned from his seductress to shaken woman to in-control doctor in seconds flat. He respected it. Respected her.

"Let me drive you." For selfish reasons he didn't want to be apart from her right now.

She gave a curt nod. "I don't have time to argue. Robert Hansen's five-year-old fell and hit his head on the corner of a table. He's got a huge gash, and there's lots of blood. I said I'd meet them at the hospital."

"Good thing I got dressed," he said, laughing.

Unfortunately, she didn't join in.

*   *   *

Holly had never been happy at someone else's expense and she wasn't about to start feeling that way now, but she couldn't deny she'd been so darn grateful for the phone call that had distracted her from Dylan's heartfelt words. Her heart pounded hard in her chest even now, as she filled out the last of the paperwork on Jason Hansen. The child had received stitches and had just narrowly missed hitting his eye on the table corner in his fall. He was one lucky little boy, she thought, signing her name and handing the clipboard in at the hospital desk.

Dylan waited for her in the lounge, where she'd have to face him and their shared afternoon. She'd started by using sex and foreplay as a distraction. A means of avoiding more serious discussion that might lead to him telling her he needed to return to L.A. But her deliberately seductive move had turned into a completely emotional one for her.

She'd wanted to give to him in a way he couldn't possibly forget. She wanted to be indelibly etched in his mind forever just as she knew that moment would be a permanent part of her, heart and soul. And now she had to live with the consequences.

She didn't doubt he loved her. It was his ability to do anything about his feelings that she didn't trust. His work would take him away from her, and the lifestyle in L.A. couldn't possibly compete with small-town life in Acton, Massachusetts. Sure, he said he was tired of the throngs of people and fans, tired of the phoniness in his world, but he'd wither and die here. And she refused to be the reason or the one he grew to resent.

Steeling herself for any discussion he might want to have, she walked back towards the small waiting room and strode through the double doors. There must have been a lull in traffic because the room was empty except for Dylan, who'd curled into the corner of the plastic couch and dozed off. A lock of his hair had fallen over his forehead, and his head rested against his balled-up leather jacket.

Her heart turned over at the sight, and she knelt down next to the couch. "Hey, sleepyhead." She nudged his arm and tried to wake him, but he'd always been a deep sleeper, so it took a few more tries before he finally jerked his head upward.

"Hey." He rubbed his eyes with his palms. "Are you all finished?"

She nodded.

"How's the kid?"

"Other than a few stitches, he's really lucky. But I doubt he'll be in the mood to wrestle with his brothers anytime soon."

Dylan laughed. "He's lucky to have you as his doctor." His voice sobered, and Holly sensed his serious mood return. "I watched you in action, you know."

Embarrassed, she shook her head. "Once I get started in an emergency, I don't see much else around me."

"I realized that." Holly's dedication and abilities hadn't come as a surprise to him, yet his respect for her had grown tremendously. And in an odd way, seeing her work had validated his decision to leave her behind all those years ago.

He rose and stretched out his muscles, which were cramped from being in one position for so long. "Are you ready to head home?"

"Uh, yeah." She seemed surprised.

They walked to the parking lot, and he slipped his arm around her shoulders. "I'm sure you're exhausted."

She nodded. "I could use a hot shower and a good night's sleep."

"Sounds like a definite plan," he murmured, and in case she wasn't sure what he meant, he nuzzled his lips against her neck and whispered what the two of them could do in that shower before she collapsed from exhaustion in her bed. With him by her side.

She laughed with him, her sexy way of agreeing to his idea. But she still seemed wary.

He guessed she was waiting for him to bring up

his comment in her kitchen earlier. He didn't plan on doing so. In fact, while alone here waiting, he'd decided to continue on as if nothing unusual had happened between them. He had little time before he had to return to L.A. for a meeting with his agent and a movie producer, which had nothing to do with superhero roles and everything to do with a part he was dying to tackle.

He wished he had the luxury of time to lay things out for Holly a little more slowly and with more care than he'd shown by blurting out his feelings in her kitchen. But what he didn't have in time, they more than made up for in emotional connection. Beyond that, Dylan had no choice but to let fate play itself out.

After their eventful night, Dylan and Holly slept late. They woke, made love and fell asleep again. The day passed in a delicious way and then they arrived at Dylan's mother's house. Dinner at the Northwood house was just like being back in high school, when life was simple and everything seemed rosy and good, Holly thought. She'd called her mother and aunt to say hi before going over to Dylan's. She missed her mother, but understood her aunt Rose had broken her hip and needed help and so Holly tried not to dwell on the emptiness of being without her own family during the holiday season. And once she arrived at Dylan's house, that emptiness began to be filled.

Dylan's mother had cooked dinner, and the house smelled delicious, warm and inviting. His sister, Amy, and her husband, Tom, and their young son, a precocious three-year-old named Matt, sat in the family room in front of the big-screen television Dylan had purchased for his mother's birthday. Typical males, Dylan and Tom talked football and took turns keeping the fire stoked and the room warm, while Amy and Matt provided the sounds of laughter and squabbling. Amy kept busy diving to keep Matt out of trouble near the hearth and away from an old black Lab that dozed in the corner and whose tail Matt liked to pull.

Holly, after being thrown out of the kitchen for attempting to help, finally settled in beside Dylan, trying desperately not to like the feeling of being part of this family too much. But how could she not enjoy and feel welcome when every so often Dylan would reach out and massage her shoulders or idly twist her hair around his finger as he talked. His family all treated her as if she belonged here, as if she and Dylan had never broken up or been apart.

But most defining for Holly was that here in his old home, Dylan's stardom and fame didn't exist, making it too easy for *her* to believe in a future. So much so that throughout dinner and dessert, she had to keep reminding herself that she'd succumbed to these fantasies once before and suffered nothing but heartache as a result.

By the time Dylan drove her home, she was stuffed from the good food and overwhelmed by memories and desire. When he turned and asked if he could come in, saying yes came as naturally to her as breathing.

Coming on top of the heavy-duty family scene, Dylan wanted to tread carefully now. Holly had relaxed in a way he hadn't seen since his return, and he didn't want to lose that mellow, comfortable mood.

"That was so nice." She dropped the keys onto the shelf in her front hall. "I love your family."

"Well, that's good, because they love you too." His gaze darted to hers, wondering if any version of the word *love* would put her on edge.

"Can I get you coffee or something to drink?"

He accepted the subject change with a nod. "A cup of coffee sounds great."

"Then make yourself at home." She smiled and gestured to the couch in the family room.

While she headed to make him coffee he didn't really need or want, he readied the room for just one of the surprises he had in store for Holly.

*　　*　　*

Thanks to a fast-brewing machine that made four cups of coffee at a time, Holly had coffee ready for herself and Dylan pretty quickly. She knew he liked his black, so she added milk and sugar for herself and walked back into her family room.

Instead of the bright space she'd left behind, Dylan had transformed the room. He'd shut off the overhead lights and turned on a small lamp in the corner along with the multicolored bulbs on her Christmas tree. From her small CD player, uplifting holiday music filled the air around them, while Dylan sat on the couch with a small wrapped box in his hand.

From across the room, she felt the heat of his stare branding her much like his heated touch. God, he was sexy. No doubt every woman who saw a similar pose from the pages of a magazine dreamed of him staring at her, wanting her, only having eyes for *her*.

He was every woman's fantasy, and for this short span of time he belonged to her. She was lucky, but she wasn't deluded by his fame. She had enough self-respect to believe that for as long as Dylan was with her, he was lucky too.

She walked inside and set the cups down on the table. "I like the atmosphere," she said softly, grateful for the thoughtful gesture.

He grinned. "I did the best with what I had." He

Carly Phillips

toyed with the ribbon on the small box, rubbing the satin back and forth between his fingers, in the same way he'd massaged certain parts of her body with gentle yet arousing care.

She swallowed hard, searching for a distraction. "What's in the box?"

"Part of your Christmas gift."

"It's early! I didn't know we were going to exchange gifts tonight. Mine isn't even wrapped yet." She had something special for him when they'd separated the day they'd been in Boston. She hadn't decided when to give it to him.

He stood and grasped her hand, pulling her down beside him on the couch. "I want you to have this and I don't want anything from you in exchange."

"Not even if it's the watch you were eyeing in the store window?" She tipped her head to the side and looked at him through not-so-innocent eyes.

He shook his head. "You noticed that? Man, you are something else. Want to know what my—what Melanie got me for Christmas last year?"

She stiffened, but he held on tightly to her hands.

"No, but something tells me you're going to tell me anyway."

"She bought me a weekend for two at a spa. Seaweed wraps, facials and full-body massages." He grimaced, his disgust with her gift evident even now, a year later.

Holly burst out laughing, her nerves over the mention of Melanie giving way to complete shock and amusement. "She really doesn't know you at all."

"No, she doesn't. Not like *we* know each other." He held out the gift box. "It's sentimental, not expensive," he said, his voice dropping low. His tone held a hint of embarrassment.

She couldn't help but smile. "I'm not looking for anything expensive. I wasn't looking for anything at all."

"I know, but this is something I want you to have." He rose and began pacing the room. Obviously something was on his mind, so she set the box aside until he could explain.

"About a month ago, I dreamed about you. Nothing unusual—I always dream about you."

Her breath caught in her throat. "You do?"

"Yeah. That time I dreamed about us exchanging gifts on Christmas Eve, and I was determined to make that dream come true again. As soon as possible."

Despite her resolve to remain strong, her throat swelled and her heart began pounding hard in her chest. "So you really came back for me?"

"I told you I did." He jerked his head towards his gift. "Open it."

She did as he asked, untying the bow and ripping off the paper. The white box was generic without a hint of what was inside. Curious, she pulled off the top and peeked inside. Her breath caught in her throat, and she lifted the gift gently in her hands.

"The angel I bought your family for their tree," she said, memories swamping her. "You're giving it back to me?"

He knelt beside her. "It's all in how you look at things, babe. I want you to hold on to this and think of why I'd give it to you, okay? How it could im-pact *us*." He took the angel from her hand and placed it on the table.

Then he swept her into his arms and into the bedroom.

Christmas Day, Holly awoke feeling warm and sated, and she tingled all over. She'd never felt as cherished and cared for as she had when Dylan had made love to her last night.

She closed her eyes and let herself remember. His warm body melding with hers, his eyes warm and giving. Most of all, she recalled the absolute feeling of fulfillment as he came inside her.

She rolled over to glance at the clock on the nightstand but the first thing she saw was her angel instead. They'd never put it on the tree, she thought. That was something they'd get to later on, she hoped, because she already sensed Dylan had left again this morning. Knowing Dylan, since he was home for a short visit, she felt sure he'd gone to see his mother.

She felt just as certain he'd be back.

Lying alone in her bed gave her time to think, maybe for the first time since Dylan's surprise visit to her office. As she let *all* her feelings wash over her, her first thought wasn't of Dylan, but of John. It wasn't so much guilt she felt as a heaviness in her heart because he was a wonderful man. But there would be time to deal with her feelings for John soon enough. Right now, she had a rare morning off and she intended to enjoy it by lounging in bed and not thinking of problems or possible solutions.

She reached for the television remote and turned on one of the morning shows, caught one segment, then dozed through the weather. She woke up again just as an entertainment reporter was dishing on the latest buzz from Hollywood.

She watched the list of stars who celebrated birthdays and heard the latest scandals before a picture on the screen caught Holly's attention. Actress Melanie Masterson's beautiful face flashed before Holly's eyes.

Curious despite herself, and compelled to watch, she sat up straighter in bed and raised the volume.

"Ms. Masterson issued a statement through her publicist announcing a New Year's Day wedding to her on-again, off-again boyfriend, Dylan North," the reporter said.

Holly pulled her knees up and wrapped her arms around her legs.

"Neither Dylan North nor his representative was available for comment, but this reporter happened to see them at a party earlier this year and they were glued together. Whatever caused their breakup obviously wasn't serious enough to keep them apart in the coming year. Diane, back to you."

Holly shook her head. "No way," she said to the television screen.

Melanie might be beautiful, but she didn't understand Dylan, not the way Holly did. And though Dylan loved his career, he wouldn't settle for a shadow of the type of woman he wanted. Then there was the fact that he'd been in Holly's bed last night. Not Melanie's. The other woman obviously had an agenda. Still, Dylan wasn't here with Holly now, and this unsettling news did nothing to relax her.

She'd lost her luxurious morning in bed, and she yanked the comforter down, rose from bed and headed for the kitchen. If nothing else, coffee would get her day back on track.

No sooner had she reached the kitchen than her telephone rang, and she snatched up the receiver. "Hello?"

"Hi, babe."

On hearing Dylan's voice, her spirits soared. "Dylan!"

"Good morning," he said gruffly.

She felt herself smile. "Good morning to you too."

"Do you have any idea how much I wanted to be there when you woke up?"

His deep voice caused a distinct warmth to settle low in her stomach. "I think I can imagine. Why'd you leave so early?"

"I went to see my mother. We have so little time, and I knew she'd appreciate a quick Christmas visit. I planned on being back before you even woke up. But—"

She gripped the receiver tight in her hand. "But what?"

"I got a call and I have to catch a flight to L.A. I'm at the airport now."

Her stomach, which had just fluttered with warmth and desire, now plummeted in disappointment. "Does it have to do with Melanie?" she asked coolly, deliberately keeping any emotion out of her voice.

"Not in the way you think. It has more to do with the movie role."

Holly drew a deep breath and tried to understand. "The role you decided not to take? Or did you change your mind?"

"No, I didn't change my mind, but the director isn't someone I want to alienate, and my agent suggested we meet with him right away and discuss it face-to-face. When I factor in travel time, I needed to leave today to make the meeting tomorrow."

She nodded. "And Melanie?"

"Wants me to take the role, and she'll do anything to get me back to L.A. to convince me," he said grimly.

"Including announcing a New Year's wedding?" Holly asked.

He muttered a succinct curse. "You know about that?"

"It was on the morning news."

His voice was cut off by an airport announcement.

"What did you say?" she asked.

"My plane's boarding. I said to remember what I told you about believing newspaper articles." She heard the pleading tone in his voice.

"I remembered." She let out a strained laugh.

"I have to go, but Holly?"

She shut her eyes and leaned against the wall. "Yeah?"

"I love you, and *I will be back.*"

"Bye, Dylan." For Holly, the trick was to find the strength and courage to believe him.

Chapter Six

Holly skipped breakfast and spent the rest of the morning playing Santa, dropping gifts off for friends and family, taking her time before returning home. When the doorbell rang, it caught her by surprise.

"Hi, Nicole." Holly forced a smile.

"That's a really grumpy 'hi' on Christmas! Good thing I came with something to make you smile." Nicole strode inside, carrying a large shopping bag.

"Let's go sit." Holly gestured towards the family room. "I stopped by your apartment, but you weren't home," she said as they settled in.

"That's because I was coming here." Nicole curled her legs Indian style beneath her, making herself at home.

Gesturing to the bag, she said, "I wanted to find a way to thank you for being so good to me since I moved here. So I made you this." She reached into the bag and pulled out a gorgeous, handmade blanket in a variety of earth-tone colors to match Holly's family room.

"Oh I *love* it. Thank you." Holly hugged her friend tight. "That was so thoughtful. I didn't know you knit!"

"My grandmother taught me."

Holly smiled. "Well, I have your present right here." She jumped up and pulled Nicole's gift from beneath her tree. "It's store bought and practical," she said sheepishly. "And nothing as beautiful as this." She fingered the soft wool, curling it between her fingers.

Nicole opened a box and pulled out a Tiffany key ring with her initial. On the key ring was a key to the office. "I thought you'd want more freedom to come and go as you please once you have the title of office manager," Holly said, hoping her friend would be pleased with the gifts.

Nicole's eyes grew wide. "Me? Office manager?"

Holly nodded. "With my new partner starting soon and him bringing in his patients from the next town over, we need a full-fledged manager. I talked to Lance—Dr. Tollgate—and he agreed to a promotion and a raise. Merry Christmas," she told her friend.

Nicole squealed and hugged Holly tight. "You're the best. Thank you."

"You're welcome."

"Okay, now that the gifts are over, where's the man?" Growing serious, she glanced around the room, obviously looking for Dylan.

"He's in L.A. Or should I say on his way back to L.A."

Nicole frowned. "That snake. I thought you had more time together."

"Something came up."

"You seem okay with it?" Nicole tipped her head to the side, questioning.

"It's not like I have a choice. Look, he lives in L.A. His career is there. His life is there. Mine is here. It's not like we could make a relationship work anyway. Assuming he even wanted something serious."

"Does he?"

"I don't know."

"Do you?"

Holly stood and arranged the blanket over one end of the couch. The colors complemented the room beautifully, and she smiled. "This is gorgeous."

"And you're avoiding my question."

Holly laughed. "That's my prerogative, isn't it?"

Nicole rolled her eyes. "You're going to have to figure things out eventually or you'll make yourself crazy. I need to get going." She rose and started for the door, and Holly followed. "What are you doing for dinner?"

"No real Christmas plans. Want to come back here and we'll have girls' night?"

"Now, that's the best offer I've had in a long time." Nicole hugged her tight. "What about this afternoon?"

"I need to see John."

Nicole sighed in understanding. "I don't envy you."

"I owe him answers." And she owed herself a lot more.

It was time to face her fears once and for all.

Later that day, Holly drove to John's and knocked on his door.

He greeted her warmly, looked into her eyes and said, "Why do I have the distinct feeling you aren't here with the news I was hoping for?"

She studied him with a fresh, new perspective. His gorgeous green gaze and handsome face would have a smarter woman than her swooning. God, she wished she were smarter because then her life would be so much less complicated.

"Can we talk?" she asked.

He gestured inside with a sweep of his arm, and once they were seated on the leather couch in his spacious den, Holly mustered her courage. "You're such a good man," she said softly.

"But you don't love me."

She shook her head. "Not the way you deserve." And the signs had been there all along. She had never given to him physically or emotionally the way she gave herself to Dylan. Oh, she had tried hard to convince herself she could love John, but the truth is she didn't. She couldn't.

She loved Dylan, and no other man would do. "I'm just so sorry it took me so long to—"

"Don't say you're sorry." He cut her off. "I'm not sorry for the time we had, and I know I learned a lot about myself. Especially about my patience level. It's too damn high," he said with a self-deprecating laugh.

Holly laughed with him before covering his hand with hers. "There's something you need to know though. While we were together I never consciously thought we couldn't have a future because of Dylan."

"I knew that or else I would have given you an ultimatum much sooner. I take it you two are back together?"

"I don't know what we are." She grimaced, unsure how to explain. "He went back to L.A.," she said, deciding that since he was asking, she'd talk to John. Old habits, she mused. They *had* been close, and she'd always confided in him.

"I caught the morning's news," he said, the implication clear.

Besides, Holly knew they watched the same channel. "Interesting stuff, huh?" She ducked her head in embarrassment.

"Is it true?" John touched her shoulder, forcing her to look up, then pinned her with his steady gaze.

"No." She shook her head. "No, it's not."

"You trust Dylan enough to say that with such certainty?"

She nodded, no hesitation in her heart.

"Then why are you in such a bad mood?" John leaned back against the couch, relaxing as they talked like old friends.

Which they were, she thought, feeling more settled than she had in a while. And he was right. She was in an awful mood.

"It sounds like you two finally have everything going for you, no?"

"Yes. No. I don't know. He lives in L.A. Not only is it across the country, but his lifestyle, the people in it, they're Hollywood. I'm small town. What kind of chance do we have?" she asked, expressing all of her doubts and fears.

Not all, a tiny voice in her head chided her.

"Listen to me," John said. "You have exactly the kind of chance that you *want*. If you're looking for excuses to bail on Dylan, I know you can be the master of avoidance. But if you want a future, you're going to have to trust him."

"I do!" She narrowed her gaze. "Didn't I just finish telling you I was certain the gossip about Melanie isn't true?"

"And that's a start. It's just not everything. When's he due back?"

She shrugged. "He didn't say. He just promised he'd return."

"Then I guess it's up to you whether you believe him or you're going to let one mistake the guy made ten years ago ruin any future you two *could* have." In that one sentence, John nailed Holly's last remaining fear.

That Dylan would up and leave her again the way he had before. The last time, he didn't know what he was running to. He had only the idea of fame and fortune beckoning to him. Now, ten years later, he knew what kind of lifestyle awaited him in Hollywood. He was America's favorite movie star.

For how long would he be content with his hometown girl?

She blinked, her eyes burning. "When did you get to be so wise?" she asked John.

"About the time I realized we were over." His lips pulled into a thin tight line.

She had to bite the inside of her cheek to keep from apologizing again. "What about you?" She asked. "Are you going to be okay?"

He nodded with certainty. "I definitely saw this coming. I've been thinking about moving to Boston," he said, surprising her.

"Really?"

"Yep. There's more of a social life there, and since I do want to settle down with the right person, I need more exposure."

"I think the women in the city had better watch out," she said, laughing.

He winked at her, assuring her that he really was going to be just fine.

Would she? Her heart caught in her chest because she realized she *would* miss him as her friend. "I admire you for making the decision and going after what you want in life."

He brushed a kiss on her cheek. "I'd like to be able to say the same thing about you. Think about what I just said, Holly."

She forced a smile. "I will."

In the coming days, with Dylan gone, she'd have plenty of time to focus on her life and make a decision about whether she was ready to put her heart on the line again. Or whether she could live with herself if she chose not to even try.

*   *   *

Three days passed in which Holly kept busy. She saw patients and readied the office for her new partner. She'd been using the extra room for personal storage, and she needed to clear her things out before the first of the year, when Dr. Tollgate started working. After tackling the boxes and moving them into her own office, she began dusting the bookshelves and desk. She found that keeping busy also helped her think. Office cleaning was akin to clearing her mind and facing what she needed and wanted out of life. What she wanted from Dylan.

He had called her two or three times a day since he'd been gone, testament to his desire to prove he'd changed. That he wasn't leaving her behind—if not without a thought, then without another word for ten years. She didn't know what more he had in mind for them, but she understood that she had to come to terms with her own feelings before he returned.

She shook her head. Her feelings weren't the issue. She loved Dylan. The problem lay with her insecurity. John had called her on it, and she knew he was right.

The door chimes startled her. Wondering if there was an emergency, she headed for the outer room to see who was there. She opened the door, looked around but saw no one. She was about to go back inside when she glanced down. A large manila envelope sat at her door. Inside was a map, a set of directions to what appeared to be someplace about half an hour outside of town and a note. In Dylan's handwriting.

Heart pounding, she stepped back into the office so she could read the letter to herself aloud. "I promised I'd be back, and here I am." She licked her dry lips before continuing. "I can't change the past, but I hope to alter the future. Stop running and meet me. If you dare."

If she dared. She shook her head, laughing and trembling at the same time. Leave it to Dylan to challenge her in the most basic way.

It was simple really. Either she trusted or she didn't. Melanie's fake announcement and her own reaction to it had proven to Holly that she believed in him. Now it was time to question whether she trusted *herself*.

Before now she'd never have pegged herself as an insecure person. Yet she was forced to admit that when it came to men and relationships, she was a complete weenie, and those insecurities dated back to Dylan's departure ten years ago. After he left, she had thrown herself into her studies. Once she'd recovered and started dating again, she'd chosen safe men, none of whom affected her emotions and none of whom gave her that sexual zing she felt with Dylan. They were all good, decent men but posed no threat to her heart.

But now Dylan was back, and he was definitely a threat, not just to the heart she'd taken such good care of, but to everything she'd become as a person. She'd always considered herself confident and capable; after all, she was a doctor who'd been making decisions about her patients for years. What about herself and choices on her own behalf?

She glanced down at the note in her shaking hands. *Stop running and meet me. If you dare.*

Did she dare? She could easily offer Dylan North her heart and maybe even trust in his promise to handle both it and her with care. But was she secure enough in herself to believe she could hold on to him this time?

There it was, her biggest fear exposed.

She could run and never know the happiness she felt certain Dylan could provide, or she could shut the door on the past forever and believe in herself at last. Holly closed the extra office door, and aware of the symbolism, she locked it up tight.

Then she straightened her shoulders, decision made. Damn straight she was secure enough to handle Dylan now. If not, she wasn't the person she thought she was.

And she'd worked too hard and come too far not

to believe in the woman Dr. Holly Evans had become.

Snow covered the ground and big flakes began to fall. The longer Dylan stood on the property he'd own as soon as the legalities had been finalized, the more time he had to convince himself that Holly wouldn't show.

He trusted Nicole to deliver the directions, so he didn't think that was the problem. No, if anything, Holly was still unsure whether she could believe in him again. He'd done everything in his power to convince her. The decision was hers to make.

He rubbed his hands together and shoved them into his jacket pocket. Closing his eyes, he envisioned the house he wanted to build on this land. The only thing was that when he pictured a wife to come home to, it was Holly he saw there. Their children playing in the yard.

In his heart he knew she shared those dreams, and he couldn't make himself believe she'd let *them* down.

"Hi, Dylan."

At first he thought he was imagining the sound of her soft voice until he opened his eyes. She stood before him bundled in a puffy down jacket, scarf and a hat with a small brim. Her eyes were wide and curious.

He was just damn glad to see her. "Hey, babe. Merry Christmas."

She smiled before she shocked him big-time by throwing herself into his arms. Dylan wasn't stupid, and he held on tight. "I missed you," he whispered in her ear.

"I missed you too." She stepped back and studied his face. "Where are we?"

This was it, he thought. The beginning or the end. "It's home." He gestured around the wide expanse of land. "Five acres of grass and trees. Of course, it needs a house and some other necessary things, like a dog and a few kids."

He tried to shoot her a cocky grin but failed. Everything he wanted out of life was on the line, and for the first time, his charm, looks and fame couldn't give it to him.

Only she could.

A dog? Kids? "Home?" Holly asked, stunned.

She blinked and glanced around. The land looked the same as much of the landscape she'd passed while driving out here. A beautiful white landscape covered in snow and ice while the sun shone overhead.

"I own it, or I will once the contract is signed. Actually—" He paused, obviously uncomfortable.

Her heart thudded so loud she was surprised he couldn't hear. He'd bought land here?

"Actually what?" Her voice cracked, she was so afraid of what came next. It was ridiculous being afraid of happiness, but it had been so long since she'd dared to hope or dream.

"Actually, I want us to own it. You and me." He grabbed on to her hands and held them in front of her. "I want to live here and raise our kids here."

"What about L.A.? Your life? Your career?"

He smiled, but it didn't reach his eyes. "I've thought this through, you know. This wasn't an impulse buy. I want you to take some time off and come with me to L.A., so you can see my life and friends for yourself. I want you to be a part of everything that I do."

She swallowed hard, daring to believe. Meeting him here had been the first step. Now she listened with an open heart as well as an open mind. "Go on."

"Then we come back here to live. I'll leave only for movie shoots and, honest to God, I'd planned on cutting back. Doing only what appeals to me creatively because financially I'm already set for life. I'll be here with you as often as I can, and you'll come to me when you can take the time. *We* can make this work. You just need to believe."

Tears dripped down her cheeks, practically turning to ice before they fell. She grasped his face in her hands and looked into his gorgeous blue eyes.

"You have no idea what your leaving the first time did to me. I withdrew, Dylan. I didn't get involved with another man who I thought could hurt me the way you did."

A muscle ticked in his jaw as he listened and replied. "I'm not sure I like where this is headed."

"Shh." She placed her finger over his lips. "You need to hear this as much as I need to say it."

He nodded slowly.

"But I also realize now that there isn't another man who could hurt me that way because there's no one I could ever love the way I love you."

He sucked in a deep breath, and when he released it, a puff of white hovered in the air. "I love you too. I never stopped, not even after I left."

"I know that now."

He brushed at her tears. "We were so young, and I was so stupid."

She shook her head. "We needed to follow the paths we did. It made us who we are."

"And who are we?" he asked.

"Two people who found their way back to each other." She laughed. "Or rather, you found me again. Either way I'm not stupid enough to turn you away." She pulled him into a long, deep kiss, savoring the warmth of his mouth and how he devoured her, as if he could never get enough.

She knew she'd never get enough of him.

Too soon, he pulled back. "You realize there'll be times I'm gone for weeks, maybe months at a time?"

She nodded.

"And you need to trust that while I'm gone, I'm still with you in here." He patted the place above his heart. "You have to know I'll be back, and you need to remember there's no one else but you." His deep gaze never left hers. "No matter what you see, hear or read. Can you do that?"

She nodded again. "Dylan, I love you. It's always been you. And not only do I trust you with my heart, I trust you to remind me not to be an idiot if those old insecurities ever arise." Because she was only human and understood she couldn't promise not to be.

Dylan met her gaze, and in her eyes, he saw everything he was, everything he desired and everything he wanted to be. "Babe, I can do that. I can do anything as long as I have you. And that angel I gave back to you? It was because I want it to top *our* tree. Because you're my Midnight Angel."

She grinned and planted a kiss on his lips. One that was warm, hot, giving and went on and on and on. . . .

Epilogue

New England Express
Daily Dirt Column

(Taken from *Entertainment Weekly*) Hollywood heartthrob Dylan North tied the knot on New Year's Day, but not with his former flame, Melanie Masterson, as previously reported. Ms. Masterson was secluded on an island retreat while Dylan North wed hometown girl and first love, Dr. Holly Evans. The two pulled off the coup of the new year, marrying in a private ceremony at a small catering hall called Whipporwill's in Acton, Massachusetts. As of now, details are sketchy, but this reporter was promised an exclusive, complete with wedding photographs of the bride and groom after they return from their honeymoon. One guest who couldn't contain her excitement reported that the desserts were all topped with Marshmallow Fluff.

Stay tuned as more information becomes available.

New York Times bestselling author Carly Phillips is an attorney who has tossed away legal briefs in favor of writing sexy, fun romances. Her first contemporary romance, *The Bachelor*, captured a spot as a Reading with Ripa Bookclub pick on *Live with Regis and Kelly*, launching her onto all the major bestseller lists. Since her first sale in 1998, Carly has sold a total of twenty-one books and continues to delight readers with her lively, fun characters. Carly lives in Purchase, New York, with her husband, two young daughters and frisky wheaton terrier who acts like their third child. When she's not with her family, you can find Carly writing, promoting and playing online! To contact Carly or for more information on this quickly rising star of romance, visit her Web site at www.carlyphillips.com.

MEET ME
AT MIDNIGHT

Janelle Denison

To Carly Phillips. It's always a pleasure to work on a project with you, and this anthology was no exception!

To Dave and Laurie Pyke, for being perfect examples of how best friends can become soul mates for life.

To my best friend, Don. I'll love you always.

Chapter One

"I've made my New Year's resolution. Care to hear what it is?"

Shane Witmer glanced up from the pepperoni-and-mushroom pizza he was sharing with his best friend, Alyssa Harte, as they sat in a booth in the back of his casual restaurant, The Pizza Joint. Having known Alyssa since they both were five years old, he'd learned long ago how to read her moods and expressions. This afternoon there was a determination about her that he'd seen many times before, and when Alyssa put her mind to something, she usually accomplished her goal.

"New Year's isn't for another four days," he pointed out as he reached for a napkin. "I've never known you to make an early resolution. What's up with that?"

"I thought I'd get a jump on things." Shrugging casually, she picked a pepperoni slice off her pizza, popped it into her mouth, then licked her fingers slowly, thoroughly, sensually. It was a habit she wasn't even aware of, any more than she realized the stimulating reaction all that licking and lapping of her tongue had on Shane's mind and body.

Swallowing hard, he forcibly pushed those too arousing thoughts from his head before they got him into trouble. Instead, he watched as she finished off the thick, doughy crust and reached for another slice. "Considering how you're enjoying your dinner, I'm guessing your resolution can't be about giving up pizza and Diet Coke like you've tried in the past," he teased.

She grinned indulgently, her blue eyes dancing with amusement. "No," she replied. "We both know that's a hopeless cause," and she took a big bite of her second piece.

Shane shook his head and chuckled. He loved her appetite and the way she enjoyed food, even if she did complain that everything she put into her mouth went straight to her hips, thighs, and butt. He thought her full breasts, lush hips, and shapely bottom were perfectly proportioned—not that he'd ever managed to convince her of that fact. She also had an innate sensuality about her that was subtle, but powerfully effective to his senses.

To him, Alyssa possessed the kind of real, womanly curves that drew a man's eyes—his gaze especially, but only when he knew for certain she wouldn't catch him admiring her voluptuous body. *Best friends* didn't do that sort of thing. He'd spent years keeping his real feelings for her buried beneath a facade of brotherly affection, a feat that was becoming more and more difficult with each year that passed.

She exhaled a resigned breath, though she was still smiling. "I've come to accept that pizza and Diet Coke are the two vices I just can't live without."

"Then I guess that means you can't live without me, because I supply the free pizza." She came by his pizza place at least a few times a week for lunch or dinner, and whenever the restaurant had any overruns on pizzas or pasta orders he dropped them by her apartment on his way home.

"You know I wouldn't be able to live without you, no matter what," she said, using the back of her hand to push away the curly blond strands of hair fluttering against her cheek. "Free food aside, you'll always be my best friend. You know all my secrets."

He laughed at that, but it was true for him as well. He'd known Alyssa for more than twenty of his twenty-six years, and from the day her family had moved into the house next to his and they'd become neighbors, he and she had been constant companions. It wasn't just that neither of them had any siblings and there hadn't been any other young children on their block. From the beginning, there'd been something special between them, a genuine closeness.

"So, let's hear this resolution of yours," he said, putting their conversation back on track and trying to ignore the way his libido stirred once again when she absently licked a smear of sauce from her bottom lip. He was also curious to know what kind of mission she'd decided upon for the coming year.

She tipped her chin up a few notches, that fortitude he'd seen moments ago flaring to life in the depths of her gaze again. "I've made the decision that this year is going to be about opening myself up to a *real* relationship with a guy, instead of breaking up with him when things start getting too intense or serious. I've got to get over being afraid of putting myself out there emotionally and getting hurt in the end."

"Okay," he said slowly, more than a little surprised by her admission. And unsettled as well.

Ever since Alyssa had started dating in high school she'd never allowed herself to get seriously involved with any man—a defense mechanism that he'd always suspected stemmed from issues surrounding her mother's inability to get past the death of Alyssa's father. It was a subject she didn't like to talk about, and therefore he knew there was much more to that emotional issue than she let on.

He leaned back in the booth and regarded her thoughtfully, wondering at the source of this very serious decision of hers. "So, what brought all this about?"

She met his gaze steadily from across the table. "I've been doing a lot of thinking lately, and I've come to realize that while I'm finally financially stable and I love my job of being a personal shopper, my personal life sucks. And it's my own fault, because up to this point I've been so commitment-phobic."

Grinning wryly, she dropped her napkin on her plate, pushed it aside, and went on. "I keep feeling like there's something important missing from my life, and I think I've figured out what it is."

Shane didn't care for the direction this conversation was heading. He felt his stomach churn with unease. "What's that?"

"Most of our friends are getting married, settling down and having families of their own, and I realize that I want that, too. I really do. I don't want to spend the rest of my life alone, like my mother has."

"And that means opening yourself up when it comes to an intimate relationship," he said. He knew she was much better about expressing her hopes, dreams, and feelings with him than with her dates, but he also knew she believed that as her best friend, he posed no real threat to her heart or emotions. Then again, she had no idea how he truly felt about her. He knew that if she ever found out, he would stand to lose the close friendship he cherished.

Bracing his arms on the table, he tried to keep his own feelings out of the equation. "So, the big question is, are you ready to put yourself out there in an intimate and emotional way?"

"I guess I'm willing to try, and that's what my New Year's resolution is all about," she said quietly as her fingers wiped away the condensation on her glass of Diet Coke. "It's past time for me to finally get over my fears and insecurities, or else I'm going to end up an old maid."

She grimaced at that notion and shook her head in dismay, which had the alluring effect of tousling those tempting spiral curls of hers over her shoulders. Her soft, lustrous hair was the object of some of his hottest fantasies, the kind that had him imagining how those silky strands would feel clutched tightly in his fists in the throes of passion . . . or caressing his heated skin as she moved above him, over him . . .

"So, enough about me and my pathetic love life," she said, waving a hand in the air between them and snapping him out of his erotic daydream. "What do *you* have in mind for a New Year's resolution?"

He couldn't even begin to wrap his mind around that particular question, especially since he was still reeling from her announcement—and how her decision might affect *them* and their relationship. *His* biggest fear was that he could lose her to another man. For good. And that possibility settled in his belly like a cold, hard knot.

She was watching him expectantly, waiting to hear what kind of changes were in store for him for the New Year. But he had no clue—and told her so. "You know, I haven't given my resolution much thought."

"Well, you should." Reaching across the table, she gave his arm an affectionate squeeze. "We need to make this next year one we'll both remember."

He was now certain it was going to be one he'd never forget, no matter what the outcome. "Tell you what. I'll give my resolution some thought and get back to you on what I come up with."

She stacked their empty plates and placed them on the small pizza tray. "Well, do it quick, because New Year's is only four days away, as you pointed out."

Shane laughed at her insistence, knowing she'd be hounding him about a resolution until he came up with one. "I hear ya. You'll be the first to know what's in store for me for the New Year."

"By the way, I received an invitation to Drew and Cynthia's annual New Year's Eve bash," she said, mentioning their mutual friends who'd recently gotten married. "I've already RSVP'd. How about you?"

He nodded. "Already done."

"Good." She grinned, her eyes taking on an optimistic glimmer. "Who knows? New Year's Eve could bring all kinds of surprises for the two of us."

Before he could reply to that, one of his waitresses came up to their table, interrupting his conversation with Alyssa. Shane was grateful for the distraction, since he didn't want to think about what kind of *surprises* were in store for his best friend, especially if it meant her pursuing the opposite sex in her quest to find a candidate for marriage.

"Shane, we need some change for the register," his employee said, gathering up the dirty dishes and silverware to take to the kitchen on her trip back.

"I'll be right there." Sliding out of the booth, he stood and glanced at Alyssa. "Can I bring you a piece of cheesecake?"

"How about one to go?" she said, not one to refuse dessert of any sort. "Work awaits me at home. I have some billing statements I need to get done for the jobs I did for the holidays."

After taking care of getting the cash for the register, Shane packed up a generous portion of cheesecake for Alyssa and gave it to her in a handled paper bag. Since it was dark outside, he walked her to her car and placed a chaste kiss on her cheek—wishing like hell that he had the right to claim that luscious mouth of hers in the kind of deep, fiery kiss that would brand and possess her and no doubt shock her senseless.

He watched her slide behind the wheel and blew out a taut breath that did nothing to ease his frustration. He summoned one of his easygoing smiles. "Be careful going home."

"I will be." She buckled herself in and started the engine of her practical Chevy Malibu. "Good night, Shane."

" 'Night." He closed the car door, waited for her to pull out of the parking lot, then made his way back into The Pizza Joint and walked to his office.

He sat down behind his desk, but instead of immersing himself in the stack of paperwork that needed his attention, he leaned back in his chair and scrubbed a hand along his jaw, wondering what the hell he was going to do now that Alyssa was so determined to put herself on the market and find Mr. Right.

For years he'd watched her date guy after guy, mostly stuffy corporate types who looked visually appealing but were much too staid for her vibrant personality. That made them very easy for Alyssa to break up with when the relationship showed signs of developing into anything significant. Alyssa's predictable behavior also made it easy for him to sit on the sidelines and be the loyal best friend she could always depend on, through good times and bad.

A part of him didn't think she'd be able to follow through with her resolution to open herself up to a guy emotionally . . . *but what if she did?* Tonight he'd seen the yearning in her eyes, the loneliness, the desire to give a real and stable committed relationship a try. Would she latch on to the next man to come into her life just because she desperately wanted marriage and a family of her own?

That possibility was enough to make him realize that he wasn't prepared to lose Alyssa to another man.

Not now.

Not ever.

And that meant it was time for him to make his feelings and intentions known—but in a gradual, subtle way that wouldn't scare her off.

A slow smile curved the corners of his mouth as an idea formed in his mind. What better way to attract Alyssa's attention than to enlist her help in turning him into the kind of sophisticated executive type who normally caught her eye and make her see that *he* was everything she was looking for in a mate?

As a personal shopper, she wouldn't be able to resist making him over; it was right up her alley. Granted, he'd always been a jeans-and-T-shirt kind of guy, and while he preferred his casual, no-nonsense attire and finger-combed hair, he wasn't opposed to changing his image if it would show Alyssa that he was the one for her—from his outward appearance to the deep emotional bond they'd always shared.

And that's when his resolution came to him. He was finally going after the girl of his dreams. And by midnight on New Year's Eve at the party that they'd both be attending, there would be no doubt in Alyssa's mind exactly how he felt about her.

Sitting in front of the computer in the small office she'd made from the spare bedroom in her apartment, Alyssa ate the last bite of the cheesecake that Shane had sent home with her, then returned her attention to finishing up the final billing statement that wrapped up the Christmas season.

December had been a great month profit-wise, and her business as a personal shopper was definitely prospering beyond her initial expectations. Her clients ranged from large corporations that needed holiday gifts for their employees and exclusive clientele list, to busy executives who didn't have time to purchase presents for their high-end accounts and colleagues, to some of Southern California's wealthier social set who were looking for that special something for friends and family members.

In the past year she'd expanded her business to include shopping for charity events, weddings, and elaborate parties and preparing gift bags for special events such as award banquets and conferences. Between perusing the Internet and hitting the local malls for specifically requested items, she was constantly busy and always challenged.

She'd long ago decided that the best part about her job was shopping until she dropped while spending someone else's money—especially since she was frugal and very practical with her own cash. She had grown up without her father, and her mother's job as a secretary had brought in only a very modest income, so there hadn't been much left over for anything frivolous. Alyssa had become thrifty by nature, which accounted for the nice nest egg she'd accumulated over the past few years.

But as she'd confided in Shane earlier that evening, despite her success with her own business there was something lacking in her life. She was gradually coming to recognize the longing to give herself over to one special person, to be able to come home to a husband and a family of her own. As much as she feared letting any man get too close emotionally because she'd witnessed her own mother's pain and heartache when her father had died, at the age of twenty-six Alyssa knew it was time for her to get past those insecurities. Hence her New Year's resolution to open herself up to the possibility of a committed relationship with the right guy.

The right guy. That thought made her think of her best friend, Shane. She smiled, because he exemplified everything she was looking for in a lifelong companion. Not only did he possess gorgeous good looks, a devastatingly charming grin, and a sometimes flirtatious personality, but he was levelheaded, insightful, always dependable, and she absolutely loved being with him. He was the standard by which she'd judged all the men she'd dated over the years, which was most likely why they'd all fallen short.

Leaning back in her chair, Alyssa closed her eyes. Shane's sexy image was already there in her mind—from his roguishly long brown hair, to those rich, seductive brown eyes of his, to that lean, athletically toned body that made him all male. Her pulse quickened, and she immediately snapped her eyes open before her sensual thoughts could drift into more forbidden territory.

She pressed a hand to her rapidly beating heart, wishing that other men had the same breathtaking effect on her as Shane did. She'd been attracted to him for years, wanted him with a secret lust and a soul-deep yearning that seemed to only grow stronger as time passed—but she'd done her best to keep her desire for him to herself. Ultimately she was afraid of giving in to those romantic feelings for her *best friend* and taking the risk of things not working out between them—thus ruining their strong, lifelong friendship.

Shane was the only stable person in her life, the one she turned to whenever she needed someone to talk to or lean on. He was her rock, the one she trusted implicitly, and she would be completely devastated if anything ever came between them— like an intimate relationship that she screwed up because of her own personal hang-ups. He was too important to her to ever take that chance, but that rationale didn't stop her from fantasizing about what could have been.

A soft *ping* sounded from her computer, and she glanced at the screen to find that a new Instant Message had appeared for her.

MEET ME AT MIDNIGHT

TheOne4You: Hi.

She didn't recognize the user name and was fairly certain that the other person had contacted her by mistake. Then again, she used her Instant Messenger for business to keep in quick contact with clients, and she supposed it was possible someone had changed their user name. She typed out a response to find out.

IshopForYou: Hi, yourself. Who is this?

TheOne4You: Someone you've known for a while now.

She frowned, curious as to why the person was being so secretive and how he'd been able to contact her.

IshopForYou: How did you get my IM address?

TheOne4You: A mutual friend of ours. And before you ask who, I swore I wouldn't tell the name of the person who gave me your user ID. It's a good friend of yours, and I can assure you they wouldn't have given it to me if I wasn't a nice, trustworthy kind of guy. <g>

She smiled, undeniably intrigued.

IshopForYou: Do *I* know you?
TheOne4You: Yes.
IshopForYou: So, we've met before?
TheOne4You: Yes. But I'm not quite ready to
    reveal who I am. For now, let's just say
    that I'm your secret admirer.

Alyssa had never had a secret admirer before, and she found the prospect of being courted by a mysterious man very sexy and exciting. She read his user name again, **TheOne4You**, and felt giddy deep inside.

TheOne4You: I want you to know that I'm
    very attracted to you and have been for
    some time now. I thought we could get to
    know one another through Instant Messag-
    ing before I meet you in person . . . if that's
    all right with you.

She grinned, her fingers automatically flying over the keyboard with a reply.

IshopForYou: Sort of like a blind date over
    the Internet?
TheOne4You: Yes. But I don't want to make
    you feel uncomfortable in any way.

MEET ME AT MIDNIGHT

She appreciated his concern and sincerity, which said a lot for his personality and gave her a bit of assurance that he wasn't some deranged online stalker. His posts so far had been amicable, and he'd given her no reason to feel threatened. In any case, he might have her user ID, but it wasn't like he knew where she lived. A lot of people she knew had made friends on the Internet. With her new resolution in place, she decided she was going to enjoy a bit of flirtatious fun with her anonymous admirer.

IshopForYou: I'm fine with this, and you don't make me feel uncomfortable at all.

TheOne4You: Good. I heard you'll be going to Drew and Cynthia's New Year's Eve party. I'll be there, too. If things work out on our online blind date, maybe we can meet in person there?

Alyssa absently chewed on her bottom lip. Even though that gave her four days to get to know him online, she wasn't quite ready to agree to anything that personal just yet. So, instead, she gave him a noncommittal reply.

IshopForYou: Maybe.

TheOne4You: Maybe is good enough for me. BTW, you have beautiful blue eyes.

Her stomach dipped at the compliment, along with the knowledge that he truly did know what she looked like. She felt at such a disadvantage.

> **IshopForYou:** Thank you. I wish I knew what color your eyes are.
> **TheOne4You:** Brown eyes and brown hair, just in case you were wondering.

She laughed out loud, but in her mind it was Shane's image that appeared—brown eyes and hair and a charismatic smile just for her.

> **IshopForYou:** Yes, I was wondering what your hair color was. You're a mind reader, too.
> **TheOne4You:** It's a gift. <g> It's late and I should let you go. Shall we meet the same time tomorrow night?
> **IshopForYou:** Sure. I'd like that.
> **TheOne4You:** Me, too. Good night and sleep well.

A shiver rippled through her, as if he'd whispered those words directly into her ear in low, masculine tones. She typed out her final words to him for the evening.

> **IshopForYou:** Good night.

He signed off first, and with a soft sigh she shut down her business accounts, then her computer. After taking her plate down to the kitchen, she returned to her bedroom, changed into the comfy pajamas Shane had bought her for Christmas, and climbed into bed. She was physically exhausted but still pumped with exhilaration after her conversation with the guy who called himself TheOne4You.

She rolled restlessly to her side and closed her eyes, wondering who he was, how she knew him, and what he looked like. He'd given her only two of his traits, and her imagination tried to fill in the blanks from there. She envisioned someone hot and sexy who had the ability to make her heart race with one glance and her body come alive with a well-placed caress.

Someone like Shane.

She moaned softly in frustration and clenched her thighs tightly together. It had been a long time since any man had been able to stir any real, deep desire from her. How ironic it was that mere fantasies of Shane had the ability to give her that kind of pleasure and sense of anticipation, without him even realizing the power he had over her body and senses.

And, unfortunately, he never would.

Chapter Two

Shane was well aware that Alyssa was a late sleeper. Neither was she a morning person, but that didn't stop him from arriving on her doorstep the next day at a quarter past eight. When he didn't get a response the first time he knocked, he tried a second time, more insistently than before. Then he rang the doorbell a few times for good measure.

Finally he heard stumbling coming from the other side of the door and knew she was looking out the peephole to see who the offender was. He grinned real big and held up the bribe he'd brought along to ensure that she wouldn't turn him away. The woman was a sucker for a hot Starbucks Caffè Mocha and a cream cheese Danish.

The door opened, and she narrowed her sleepy-eyed gaze at him. "You're cruel, you know that?" she grumbled good-naturedly.

He gave her a look of mock offense. "I come bearing some of your favorite gifts, and you have the audacity to call me cruel?"

"It's barely eight in the morning," she complained, and relieved him of one of the large coffee cups he was carrying in his hands. With a grumpy frown, she shuffled into the adjoining living room, knowing he would follow her into the apartment and shut the door behind him, which he did. "You could have at least called and given me some time to wake up before you got here."

He rolled his eyes at that. "You would have ignored the phone."

"Okay, you're right." She sat down on the couch and pushed her unruly, disheveled curls away from her face with her free hand. She wasn't wearing an ounce of makeup and yet she looked beautiful, her complexion smooth and still flushed from slumber. "I tried to ignore the door, but you were making my head pound with all that banging."

A huge exaggeration he didn't bother to dispute. "Late night?" He settled in beside her and took a drink of his coffee—straight-up black and strong, without anything froufrou in it like hers.

"No, not really. Just a busy one getting all of December's billings and statements done. But I'm pretty much caught up for the month, so I'm happy."

That news worked well into his plans, since he

would be spending a lot of time with her over the next few days if she agreed to help make him over into a metro-male.

Tucking her legs beneath her on the couch, she wrapped her hands around the paper cup, took a sip of her warm drink, and moaned her appreciation. Then a smile slowly curved the corners of her mouth, revealing that she was gradually waking up—at least enough to enjoy her sweetened coffee.

"Okay, I'm close to forgiving you for getting me up so damn early. This Caffè Mocha is delicious."

"And what do I get for this cream cheese Danish?" Waggling his brows temptingly, he dangled the pastry bag just within her reach.

"How about a sincere thank-you?" she asked hopefully and licked her lips in anticipation.

He contemplated that for a moment as a dozen other arousing payments came to mind. "I guess that's good enough for now." He gave her the breakfast roll, and while she took a big bite of the flaky confection, he leaned back against the sofa cushions and took in her morning attire.

"By the way, nice pj's." Nicer still was the way the top clung to her full breasts, which was a bonus he hadn't counted on when he'd bought the pajamas for her.

"Yeah, my best friend has pretty good taste and

knows exactly what I like." Grinning at him, she set the Danish on the paper bag she'd smoothed out on her lap to use as a makeshift plate and prepared to pull the pastry apart to eat in bites. "Nice comfy cotton."

Oh, yeah, he'd learned long ago what her preferences were when it came to sleepwear. When he'd walked into a department store to buy her Christmas presents a few weeks ago, he'd forgone all the racy, sheer, silk and lace nightgowns and teddies in favor of utilitarian, full-coverage pajamas—but not before he'd spent a few decadent moments imagining her in a couple of those wispy, barely there outfits that she insisted were more for seducing a man than for any real sleeping comfort.

Yep, that was his practical, sensible Alyssa, all right.

Seriously, though, he was probably the only guy in a hundred-mile radius who thought she looked downright enticing in a plain pink pajama top and a pair of striped drawstring pants that were warm and soft and as functional as nightclothes were supposed to be. There was nothing provocative about what she was wearing, but it was the whole sleepy, mussed-hair, I-just-rolled-out-of-bed concept that did it for him in a major way.

"So, what brings you by at such a gawd-awful

hour in the morning?'' she asked, then licked the sugary glaze from her fingers in that sensual way of hers.

Heat pooled in Shane's belly, and lower, and it was all he could do to just sit there and watch her tend to her sticky fingers instead of taking over the job for her with his own lips and tongue. He took a drink of his strong coffee, hoping for a much-needed jolt of caffeine before giving her an answer in a voice that he hoped was steadier than he felt.

"I figured out what my New Year's resolution is going to be."

"Yeah?" She glanced up at him, her blue eyes wide with curiosity. "Do tell."

He inhaled a deep breath, hoping like hell that the idea he'd concocted didn't backfire on him in any way—because her agreement to help him hinged on the success of his entire plan to make her view him as something more than just a best friend. "Seeing that you're ready to open yourself up to the possibility of a serious relationship, I figured it's time that I did the same thing."

Surprise flashed in her eyes, along with another emotion he couldn't fully define. "Really?"

He shrugged, doing his best to keep his demeanor casual and relaxed. "Actually, there's someone I've been interested in for a while, but the timing hasn't been right until now."

A small frown formed between her brows. "Oh," she said quietly. "Why didn't you tell me this before now?"

Since they discussed just about everything, he'd been prepared for that question, and his answer came from his heart. "This woman isn't even aware of my interest in her, and I didn't tell you about it because I didn't think it had a chance of developing into anything significant."

She searched his features, for what he wasn't sure. "And now you do?"

"I honestly don't know, but it's time I put myself out there like you're going to do and find out where things stand between us," he said, choosing his words carefully so he didn't give anything away— like the fact that *she* was the woman he was after. "If it's not what I thought it was and the feelings aren't reciprocated, then at least I'll know I tried."

She nodded and glanced away instead of offering him her opinion on the matter like he'd given her last night at his restaurant when she'd told him about *her* plans for the New Year. Instead, a strange silence descended in the room as she took a drink of her coffee. He wished he knew what was really going through that mind of hers. Normally he could read her expression fairly well, but not today, and that lack of insight frustrated him to no end.

Setting her paper cup on the end table beside the

couch, she pulled off a chunk of Danish, popped the piece into her mouth, then cast him a speculative glance. "So, who is this mystery woman?"

He paused, but he knew there was no easy way to answer that question either. "I'd rather not say. At least not yet."

Her delicate brows arched high, but not before he'd witnessed the spark of hurt that flashed in her gaze because he wasn't willing to share something so monumental with her. "That serious, huh?"

"No. Not at all," he said gently. "I just want to get used to the idea of finally making my feelings known to this woman before I tell anyone who she is."

"I understand," she said, but he could tell by her quiet tone and the way she wouldn't meet his gaze again that she didn't understand at all. Because she wasn't just *anyone*.

God, he hated being so secretive with her, but it was necessary. In a few days she would look back on this conversation, realize his reasons for being so vague, and—he hoped—forgive him for being so closemouthed about the woman in question.

"Now that I've decided to go for it, so to speak," he went on, attempting to add some humor to break up the odd tension between them, "I need your help with something."

"Sure. Anything. You know that." She gave him only a semblance of her normally sunny smile.

"This woman is going to be at Drew and Cynthia's New Year's Eve party, and I really want to make a good impression, since that's when I plan to let her know how I feel about her." Again Alyssa glanced away, focusing on the Danish on her lap to keep from looking at him. Or so it seemed. "I was hoping you could help me spruce up my image a bit. You know, make me look more like one of those clean-cut executives you date."

That snagged her attention, and she cut her gaze to his. "Is that what she's into?"

"Seems to be." He spread his arms out wide, indicating his casual everyday attire. "Besides, it wouldn't hurt to give my current wardrobe an overhaul so I look more presentable for the party—like trading in my jeans for a pair of nice slacks or khakis' and my cotton T-shirts for some dress shirts and ties. And my hair could definitely use a trim."

When she didn't reply, he stretched his arm along the back of the couch and brushed back the hair that had fallen over her shoulder, loving the way those soft curls wrapped themselves around his long fingers, ensnaring him in more ways than one. His knuckles grazed the side of her neck, and he felt her shiver from his touch.

Something was very wrong. He didn't know exactly what, but he could *feel* her subtle withdrawal, more than she'd ever displayed with him before. He got the distinct feeling that her emotional retreat ran deeper than just the issue of his not telling her about this "other woman" before today. There was more going on in that beautiful head of hers, he was sure.

He squeezed her shoulder affectionately. "Are you okay, Alyssa?"

As if realizing how silent and pensive she'd become, she shook off her mood. "Of course. I'm fine. Just great." Her voice rang with false, unconvincing certainty and did nothing to reassure him. "This just seems so sudden, that's all. But of course I'll help you out. We could even go shopping for new clothes today and hit some really good after-Christmas sales. I'll see if my hairdresser can fit you in for an appointment for a cut and trim sometime tomorrow."

"That would be perfect." He smiled, relieved to have finally gained her cooperation, because convincing her to help him had been iffy there for a while. "Consider me yours for the next two days."

She shoved the last bite of Danish into her mouth, and a large crumb fell on her pajama top, coming to rest right on the upper swell of her breast. She seemed completely unaware of the mess she'd made, until he reached over and picked up the morsel for himself. He deliberately let his touch linger on the soft, voluptuous curve of her breast a bit longer than was *friendly*, and his fingers lightly grazed the nipple that had automatically tightened from that forbidden caress.

Her eyes grew round at the intimate contact, her sweet, moist lips parted, and she sucked in a startled breath.

Pleased that he'd gotten such a promising response out of Alyssa, he popped the crumb of Danish into his mouth and winked at her. "Ummm, good stuff," he murmured huskily—and could have been referring to the pastry, or the way her soft breast had felt against his fingers. Like pure, unadulterated heaven.

What had just transpired between them could have been construed as innocent fun—he'd certainly touched her before in playful situations—but much to Shane's own surprise he watched her cheeks flush and her eyes darken with *desire*. His own body responded with a jolt of sizzling awareness. Time seemed to stand still as he slowly dropped his gaze to her lush, kissable mouth and thought of all the erotic pleasure to be had between those soft, tempting lips.

Abruptly, she stood, shattering the intimate moment and leaving him to wonder if he'd just imagined the liquid heat in her gaze, the wanting . . .

But then she turned around to face him. He saw the residual longing still in her eyes and the pulse beating wildly at the base of her throat, and he knew what he'd seen and felt between them had been *very* real.

And it was just as obvious to him that she wanted to pretend that it had never happened.

Self-consciously, she tugged at the hem of her pajama top, which served only to stretch the cotton fabric tighter over her peaked nipples—which he was sure she hadn't meant to do. Then she shifted anxiously on her feet, her gaze darting from him to something over his shoulder. Anywhere but at him.

"I'm, uh, going to go and take a shower and change, and then we'll go shopping." She bolted from the room as if the devil himself were nipping at her heels.

Once she was gone, Shane dropped his head against the back of the sofa, closed his eyes, and exhaled hard and deep. Who would have thought that he and Alyssa could generate such hot chemistry together? He could only imagine what would happen if it was ever fully ignited—spontaneous combustion was what came to his mind.

With a touch, a look, he'd managed to prove that

there was definitely something going on between them, something neither one of them had been willing to acknowledge until this morning—even if *she* wouldn't admit it or face the attraction that was simmering beneath their friendship.

But she would, soon.

He'd crossed a few boundaries with her and had been rewarded with a glimpse of what could be. He grinned, fairly certain he was going to cross a few more lines with Alyssa before the week was through.

Alyssa stripped off her pajamas and stepped beneath the shower head, praying that the hot water would dispel the crazy, wild fluttering in her stomach and the tingling in her breasts. Butterflies, that's what they were—and it had been forever since she'd experienced that light, tickling sensation in the pit of her belly that occurred when she connected on a physical, sexual level with a man.

And today that man had been Shane.

She groaned in dismay and tilted her head back to douse her hair. What in the world had happened out there in the living room? They'd gone from having a teasing conversation about her grumpy morning mood, to a more serious discussion about Shane wanting to improve his appearance for some woman he was interested in, to her getting turned on when he'd accidentally touched her breast and nipple. From there, things had escalated into a far more sensual moment, taking her completely by surprise.

Her body still trembled deep inside, her mind was spinning like a top, and she could hardly process all that had just transpired. She was confused and appalled, and if she was honest with herself, she was still bothered over the fact that Shane was interested in someone but didn't feel inclined to share who. At least not yet.

She snorted at that as she shampooed her hair, silently berating herself for having double standards where Shane was concerned. It wasn't as though she'd come right out and told him about her secret admirer either. So, in truth, she really didn't have the right to be so upset with him.

But, dammit, she was. Not to mention envious and jealous, too. And those were emotions she wasn't used to dealing with.

The thought of losing Shane, her best friend, to another woman sent a shaft of panic racing through her, because she feared if that happened, he'd no longer be there for *her* when she needed him the most. Or that possibly another woman wouldn't understand, or tolerate, their close friendship.

Maybe her fear of losing Shane was the reason why she'd allowed her deeper feelings for him to surface this morning—like the desire and attraction she'd managed to keep buried for so long. It *had* to be a subliminal thing that had coaxed those intimate yearnings out into the open now, but whatever the reason she didn't plan on letting it happen again!

She finished up with her shower, and by the time she'd blow-dried her hair and changed into jeans and a blouse, she was ready to face Shane and the day ahead with a new attitude and outlook. Even if that meant helping him to impress another woman.

Chapter Three

Shane stepped out of the dressing room and into the private viewing area where Alyssa was waiting for him to model one of the outfits she'd selected for him.

"Well, what do you think?" he asked.

"Wow, you clean up pretty well, Mr. Witmer." She walked up behind him and smoothed her hands along his broad shoulders, then turned him to face the three-way mirror that gave him a better overall view of his new appearance. "But the real question is, what do *you* think?" She bit her bottom lip expectantly.

Shane glanced at his reflection and was instantly pleased with the new sophisticated image he saw staring back at him. The long-sleeved burgundy suede dress shirt and black double-pleated slacks Alyssa had picked out for him were something he never would have chosen for himself, but he had to admit the outfit made him look hip and much more sophisticated than his jeans and T-shirts ever had. She'd also accessorized the look with a thin leather belt with a small silver buckle and a comfortable, and very expensive, pair of Italian loafers that looked and felt fantastic on his feet.

He met her waiting gaze in the mirror and gave a nod of approval. "I like the entire package. A whole lot."

"Good." She came around to stand in front of him and straightened the black tie with a swirling burgundy pattern on it, her fingers absently grazing his chest as she smoothed the strips of silk down along his torso. "This outfit will be perfect for the New Year's Eve party."

Shane liked having her fuss over him. He liked her hands on him even better. "You think so?"

Taking a step back, she eyed him critically one more time, then smiled. "Absolutely. You can also wear the shirt open at the collar and without a tie if you want to go for a more casual look instead. So you have a few options."

He propped his hands on his hips and slanted her a curious glance. "Would an outfit like this on a guy turn *your* head?"

Her gaze traveled from his chest, all the way

down to his shoes, and up again. "Yeah, I'd definitely give you a second glance," she admitted with a playful grin. "You look hot."

And that was all Shane needed to hear to make his decision—because ultimately it was having *her* eyes on him that mattered the most. "In that case, I'll take everything I'm wearing."

She laughed and quickly stepped away from him. It wasn't the first time he'd noticed how she was trying to keep things between them low-key after that intimate moment in her living room that morning. He let her have her way because he didn't want her to feel threatened by all the new feelings developing between them.

"That's only one outfit," she said as she skimmed through the other clothes she'd selected for him, which were hanging on a wire rack against the wall. "You need a few more coordinating pants and shirts for other things, like an evening out with friends, or when you go out on a date with . . . well, with the woman you're interested in."

She stumbled over that last part but quickly recovered, which he was glad to see. Pulling a tan shirt with an abstract design on it from the rack, she turned and showed it to him. "What do you think of this one?"

Again, it was a far departure from what he would have picked on his own, but he liked the colors and the style. "I can't say until I try it on. Do you have a pair of pants to go with the shirt?"

"Hey, I'm impressed," she teased as she selected a pair of tan, casual-looking khakis to go with the short-sleeved shirt. "You're catching on to the whole concept of coordinating your clothing. Who would have thought you'd even want to do such a thing?"

"Yeah, imagine that," he said dryly. "Are you going to let me buy at least one pair of jeans today, just so I don't feel totally out of my element?"

"Sure." She paused thoughtfully, then grinned. "Just so long as there are no rips or tears, or faded patches and spots. I think a pair of Diesel jeans in a dark blue indigo could work for either casual or semicasual occasions, if paired with the right kind of shirt."

"Diesel jeans?" He'd never heard of the brand, but they sounded expensive. "Why do I get the feeling that's the only compromise you're going to allow?"

"You're a smart man, Shane." She patted his cheek playfully. "You're the one who asked for this makeover, not me."

"All right, all right," he conceded and disappeared into the dressing room to change into what ended up being the second of at least a dozen different coordinating pants and shirts.

By the time they were done shopping, they were both loaded down with department-store bags filled with clothes and accessories for him, and he'd spent a small fortune. Not only did he now have a new wardrobe fit for an executive, but Alyssa had also taken him over to the cologne department and had him purchase a brand-new men's fragrance that she insisted would drive any woman crazy with desire.

The only one he was interested in driving crazy was her, and the cologne seemed to do the trick there as well. She'd spritzed his wrist with the woodsy scent, inhaled deeply, closed her eyes, and moaned like a woman in the midst of an orgasmic experience.

And that was all it took for him to plunk down his credit card and buy a large bottle of the stuff.

They reached his SUV and tossed the bags into the back of the truck. After climbing behind the wheel, and with Alyssa in the passenger seat, he pulled out of the mall parking lot and headed onto the freeway.

He'd had such a great afternoon with her that he hated for their time together to end. "Would you like to come back to the restaurant with me and get a pizza or a pasta dish?"

She shook her head. "Actually, I can't. I have a bunch of party favors for a client's New Year's Eve party that I need to pick up and deliver before five today."

He took the turn off the freeway that led to her

apartment. "Okay. If you change your mind or want to stop by The Pizza Joint after your errands, I'll be there."

"I think I'll pass tonight." She softened the rejection with a genuine smile. "I had a great day with you, though. It was tons of fun dressing you up. And tomorrow you get your hair cut." She reached across the console and ruffled the unruly strands with her fingers.

He admitted to having a few reservations about her stylist messing with his hair. Usually he went to a barber, and he had no idea what to expect tomorrow. "By the way, no buzz cuts."

"Giving you a buzz cut would be a crime. You have gorgeous hair." She ran her fingers through the thick strands again, this time seemingly measuring the length in different places. "A bit of layering on the top and a trim around the ears and neck, and you'll be good as new. It'll be painless. I promise."

Amused laughter escaped him, and he brought his SUV to a stop in front of her apartment complex. "Are we still on for our date tomorrow night?"

She looked at him in confusion. "Date?"

"The annual *Twilight Zone* marathon. Remember?"

She groaned. "I can't believe I let you sweet-talk me into watching all those creepy reruns with you every year. You know how much I hate scary movies and shows."

But he loved the way she inevitably curled up to him on the couch whenever she got spooked or frightened while they were watching the shows. "Hey, it's become a tradition. You can't back out on me now."

She released a long-suffering sigh. "All right, I'll be there. Can we do Chinese takeout for dinner?"

He'd give her anything she wished. "You got it. Chinese takeout it is."

She leaned over and kissed him quickly on the cheek. "Consider it a date, then," she said, then got out of the truck and headed up the walkway to the complex.

Shane sat there in his truck to make sure she made it into the building safely—while enjoying the backside view of her curvy hips swaying provocatively every step of the way.

Alyssa sat at her computer that evening, searching the Internet for the best pricing on floral arrangements for an upcoming fiftieth wedding anniversary party one of her clients was hosting for her parents. The woman wanted bouquets of cattleya orchids and white roses in the center of each table, and they certainly didn't come cheap.

She went through her normal sources, trying to find the best cost she could for her client, and after an hour of Instant Messaging back and forth with a floral designer, she finally nailed down a price she was happy with.

She typed up an estimated cost sheet for her client and e-mailed it off, then leaned back in her chair and extended her arms over her head to stretch the kinks from the muscles along her shoulders and back. The day had been a long one—with Shane's early-morning visit, their shopping spree, and the last few hours she'd spent in front of her computer getting work done.

She thought back to her afternoon with Shane and the drastic changes he was willing to make for this woman he was interested in. It was a first for him. Over the years he'd dated plenty of women on a casual basis, but she'd never seen him so intent on making such a significant impression on any of them. And the fact that he was so willing to change his image to catch a woman's eye now led her to believe that it had to be very serious for him.

Her stomach knotted with envy, just one of the many emotions she wished she had more control over. The others were more of the sexy variety. Even though she'd tried to act like everything was normal between them today after this morning's fleeting but very sensual encounter, she couldn't deny her escalating feelings for Shane. The desire was becoming more pronounced when she was with him, and she could sense it pulling at her more and more often, in a way that was getting increasingly difficult to resist.

Blowing out an upward stream of breath, she pushed away from her desk, frustrated at herself and the entire situation. Her feelings for Shane couldn't develop into anything sexual—no matter how physically attractive she might find him—and she'd do well to keep that first and foremost in her mind. Years of friendship were at stake, not to mention that it would probably shock the hell out of him if he found out that he'd become the object of some of her most tantalizing fantasies.

Standing, she headed into the kitchen to make herself a late-night snack, hoping that would help snap her out of her current funk. She poured Rice Krispies into a bowl, added milk, and headed back to her office. She would eat her cereal, play a game of Free Cell, then shut things down for the night and go to bed. But when she glanced at her computer screen, she saw an Instant Message waiting for her.

TheOne4You: Hi, beautiful.

Her secret admirer. She'd been so wrapped up in her search for flower arrangements and then in her troubling thoughts of Shane that she'd forgotten they'd agreed to chat again tonight. Smiling at his flirtatious greeting, and welcoming the distraction, she set her bowl of cereal aside and typed out a response.

IshopForYou: Hi, yourself. How are you?

TheOne4You: Great, now that I'm talking to you. How was your day?

IshopForYou: It was good. I was out most of the day shopping with a friend. He ended up buying himself a new wardrobe, which is a rarity for him.

TheOne4You: This is a *guy* friend?

She raised her brows at his question as she ate a bite of her cereal. Was he jealous? she wondered. She found that notion amusing.

IshopForYou: Yes, a guy friend.

TheOne4You: Do I have to worry about him being any kind of competition for me?

She laughed out loud and shook her head.

IshopForYou: No, he's been my best friend since I was five. He's a great guy. I don't think you have anything to worry about.

TheOne4You: You sure about that?

IshopForYou: I'm sure. He's interested in some other woman, which is why he spent a for-

tune on new clothes today—so he can impress her.

TheOne4You: And do you think he will? Impress her, I mean.

She mulled over that question as she ate another
spoonful of Rice Krispies, recalling the various
outfits Shane had tried on and bought. He'd
looked sharp and gorgeous in designer duds, literally head-turning. But she had reservations about
him changing his image for another woman when
being a metro-male wasn't at all who he really
was. If she had the choice, she preferred the laid-
back, jeans-and-T-shirt Shane over the polished
style he was so adamant about incorporating into
his wardrobe.

IshopForYou: I think that my friend's personality is what will win this woman over, not
what he's wearing. He can be very charming and charismatic when he wants to be.

TheOne4You: Enough about your friend. Let's
talk about you for a while.

IshopForYou: Okay. What would you like to
know?

TheOne4You: What are some of the traits you
look for in a guy?

Her mind filled with images of Shane. He was the epitome of what she considered the perfect guy—inside and out.

IshopForYou: Honesty is a biggie. He also needs to be interesting and entertaining, and it's always great if he's fun and likes to have a good time. Being spontaneous is a good thing, too.

And just because she was feeling a bit impetuous, she tossed in her other requirement when it came to dating a man more than once.

IshopForYou: He also needs to be a good kisser.
TheOne4You: Hmmm. That's good to know. What do you consider a good kiss?

She bit her bottom lip, debating how far to take this particular conversation, which had the potential of becoming very personal and risqué—but only if she allowed it to go in that direction. In the scheme of things it really was a harmless question, and she supposed it wouldn't hurt for her admirer to know what she preferred.

IshopForYou: I like warm, soft lips and slow,

sensual kisses. Though deep, passionate kisses definitely have their time and place, too, LOL. I think any good make-out session should start with those leisurely kisses and build from there.

TheOne4You: I agree. Kissing is the best part of foreplay. I don't like to limit kissing to just the mouth, either. There are just so many other sensitive, erotic spots to enjoy with your lips and tongue and teeth.

IshopForYou: Like where?

Oh, Lord, had her trigger fingers really typed that? His instant response confirmed that they most definitely had!

TheOne4You: A woman's neck is my favorite place to nuzzle and kiss. So is the upper curve of her breast, and her belly right below the navel. And then there's the soft, tender skin of her inner thigh.

Alyssa squirmed in her chair as she read his arousing comments. Oh, wow. The man had a way with words that affected her not only mentally but physically as well. Warmth surged through her, her pulse quickened, and she felt restless and breathless and very, very hot all of a sudden.

MEET ME AT MIDNIGHT

It had been a long time since a man had taken that kind of time and care with her during foreplay or sex. It was nice to know that there was a guy out there who appreciated all that seductive petting, caressing, and kissing just as much as she did. However, if they didn't stop talking about sex, she knew she'd never be able to sleep tonight.

She groaned out loud. Hell, who was she kidding? She was fairly certain she would have a tossing and turning kind of night, thanks to her secret admirer's very steamy dialogue.

IshopForYou: I think we got a bit off track for a minute there.
TheOne4You: It was fun, don't you think? <g>

She laughed at his blatant attempt to get on her good side by showing her just how *fun* he could be.

IshopForYou: Yes, it was fun. You scored extra points by showing me just how entertaining you can be.
TheOne4You: And spontaneous.

She bit back another laugh.

IshopForYou: Yes, that too.
TheOne4You: I aim to please.

She was beginning to have little doubt of that.

TheOne4You: So, in getting our conversation back on track, does the guy you date have to be good-looking?

IshopForYou: No, not necessarily. I think finding a man attractive comes from what's inside. A guy's ability to make me laugh is more important to me than how he looks.

And he'd managed to give her a few chuckles tonight, so he had lots of potential in her book.

TheOne4You: I love your laughter. It's husky and sexy.

The fact that he'd been close enough at some point to hear her laugh momentarily took Alyssa aback. Her heart pounded hard and fast in her chest, and her mind tried to conjure up *his* face, but she honestly had no idea who her secret admirer was.

IshopForYou: You've made me laugh?
TheOne4You: Maybe.

She groaned at that vague answer, though she wasn't surprised that he was being evasive and mysterious, since that had been his MO thus far.

IshopForYou: You're killing me, you know that?
TheOne4You: It's called creating and building anticipation.

And sexual tension. He'd managed to instigate plenty of that between them tonight.

TheOne4You: Shall we meet at the same time tomorrow night?

She was about to type *yes*, until she remembered she already had a date.

IshopForYou: I'm sorry. I can't. I have plans with a friend and it will probably be a late night.
TheOne4You: Your guy friend, by chance?

She was amazed at how intuitive he was. Or maybe it had just been a lucky guess.

IshopForYou: Yes. I promised I'd watch the *Twilight Zone* marathon with him, and it's an all-nighter thing.
TheOne4You: Sounds like a fun evening.

She thought about how Shane teased her about being a chicken because she covered her eyes during the spooky parts. Inevitably he tried to scare her at some point during the night. He took great pleasure in making her scream and jump in fright, the rogue.

IshopForYou: Yeah, we have a good time. It's something I wouldn't miss, even though I don't like creepy movies or shows.

TheOne4You: Your friend is a lucky guy to be able to spend the night with you.

Alyssa caught the sensual connotation in his reply but chose not to pursue the direction of yet another sexy conversation with him. As much as she'd enjoyed their discussion about kissing, she figured that was enough intimacy for their first online blind date.

TheOne4You: Since you won't be around tomorrow evening, I'll catch up to you at some point in the next day or so. New Year's Eve is only two days away.

IshopForYou: I know. I'm looking forward to meeting you.

She genuinely liked him, enjoyed their conversations, and she was undeniably curious to find out what he was really like in person. With Shane meeting his own date on New Year's Eve, she was glad she'd have someone special of her own to look forward to.

> **TheOne4You:** If I was there with you now, I'd
> kiss you good night.

Her body heated at his words, and even her breasts reacted, her nipples tingling. She was fairly certain that if he had been standing here in the flesh she would have given in to the warm, damp touch of his lips on hers. However, because she didn't want him to think she was that easy, she played hard to get.

> **IshopForYou:** It's only our first date. What
> makes you think I'd *let* you kiss me?
> **TheOne4You:** Because right now, at this mo-
> ment, you want me to kiss you. And now
> that I know how you like to be kissed, you
> can bet I'm going to use all that knowledge
> to please you when the opportunity arises.

He was all but stating that it was just a matter of time before she succumbed to his charms. The man was something else, but if she was honest with herself, she had to admit that his confidence excited her on a purely female level. She loved strong, self-assured men who weren't afraid of going after what they wanted.

And he obviously wanted her.

TheOne4You: Good night, Alyssa. Have sweet dreams.

He signed off, and she sighed, certain that her dreams were going to be anything but sweet tonight after their suggestive exchange.

Later, as she settled herself in bed, she thought about those erotic kisses he'd described and tried to conjure up his features and what he might look like. But as she gradually drifted off to sleep, her secret admirer took on the face of her best friend, Shane Witmer.

Chapter Four

"I feel naked."

Arms crossed over her chest, Alyssa leaned against the bathroom doorframe that connected to Shane's bedroom and grinned at her best friend, who was examining his new haircut in the mirror above the vanity. Despite his claim, he was fully dressed in one of his new collared knit shirts and a pair of navy Dockers—darn it. But she did have a moment of fun imagining that lean, toned body of his without any clothes on.

"Trust me, you certainly don't look naked," she told him.

He slanted her a wry you're-such-a-comedian kind of look as he ran his fingers through the much shorter strands, which had been shaped and layered to fall right back into place. And they did, much to his chagrin.

"You know what I mean," he grumbled at his

reflection. "I'm used to having hair around my ears and neck, and now there's . . . nothing."

"There's plenty, and it's trimmed nice and neat, just how you wanted." She tried to soothe his ego with a calm, placating tone, because it was becoming increasingly obvious that he was having a hard time adjusting to this new look of his. "You'll get used to it."

His gaze met hers again, direct and curious. "What do *you* think of the cut?"

It was a definite change for him; he looked every bit like a clean-cut, hip, urbane male. But she'd be lying if she didn't say she already missed his longer, always mussed hair which had given him a bit of a bad-boy appeal.

"It's very stylish." And without his hair falling over his forehead or his ears, his gorgeous features were now more pronounced. Even his rich brown eyes had taken on a darker, sexier, more compelling gleam.

"Stylish is good, right?"

A hint of uncertainty had crept into his voice, which didn't happen often with Shane, who was usually so secure in his masculinity. She was realizing that he was having a few regrets about getting rid of his longer locks, and she found that bit of vulnerability endearing.

"Stylish is *very* good, and the cut goes with your

new image," she assured him. "In fact, I think you're ready for tomorrow night at the New Year's Eve party."

"Thanks to you."

They headed into the kitchen, where dinner awaited them. On their way to Shane's place after his haircut they'd picked up Chinese takeout and some snacks for the *Twilight Zone* marathon, which was due to start in about an hour.

At the kitchen's bar area, where they ate all their meals together, they sat across from one another with boxes of their favorite entrées and paper plates set out between them. Shane grabbed one of the boxes, opened it up, and piled his plate with orange chicken before handing the box to her.

"So, what are you wearing tomorrow night?" he asked as he added a heaping serving of chicken chow mein to his plate.

Picking up a pair of the wooden chopsticks, Alyssa broke them apart and rubbed them together to smooth out the edges before eating with them. "I honestly hadn't given it much thought. Since I'm done with you, I'm free tomorrow during the day. I'll probably go shopping for something then."

"Are you going sexy or sedate?" He waggled his brows at her as he started in on his moo-shu pork, obviously hoping for the former, which she found amusing.

"You know that sedate is more *my* style." She didn't have one of those cute centerfold figures that she could squeeze into a slinky, revealing dress. No, she was better off in something practical and far less form-fitting.

"I was thinking we could drive to the party together if you like."

The piece of orange chicken she'd been swallowing nearly choked her. How did she explain to Shane that she, too, was meeting someone at the party, and going together might not be the best idea, depending on how the evening ended for each one of them?

Which she reminded him of. "You know, I really don't want to cramp your style if things work out with you and your lady friend." Whom she was absolutely dying to meet.

He looked completely unconcerned about that. "If things work out, we'll make other arrangements, and if things don't work out, then you can be my excuse to leave."

She sighed and absently twirled the chow mein noodles around her chopsticks. It was time to fess up to him about her secret admirer. "Shane, there's something I need to tell you."

"Okay." He took a drink of his soda and pushed his fork through his chicken. "What's up?"

She told him before she lost her nerve. "I'm meeting someone tomorrow night, too."

"You are?" he asked in surprise. "Why didn't you tell me?"

At least she had some ammunition to use against that line of questioning. "I didn't say anything for the same reason you're not telling me who this mystery woman of yours is—because I have no idea if anything is going to come of his interest."

He processed her response for a few quiet moments as he finished off his chow mein, then asked, "So, who is he?"

She gave him a sheepish smile. "The funny thing is, I don't know."

"You don't know who he is?" he repeated incredulously. "How can you not know who he is?"

She realized how bad that sounded and winced. "What I meant was, I haven't met this guy face-to-face yet. Well, he says I know him—but he hasn't told me *who* he is. He's contacted me a few times through Instant Messaging, and he seems nice enough. He told me he was going to be at Drew and Cynthia's party, and I've agreed to meet him there."

She waited for a reaction from him, some kind of protective instinct to kick in, or maybe even a bit of male jealousy. To her disappointment, he remained cool, calm, and unaffected.

"Well, we can still drive together," he said, and started in on second helpings of the pork and chicken. "We can be each other's excuses to leave the party if things don't work out with our respective dates and we need the outlet."

She appreciated that safety net of knowing Shane would be there for her if she needed him, because she really didn't have any idea what to expect from her date. "Okay," she agreed. "I'll be ready by six."

She finished up her dinner and watched Shane polish off what was left of the Chinese food. The man had a big appetite. When he was a young boy and a teenager, his mother made huge meals for Shane and his father. Alyssa had always been amazed when they'd devoured the meals with no problem.

Alyssa smiled to herself as those fond recollections filtered through her mind. She'd spent many evenings and weekends at the Witmer house. She'd been so young when her own father had passed away, and her mother had never remarried, but there had been a sense of security, comfort, and family unit at the Witmer home that she'd loved. Because of an emergency hysterectomy, Shane's mother hadn't been able to have any more children after her son was born, and she'd always treated Alyssa like the daughter she never had.

Setting her chopsticks on her paper plate, she

folded her arms on the counter. "Have you heard from your parents since they left for their holiday vacation in Cancún?" she asked. The couple owned a time-share at a luxurious Mexican resort, and now that they were both retired, they spent a few weeks out of the year relaxing and golfing at the sunny retreat.

"Just once," he said, and she heard the relief in his voice. "My mom is getting better about not checking up on me as often as she used to."

"She means well." Alyssa gathered up their paper plates and stacked the empty takeout boxes together. "Regardless of how old you are, you're still her baby."

Shane groaned at that. "Do you think that being an only child tends to make our mothers more clingy and protective?"

She dumped the trash into the wastebasket beneath the sink and laughed lightly. "No, it's strictly *your* mother who's that way."

Alyssa had long ago stopped wishing that her mother had given her the kind of unconditional attention that she'd yearned for as a young girl, and even now as an adult. Unfortunately, her mother had let the grief of losing her husband consume all of her emotions, and there hadn't been a whole lot left over for Alyssa.

After spending years watching her mother mourn

her deceased husband, Alyssa had come to the conclusion that she would never give herself over so completely to any one person and set herself up for that kind of deep, everlasting pain, which was the reason why her relationships never lasted long. Nor did she open herself up enough to any man to constitute anything serious.

But come the new year, she was going to try to change all that and finally break the vicious cycle that had ruled her emotions and relationships since she'd started dating at the age of sixteen.

"Did you talk to your mother on Christmas Day?" he asked.

"Only because I called her," she answered.

"Again?" His incredulous tone belied the fact that he knew how withdrawn her mother had become. But he wanted her to know he thought it wasn't right.

"I made plans to see her on New Year's Day so we can watch the Rose Parade together, like we do every year. But it's my doing, not hers."

"Damn, Alyssa." He slipped his hands around her waist from behind, surprising her with the warm, comforting, and unexpected hug. "It shouldn't be that way."

She closed her eyes, relishing the gentle way he was holding her, the way his face was pressed to the side of hers and his hands were clasped against her belly—which tumbled with sensual awareness.

She swallowed hard, ignoring the physical, arousing sensations making themselves known where Shane was concerned. "It's always been that way. I'm okay with it." She might have come to accept the situation, but she'd never grown used to her mother's indifferent behavior.

Sidestepping him, she grabbed the jumbo-sized bucket of Red Vines licorice that was their snack of choice for the *Twilight Zone* show. She turned to him with a bright smile, refusing to let a too serious moment spoil their evening together. "Come on. We have a marathon to watch."

Five hours and more than ten *Twilight Zone* episodes later, Shane and Alyssa were reclining on the wide sectional couch next to one another—shoulder to shoulder, hip to hip, with Alyssa occasionally turning toward him when something from one of the shows scared or startled her. Which, lucky for Shane, was more often than not.

He'd turned off all the lights earlier so that the room was dark and eerie-looking. The shadows flickering on the living room walls from the glow of the TV added to the ominous ambience. He glanced toward Alyssa and found her gaze completely focused on the current episode, "Nightmare at 20,000 Feet," which was one of his favorites because it never failed to give her a good scare.

Her eyes were wide. Her body was rigid with anticipation, and her expression intense as she watched the story unfold, about a man on a plane who believed he was seeing a hairy monster figure standing out on the aircraft's wing during a very heavy rainstorm. And just because Shane felt like breaking up the tense moment, he leaned toward Alyssa and tickled her in the ribs while growling in her ear, effectively terrifying her.

She screamed and jumped, then glared at him and punched him in the arm. "Dammit, Shane, you know how worked up I get over this episode."

"Yeah, I do, which is why scaring you is so much fun," he said, chuckling. "And here comes your favorite part."

Actually, it was one of the scenes she dreaded the most, where the delusional passenger opened the curtain covering the aircraft's window, only to find the gremlin pressing his ugly piglike face against the glass.

Another small scream caught in her throat, and she rolled toward Shane and buried her face against his neck so she didn't have to look at the little demon. "God, I hate that evil gremlin monster," she said as her body shuddered along the length of his.

"I'm not watching any more of this episode. It's absolutely horrid. Tell me when it's over."

He slid his arm along her shoulders and tucked her closer to his side, so that their bodies were nearly entwined intimately. "You big chicken."

She pinched him lightly on his belly for that. "I only put myself through this torture once a year for *you*, you ungrateful oaf."

"I appreciate your sacrifice," he said solemnly. He also liked the way she splayed her hand on his stomach. "Now be quiet so I can watch the rest of the episode without you yammering in my ear."

She huffed in response to his playful insult, and her warm, damp breath wafted against his neck— which he felt like an electrifying caress all the way down to his groin. He sucked back a groan, and it took monumental effort to concentrate on the show instead of the perfect way Alyssa fit against him.

The episode continued, with the gremlin wreaking havoc on the aircraft's propeller and engine and freaking out the man in the process. In a fit of panic, the guy managed to secure a gun, and after opening the auxiliary exit and getting himself sucked half-way out of the plane, he shot at the monster, in his mind killing it. The bizarre encounter sent the man into a mental breakdown and left the audience wondering if it had all been real or was yet another wacky trip through the Twilight Zone.

173

With the episode over, Shane's attention returned to Alyssa, who was still snuggled up against him, her body completely relaxed and her breathing deep and even. Realizing she'd fallen asleep, he grinned to himself and threaded his fingers through her soft, spiral curls. He caught the floral scent of her shampoo, which went straight to his senses. He thought about waking her up to watch the next show, but instead decided to let her rest a little longer while he played with her hair and enjoyed the feel of her lush breasts pressed so enticingly against his chest.

He was halfway into the next episode when Alyssa murmured something in her sleep and shifted closer, so that her thigh slid in between his legs and she was half on top of him. She nuzzled his throat, and her soft, moist lips trailed along the underside of his jaw, sending a flash of heat rippling through him.

His body hardened in a rush, his pulse quickened, and he didn't dare move, because he didn't want this erotic moment to end. When her hand started wandering lower, toward the waistband of his khakis, the erection straining the fly of his pants throbbed in anticipation.

But instead of stroking along that taut, confined ridge of flesh, her palm changed directions. Her fingers found the hem of his T-shirt, slipped beneath it, and stroked and caressed his stomach, his chest, and all the way up to his taut nipples.

Unable to help himself, and needing to touch her too, he gently slid his hand over the sweet swell of her hip, then dared to skim higher, until her plump breast filled his large palm and his thumb rasped over the tight nipple beading against her top. She moaned softly and arched into him. Shane was certain she was still sleeping and in the throes of a very pleasurable dream that was beginning to mingle with something far more tangible.

He really should wake her before this encounter went any further, but that thought fled his mind when her mouth settled against his, tempting him beyond reason. Lost in the seductive moment, he flicked his tongue along the seam of her lips, and when they parted for him he delved deep inside, engaging her in the kind of slow, soft kiss he'd fantasized about for years.

Except reality was so much better. So much sweeter. She tasted like honey and heat and his most treasured wish come to life. He couldn't get enough of her.

Gently, he eased her beneath him and his erection found a home at the crux of her thighs. Tangling one of his hands in her tousled hair, he kept on kissing her . . . deeper, and deeper still. He was getting drunk from the feel of her, and her uninhibited response was like a drug to him, dragging him under and pushing him to the point of no return.

And that was a line he refused to cross without her being completely and totally aware of who she was about to make love to.

He slowly, gradually, broke the heated kiss. His breathing was shallow and ragged, his body rioting with the need to be inside of her. Ignoring those demands, he grazed his lips along her cheek, her jaw, then lower to the fragrant skin of her throat.

A soft, purring sigh escaped her, along with his name, which surprised the hell out of him. Either she was more cognizant than he'd originally thought or she'd just let slip her true and intimate feelings for him.

She stirred beneath him, and he lifted his head just in time to watch her lashes drift open. Even with only the soft glow of the TV for illumination he could see that her lips were swollen from his kisses, and her eyes were hazy with desire.

She frowned up at him for a handful of seconds, until the confusion in her gaze gave way to the realization of what they'd just done, that what she'd just experienced hadn't been a dream after all. Then, with a physical jolt he felt to his soul, she panicked.

"Oh, God, no," she said in a raspy, frantic whisper and started pushing him off of her.

He immediately moved, and as soon as he let her

up she bolted off the couch to put some distance between them. She stared at him, horrified. "What were we doing?"

He sat up, braced his forearms on his thighs, and tried not to think about the aching erection still making itself known. Her question was a silly one, because he knew that she fully realized what had just happened between them. But just in case she needed him to confirm their actions, he gave it to her straight. "I believe we were kissing."

She moaned, a low, keening sound that told him she wasn't at all pleased to hear him verify that particular truth.

"It's not a big deal, Alyssa," he said, trying to soothe her.

"Yes, it is!" she wailed and waved her hand wildly in the air in her near hysteria. "You're my *best friend*!"

He tilted his head and regarded her calmly. "And?"

She looked at him as if he were insane. "And best friends don't kiss like that. Those kind of kisses can change *everything*."

Exactly, he wanted to say, but didn't, because it was obvious to him that she had a big problem when it came to accepting any kind of change in their *friendship*. No matter that she'd just shown him how much she wanted him minutes ago. She wasn't ready to admit that things had, indeed, already changed between them.

"Look," she said, her tone pragmatic and much calmer now. "We were obviously both asleep and not thinking straight, so let's just chalk it up to a mistake and forget it ever happened. I need to go to the bathroom. We'll finish watching the marathon when I get back."

He watched her leave the room, and as soon as she was gone he cursed beneath his breath, hoping that he hadn't just ruined all the headway he'd made with her over the past few days.

One way or another, tomorrow night, New Year's Eve, he would find out.

Chapter Five

Alyssa was on a mission—to find the perfect New Year's Eve party outfit and to forget all about the hot, melting kiss she'd shared with Shane the night before.

With her arms loaded down with an array of outfits, she made her way to the boutique's dressing room, still shaken by how far things had gone between the two of them. Now, knowing just how weak she was when it came to resisting Shane, she was more driven than ever to date other men and force herself to get over her intimate feelings for him.

As she'd told Shane last night, giving in to a physical attraction would change everything between them. What scared her the most was the thought of not being able to live up to his expectations. She also feared she wouldn't be able to give him what he needed from a committed relationship when she'd never been able to sustain anything remotely serious or lasting with a man. The risk of losing Shane for good because of her inability to open herself emotionally wasn't a chance she was willing to take with him.

Her worries were probably for nothing, considering that he was interested in another woman. Their kiss had most likely been a fluke. A spur-of-the-moment passionate embrace that had gotten out of hand and never should have happened. What she needed to concentrate on was her own secret admirer and grabbing *his* attention tonight.

With that thought in mind, she decided to hell with being sedate and practical. Tonight she was going to throw sensibleness right out the window and wear something sexy, sultry, and fun. An outfit certain to attract her own fair share of attention.

Half an hour later she left the boutique with a sparkly white dress that was flirtatious and more form-fitting than anything she'd ever worn before. She'd also purchased sheer, lacy, barely there lingerie to wear beneath it, and a pair of strappy high-heeled shoes that made her legs look slender and endlessly long.

She stopped at the beauty shop and treated herself to a manicure, pedicure, and facial, which was a rarity for her. By the time she arrived back home and indulged in a fragrant bubble bath, she was feeling upbeat and optimistic about the upcoming evening.

With a few hours still left to go before Shane picked her up at six, she wrapped her damp hair in a towel and slipped into her well-worn terry robe until it was time for her to get ready for the party. She went into her office, booted up her computer, and did a bit of work and Internet research on a few open projects. Since she hadn't heard from her secret admirer yesterday because of her busy schedule, she was hoping he would contact her one more time before they met face-to-face tonight at Drew and Cynthia's.

He didn't disappoint her. His Instant Message appeared on her screen, blinking with a greeting.

TheOne4You: I can't wait to see you tonight.

She bit her bottom lip, wishing she was more excited about the prospect of meeting him, too. Sure, she was curious about who he was, and she'd enjoyed their correspondence over the past few days. But she lacked that sense of exhilaration and anticipation that usually came with dating someone new. And she had a feeling her sizzling kiss with Shane was to blame.

Still, she was determined to give this guy a chance.

IshopForYou: Are you going to tell me who you are before we meet tonight? Like at least your name?

TheOne4You: A name isn't necessary. I promise you'll know me when you see me, and you won't need an introduction.

She arched a brow as she read his evasive note and wondered why he felt the need to be so secretive.

IshopForYou: You like to draw out the suspense, don't you?

TheOne4You: Yes, I do. <g> Meet me at midnight tonight out in Drew and Cynthia's backyard, by the rose garden, and you'll learn everything you need to know about me.

After that short and to-the-point message, he immediately signed off, before Alyssa could post a response.

She blinked at the computer screen, feeling frustrated and confused. That was it? Meet him at midnight? After all their Instant Messaging, she had to wait until the end of the evening to finally find out who her secret admirer was?

Unbelievable, she thought with a shake of her head.

But she had no choice but to be patient and wait for the stroke of midnight to appease her curiosity, because she didn't have a clue as to who her mystery man was. And since she was dying to discover his true identity, she knew she'd be in the rose garden, as he'd asked.

Shane's jaw nearly dropped to the floor as Alyssa opened the door to her apartment when he arrived to pick her up for the New Year's Eve party. He'd never seen her look so blatantly sexy. She literally took his breath away.

"Do you like my new dress?" she asked, twirling around so he could inspect her from all angles.

Like it? God, he was in awe of how the shimmering white fabric clung to her generous breasts and molded to her waist and hips, showing off her voluptuous figure. The plunging neckline displayed more cleavage than he'd ever seen on Alyssa, and the hemline hit her mid-thigh, baring her long, smooth legs to his gaze.

Then there was her hair, which she'd piled on her head in a mass of tousled spiral curls, some of which had escaped to wisp against the nape of her neck and along the sides of her face. Her makeup was lightly applied, but the soft pink and beige hues she'd used brought out the deep blue of her eyes, and her glossy lips looked as sweet and ripe as a juicy peach.

He swallowed hard. "You look . . . *wow!*" It was the only word he could find to describe just how incredible this transformation of hers was. "I'm sure I'm going to have to beat the guys off with a big club tonight."

She laughed, the husky sound increasing his internal temperature a few notches. "I'm feeling pretty good, and I'm determined to have a good time tonight." She stepped toward him and straightened the collar of the burgundy dress shirt he'd worn, then tipped her face up to his. "By the way, you look pretty 'wow' yourself. Your lady friend might not recognize you all dressed up like this," she teased.

He nearly groaned as her hands trailed briefly down his chest before falling away, and he had to resist the strong urge to wrap his arm around her waist, pull her tight against him, and kiss her like he was aching to.

But resist that particular temptation he did. They both had a big night ahead of them, and remembering too well how she'd panicked on him last night after their heated embrace, he wasn't about to spoil her good mood with a spontaneous kiss now.

So he took a step back and smiled. "Are you ready to go?"

"As ready as I'll ever be." She grabbed her small purse and a shawl, then hooked her arm through his and returned his smile with a dazzling one of her own. "Let's go meet our dates."

By nine that evening the party was in full swing, with champagne and drinks flowing freely, a buffet of food set out for guests, and music drifting from the speakers flanking the large backyard patio, which had been turned into a dancing area. One of the nice things about living in Southern California was the weather—even on the last night in December the evening was gorgeous, with a clear, moonlit sky, stars glittering overhead, and just a hint of a chill in the air.

At least thirty-five people were celebrating New Year's Eve with Drew and Cynthia, and they wandered from inside the house, where it was warm, to the backyard, where it was cool. Alyssa found herself circulating through the throng of guests as well, talking to friends she hadn't seen in a while and also sizing up every single guy as someone who potentially might be her secret admirer.

But so far she hadn't experienced any kind of spark or chemistry with the few men who'd expressed an interest in her, and she still had three hours to go before she would discover her admirer's identity.

She also found herself keeping an eye on Shane during the course of the evening. She watched every female in the room who approached him, or that he conversed with, always wondering if she was "the one." Her emotions ran the gamut from flashes of jealousy when he paid too much attention to one particular woman, to extreme relief when he moved on to another group of friends, leaving the lady behind. She felt like she was on an emotional roller coaster with no end in sight.

At the moment, Shane was standing with Drew and Cynthia. Alyssa made her way across the room toward them, thinking that Shane looked incredibly handsome in his new clothes and his shorter hair style. He looked like he'd just stepped straight out of the pages of a *GQ* magazine. But despite how he'd changed on the outside to impress his lady friend, Alyssa hoped the woman appreciated the genuine man beneath those clothes even more. Shane was one of a kind, and he deserved a woman who treated him like the true catch he was.

As if he could sense that her thoughts were centered on him, Shane glanced at her as she approached, his gaze slowly sliding down the length of her dress, then back up again. The sexy, disarming grin that pulled up the corners of his mouth and the heat that filled his eyes made her heart skip a few beats. She'd yet to see him smile like that at any of the women at the party tonight, and it gave her a bit of a thrill to have captured his attention with the dress she'd worn.

Alyssa came up beside Shane and lifted her nearly empty glass of champagne to the happily married couple in a toast. "Great New Year's Eve party, as always."

"I'm glad you're enjoying yourself." Cynthia's eyes sparkled with delight, and her complexion glowed in a way that Alyssa had never seen before. "You look absolutely *amazing* in that dress."

A warm blush swept across Alyssa's cheeks at the compliment, making her realize that she really ought to dress up more often. "Thank you."

Cynthia touched her husband's arm and glanced up at him adoringly. "Drew and I were just about to tell Shane some exciting news, and we're glad you joined us."

Whatever it was, Alyssa could feel their excitement.

"What's up, you two?"

"We're going to have a baby," Drew announced, puffing his chest out proudly.

Alyssa gasped in surprise and hugged Cynthia,

while Shane shook Drew's hand. "Oh, my goodness! Congratulations! I'm so happy for you both," they said.

"We're pretty thrilled, too." Cynthia placed her hand on her still-flat belly. "We're going to go spread the good news, but we wanted the two of you to be among the first to know."

Alyssa sighed as the couple moved on, a little envious—okay, a whole *lot* envious—over their close, loving relationship. They were such a great pair, and she experienced a deep pang of loneliness thinking about how all her friends were getting married, having families, and moving on with their lives. She was still hopelessly single and so afraid of making the kind of commitment it took to sustain a lasting relationship.

Refusing to allow such depressing thoughts to get her down tonight, she returned her gaze to Shane. "So, where's your mystery woman?"

"I'm not meeting her until later," he replied easily. "Where's your secret admirer?"

She finished off her champagne and set it on a nearby passing tray. "The thing is, he *could* be here, right in plain sight, and I wouldn't even know it." And that possibility frustrated the heck out of her.

He slid his hands into the front pockets of his slacks, his brown eyes seemingly searching her expression. "So you haven't seen him yet?"

"No." She shook her head. "I'm not meeting him until later, too, out by the rose garden at midnight." Then she grinned wryly. "Maybe our dates are hanging out together until later."

His low, deep laughter curled through her. "In that case, why don't we do the same thing?" He held his hand out to her. "Care to dance?"

It sounded like a wonderful distraction to her. She placed her fingers in his warm palm, which felt so perfectly right. "I would love to."

He led her outside to the patio, where the music was playing and the mood was festive. The next few hours passed quickly as they danced, perused the buffet, drank another glass of champagne, and then danced some more.

When a slow song came over the speakers, Alyssa turned to walk off the dance floor, but before she could escape Shane grabbed her hand and gently whirled her back around to face him. Before she could protest, he wrapped one arm around her waist, gathered her close, and secured her other hand in his.

He raised a teasing brow at her. "You thought you were going to get away, didn't you?"

She wasn't about to admit that yes, she'd been trying to avoid this kind of close contact with him. Her hormones just couldn't take the feel of his hard, warm body pressed so intimately against hers.

"What if our dates are watching us?" she asked, using that as an excuse for him to let her go.

"Who cares?" he said, shrugging those broad shoulders of his. "I'm not letting you go until the song ends, so relax and enjoy yourself."

How in the world was she supposed to relax when every single one of her feminine nerve endings was tingling with sexual awareness? She exhaled a deep breath that didn't do much to dispel the tension humming through her veins.

As they swayed to the music, their bodies seemingly melted into one another, aligning in a way that was very seductive and arousing—as was the slow, rhythmic way his hips moved against hers. He slid a hand down her back and let his warm palm come to rest at the base of her spine. A hard, masculine thigh pressed between her legs, her breasts grew heavy, and her sensitive nipples peaked against the lacy cups of her bra.

Her pulse quickened, and she bit her bottom lip to hold back a groan of pure pleasure.

And still he continued to torment her.

He pressed his cheek lightly to hers. She felt his damp, heated breath caress her skin and could smell the warm male scent of his cologne, which did crazy things to her insides. Her knees went weak, as did her resolve to keep things platonic between them.

His lips grazed her jaw, then trailed down the side of her neck. She closed her eyes as a shiver rippled through her, bringing with it a need and hunger so strong that it threatened every one of her defenses against this man who was her very best friend.

"You really do look beautiful tonight, Alyssa," he murmured, his voice husky and rough around the edges. "Your secret admirer is one hell of a lucky guy."

She didn't know what to say, because at the moment she didn't give a damn about her secret admirer, or what *he* might think about the way she looked. Shane made her *feel* beautiful, and sexy, and she wanted him like no other man she'd ever been with. If they hadn't been surrounded by other people in the midst of a party, she feared she would have given into that desire right then and there.

That startling thought was enough for her to put an end to their slow, tantalizing dance even before the music ended. She tried to ease from his embrace, but he didn't completely let her go.

She couldn't look him in the eye, afraid that he'd be able to see just how affected she was by him. "I, ummm, I need to go."

"Go where?" he asked, his voice too damn alluring.

"To meet my date." She dared to finally look at

him and found him staring at her with unnerving intensity. "It's almost midnight."

This time when she moved away from him, he released her, much to her relief, because she needed the physical distance. She went inside to get her shawl, saw that there was less than ten minutes until twelve o'clock, and made her way out to the rose garden to regain her composure and clear her head before her secret admirer arrived.

Drew and Cynthia's backyard was large and beautifully landscaped. While Alyssa could hear the guests up at the house, it was quiet where she was, with only the bright moonlight offering her any source of illumination. She breathed slowly and deeply and paced restlessly along the short walkway, welcoming the cool evening air wafting over her overheated body.

Minutes later she heard someone approaching from behind, and with her heart pounding hard and fast in her chest she turned around, fully expecting her secret admirer to be standing there. Instead she found Shane. While she was surprised that he'd followed her out to the rose garden, she didn't think her date would appreciate Shane's being there when he arrived. *If* he even showed up.

"What are you doing out here?" she asked cautiously.

He came up to her and gently brushed away

wisps of hair tickling the side of her face. "I just wanted to make sure that you were okay."

"I'm fine," she said, all too aware of the butterflies that had hatched in her stomach upon seeing him again. "Though I'm beginning to think we both got stood up tonight."

He smiled at her, his dark eyes indulging her. "No man in his right mind would stand you up, Alyssa."

She trembled deep inside, and she wasn't so sure that it was the chilled air that had caused the reaction. Rather it was the rich, sincere tone of Shane's voice.

"I'm starting to have my doubts about that." She tugged her shawl tighter over her shoulders, using it for warmth and a protective shield from her response to Shane's nearness as well. "I just heard someone up at the house yell that there are only two more minutes left until midnight, and here I am standing in the rose garden with you, not my date, and I have no idea who he is."

He pushed his hands into the front pockets of his slacks, his casual stance belying the direct and purposeful way he was watching her. "Don't you think you'll know him when you see him?"

Startled by his choice of words, she narrowed her gaze at him. "What do you mean by that?"

"The guy you're waiting for could be standing right in front of you."

You won't need an introduction, her secret admirer had told her. "Is he?" she whispered.

Shane's expression never changed. "What do *you* think?"

Her head spun as bits and pieces of her online conversation with him filtered through her mind, fast and furiously. *I want you to know that I'm very attracted to you and have been for some time now. . . . You have beautiful blue eyes. . . . I love your laughter. It's husky and sexy. . . . Your friend is a lucky guy to be able to spend the night with you.*

She grew dizzy over the probability that Shane had been her secret admirer all along.

"Oh, God," she breathed in shock. "You're . . ."

"The One for You," he finished before she could, giving her the screen name he'd used over the past few days.

And now it held a deeper, more intimate meaning.

She shook her head wildly, feeling so over-whelmed and confused. "I don't understand. What about the woman you're trying to impress?"

Finally a slow, hopeful smile lifted his lips. "You're that woman, Alyssa."

"You made all those changes for me?" she asked in disbelief. "Your clothes, your hair, this new image of yours . . ."

He nodded. "Because I hoped that those changes

would show you that I can be everything you're looking for in a man, inside and out."

Her heart squeezed tight and tears burned the back of her throat, because she so *wanted* him to be the man for her. But she didn't know if she could be the kind of woman he needed in his life. And she didn't give a damn about his nice preppy clothes and clean-cut image. She loved him just the way he was, *before* his transformation.

Oh, Lord, *she loved him.* More than the sibling she never had. More than the best friend he was. She loved *everything* about Shane Witmer.

They could hear the countdown for the stroke of midnight begin up at the house. In ten more seconds it would be New Year's Day.

She stared at Shane, who was standing in front of her so patiently, waiting for her to make a decision—to say or do something to let him know where he stood with her now. But she couldn't bring herself to speak. He'd gone all out to be her secret admirer and change his appearance to please her. He'd made himself vulnerable for her and was now facing the possibility of her rejecting him.

As shocking as it was even to her, she had no intention of turning him away.

She was merely a woman, with a woman's heart and needs, and she was only so strong. She didn't want to be alone tonight. Didn't want to go home to an empty bed and dreams of Shane. She ached for him, and it was a need she could no longer deny.

The guests at the party hooted and hollered and started singing "Auld Lang Syne" as the clock struck midnight.

"Happy New Year, Alyssa," Shane said, but he made no move to hug her as he normally would.

No, she realized, he was waiting for her to make the first move, whatever it might be.

Her mind told her to get the hell out of there before she did something she would regret later, but her emotions . . . oh, Lord, they were telling her to follow what was in her heart. What had been there for years.

Before she lost her nerve, or came to her senses, she closed the distance between herself and Shane, curled a hand around the nape of his neck, and brought his mouth down to hers for a hot, deep, and wholly passionate kiss. And nothing in that moment mattered but kissing this man, who meant everything to her.

Shane didn't hesitate to respond. His warm palms framed the sides of her face, and he angled her head for a deeper, more demanding possession. Their tongues touched, entwined, mated, and she moved in closer, drawn to the heat of his body. Their hips aligned. He was already hard and thick, and her own body softened, growing damp with desire, burning up with need.

Too soon he ended the kiss and stared deeply, steadily, into her eyes, so that there was no mistaking the depth of his feelings for her. "I want you, Alyssa."

"I know." Her words were hushed, almost a whisper, and it was a major battle to keep her fears out of the equation. "Even though I know I shouldn't, I want you, too."

"Be with me tonight."

His request was simply, eloquently stated, leaving no doubt in her mind what he was asking.

Her answer was just as meaningful. "*Yes.*"

Chapter Six

Alyssa had been in Shane's bedroom many times before, but never under such intimate circumstances. They stood beside his bed, which he'd turned down. He gently clasped her hands in his much larger, warmer ones. They were both still fully clothed, but she couldn't remember ever feeling so bared and vulnerable in her entire life as she did in that moment.

"Are you sure about this, sweetheart?" he asked as he tenderly rubbed his thumbs over her knuckles.

Sweetheart. That was an endearment he'd never used with her before. Already there were subtle changes happening in their relationship, and they hadn't even slept together yet. She didn't want to think about the more devastating changes that might occur between them come the morning.

She reached up, pulled the pins from her hair,

and let it tumble around her shoulders in a mass of disheveled curls. "Don't ask me that question right now, Shane," she said. If he gave her too much time to contemplate the answer, he wouldn't like what she had to say. The only thing she was certain of at this very moment was wanting this one night with him. She would deal with everything else tomorrow.

"I don't want to think about anything right now except you and me, together." Smoothing her hands up his chest, she went to work on the buttons of his shirt. He'd removed his jacket and tie as soon as they'd walked into his house, which made her job of undressing him that much easier.

"Tonight, I just want you to make me *feel.*"

He charmed her with one of his devastatingly sexy grins. "Oh, I plan to."

She wanted to make him feel, too, and set out to do so. As she bared his throat, she pressed her nose to his neck and inhaled his warm, male scent. When all the buttons on his shirt were unfastened, she pushed the fabric over his broad shoulders and down along his arms while planting soft, warm kisses down his muscular chest.

He groaned raggedly and threaded his fingers through her hair as she flicked her tongue over one rigid nipple, then the other. Her mouth came back up to his for more of his slow, soft, sensual kisses

199

while her hands unbuckled the thin leather belt at his waist. He reached behind her, unzipped her dress, and with a firm tug it slithered down her body and pooled on the floor at her feet. His slacks joined the array of clothing, leaving him clad in only his boxers and her in a sheer, lacy bra and silky panties.

Lifting his lips from hers, he took a step back and looked his fill of her, his eyes darkening with a hungry heat as he traced a finger along the upper swells of her breasts, then into the full cleavage, where he found the front clasp to her bra and deftly unsnapped it. The cups fell away, releasing her heavy, swollen breasts to his gaze.

He pushed her bra straps over her shoulders and down her arms. "I've been waiting a lifetime to see your breasts, to touch them," he murmured as he delicately plucked the stiff peaks, then filled his palms with the mounds of flesh.

The heat and pressure of his hands on her breasts felt so good, as did the scrape of his calloused thumbs across her nipples. She ran her hands down his smooth back, let her fingers slip beneath the waistband of his underwear until she cupped his firm buttocks in her palms. Then she leaned into him so that her breasts were flattened against his chest and began kissing her way down his torso, until she was kneeling before him, at eye level with the impressive length straining against his snug boxers. She nipped at him through the cotton, heard him growl deep in his throat, and started dragging that last barrier downward so that she could touch and taste him for real.

He fisted her hair in his hand and gently tugged her head back so she was looking up at him. "Alyssa . . . you don't have to do this."

She licked her lips. "I want to."

In the next instant his underwear dropped to his feet, and she was graced with the beauty of his completely naked body, hot and aroused for her. She wrapped her hand around his erection and brushed her thumb over the moist tip. His hips bucked toward her, and she smiled as she slowly took him into her mouth, every single hard inch of him. He tasted smooth against her tongue, the shape of him exotic and all male, and it didn't take her long to discover the rhythm and friction that pushed him close to the edge.

He shuddered, and his fingers tightened in her hair to pull her back up. Because she wanted him inside her when he came, she followed his silent command.

"God, you have such an incredible mouth," he said as he grazed his thumb along her still-damp bottom lip. "Now it's my turn. Lie down for me."

She moved onto the bed, still wearing her panties.

Shane crawled up over her, with his knees bracketing her thighs and his hands braced on the mattress by her head. His eyes were dark and hot as he stared down at her. "Do you remember what I told you during one of our online conversations about kissing being the best part of foreplay, along with all those sensitive, erotic spots I enjoy kissing?"

Her neck, her breasts, her belly, her thighs. Each body part began tingling in anticipation. "Yes."

"Good, because I'm going to kiss you in every one of those spots."

And then he made good on his promise. He started with her mouth and slanted his lips across hers, letting one kiss melt inevitably, enticingly, into another, until her entire body grew soft and pliable and anxious for his mouth to move on to those other erogenous zones.

In his own sweet time, he nuzzled her neck and grazed his lips and tongue and teeth down her throat to her breasts. She gripped the sheets in her hands, writhing impatiently beneath him, and nearly sighed in relief when he closed his lips over a nipple, sucked it into his warm, wet mouth, and swirled his tongue along the sensitive tip.

He followed the curve of her breast with his lips, marked her with little love bites here and there, and pressed kisses along each of her ribs before dipping his tongue into her navel. By the time he reached the waistband of her panties, she felt as though she was going to come right out of her skin.

But Shane had more pleasurable pursuits in mind, and after stripping away that last scrap of material he settled between her legs, using the gentle pressure of his hands to spread her wide. He smoothed his flattened palms up her thighs, followed by soft, openmouthed kisses, until both met up at the most feminine part of her. His thumbs delved along her sex, then parted her flesh. She felt the heat of his breath first, the slow, languid stroke of his tongue second, then two fingers push deep, deep inside her as he closed his mouth over her, giving her the deepest, wettest, hottest kiss yet.

The moan that escaped her was long and satisfying. Lost in the ecstasy of his selfless giving, she pushed her fingers through his shortened hair and lifted her hips, deepening his penetration. Her orgasm hit, strong and powerful, and she surrendered to the incredible, mind-blowing release with a low, keening cry.

She panted, trying to catch her breath, her rushed climax leaving her weak and pliable. When she finally came to her senses again she found Shane sheathing his shaft with a condom, then he was sliding up and over her body and lacing their fingers together at the sides of her head. Instinctively, she wrapped her legs around his waist and closed her eyes when she felt the head of his sex start to push inside her.

"Open your eyes and look at me, Alyssa," he demanded in a rough, barely restrained voice.

Unable to deny him anything, she did as he asked and felt her heart leap at the emotion shining in his eyes.

"I love you," he said, and then he lowered his head and kissed her tenderly at the same time he thrust into her, claiming her body as surely as he'd stolen her heart.

As he made love to her in every sense of the word and she shattered once again in his arms, Alyssa knew she would never be the same.

And neither would their friendship.

Shane fell asleep with Alyssa curled up to his side, with her arms around him and their legs entwined. He woke up in the early-morning hours to find her attempting to slide quietly out of his bed so as not to disturb him.

As she stood and turned to look at him, he closed his eyes again, knowing without a doubt that she had every intention of leaving him before he had a chance to wake up. She was trying to avoid an awkward morning-after scene, and he wasn't about to spoil her plans with a confrontation that would cause her to shut him out completely and emotionally. He knew her well enough to know that was her method of operation, and he was a fool for thinking that his declaration of love last night would change anything between them this morning.

He listened to her move around the room and pick up her clothes, disappointed at her covert exit, but not surprised. He heard her head down the hall to the living room and quietly make a call to a cab company to pick her up. Then she came back to his room again.

He sensed her standing by the side of the bed, and it took every ounce of control he possessed not to open his eyes and beg her to stay.

He heard what sounded like a soft sob. Then she whispered in a soft, aching voice, "I love you, Shane. So much it hurts."

And she obviously didn't know what to do about those feelings. She was afraid of being in love, afraid of letting those emotions consume her to the point that if something should happen to the person she cared for she would never be able to fully recover from the loss.

Shane had given Alyssa everything last night, his heart and soul, and there was nothing left that he could do or say to convince her that they could have a future together. It was up to her to believe in herself. And in him. She had to come to him on her own and be willing to meet him halfway.

Mostly, she had to be willing to trust in him and what they shared together.

But until then, all he could do was be the best friend that he'd always been to her—even if that wasn't enough for him any longer.

Alyssa returned home from spending the night with Shane, feeling guilty for the cowardly way she'd snuck out on him that morning. But a sense of panic had driven her, and she'd needed the time and space away from him to deal with the fact that they'd slept together . . . and just how in love with him she truly was, and what all that meant to their friendship and future.

She knew she couldn't avoid the inevitable discussion forever, or pretend as though last night had never happened, and she didn't intend to do either. She'd made a clear and conscious choice to make love with Shane, and she took full responsibility for that decision and her actions, no matter what the eventual outcome.

She jumped in the shower and changed for the day, then drove over to her mother's place to watch the New Year's Day Rose Parade with her—an annual tradition that Alyssa had started years ago as a way of instigating some quality time between them, because if she didn't make the effort, it most likely wouldn't happen.

Twenty minutes later, she walked into her mother's house carrying a box of muffins for breakfast and headed toward the kitchen, where she could hear her mother going through the cupboards. She turned around when Alyssa entered the room and set two coffee cups on the counter by the percolating coffeepot.

Alyssa came up to her mother and kissed her on the cheek. Even in her mid-fifties, Beth Harte was still a beautiful woman, and Alyssa thought it such a shame that she'd never remarried. "Hey, Mom. Happy New Year."

"Same to you, dear." Her mother smiled, poured them each a cup of coffee, and added cream and sugar to the mix. "It's always nice to see you, but you know you really don't have to spend the day with me today."

Alyssa set the box of muffins on the counter and rolled her eyes. "What if I *want* to?"

Her mother shrugged. "I'd just think you'd have better things to do than to babysit me on New Year's Day."

"I've never thought of my visits as babysitting you." Alyssa grabbed two small plates and put one of the blueberry streusel muffins on each dish. "Do you ever think that maybe I want to spend time with you?"

The look her mother slanted Alyssa's way was

207

filled with a hint of warmth. "Well, I do appreciate it, you know."

No, Alyssa *hadn't* known, and she felt her spirits lift at the thought that her visits might make even a tiny bit of a difference to her mother.

They took their early-morning breakfast out to the living room and sat down on the couch next to one another. They watched the Rose Parade while eating their muffins and drinking their coffee and commented on all the beautiful and unique floats on display this year. As always, their conversation was light and superficial—more like acquaintances than mother and daughter.

Alyssa sighed inwardly and glanced around the living room. She was reminded of the solitary life her mother had led since her father's death so many years ago. Her mother still lived in the same house she and her husband had bought after they'd married, the same house in which she had raised Alyssa on her own. Not much had changed in the way of updating the place.

The furniture had remained unchanged, as had the old pictures of her father, and even of herself. It was as if time had stopped for her mother the day her husband had died. As always, the curtains across the windows were drawn, as if her mother was trying to preserve the old memories and feared that if she opened the drapes they'd all disappear as the room was exposed to bright, cheerful sunlight.

Her mother was so wrapped up in the past that she couldn't see the present, and it struck Alyssa in that moment that she wanted, and needed, to let the past, and her own hang-ups and insecurities, go. If she didn't, she was going to end up just like her mother—all alone, detached from friends, allowing pain and fears to rule her life.

After such a momentous night with Shane, the revelation was huge, and she tried to absorb the stunning realization. Now Alyssa was at the point where she needed answers to questions she'd never had the courage to ask her mother before today. She hoped that whatever explanations her mother had to offer would give her a better insight into her own personal insecurities and fears.

She glanced from the parade on TV to her mother, who seemed to be enjoying the New Year's Day festivities.

"Mom, why haven't you dated anyone seriously since Dad died?"

Her mother looked momentarily surprised by the question and then grew quiet, for so long that Alyssa didn't think she was going to give her an answer.

Then a bleak sadness filled her mother's eyes. "Because for me, I met and married my one true love. And when he died I never fully recovered from that loss."

Witnessing her mother's devastation firsthand had made Alyssa consciously avoid experiencing that kind of pain for herself. But as a result her life was empty, when she wished it was much, much fuller.

Still, Alyssa was curious about a few more things. "Do you ever wish you'd never gone through something that brought you such heartache, like Dad's death, and as a result you couldn't bring yourself to love like that again?"

A wistful smile softened her mother's features. "I have no regrets about loving your father the way I did. The way I still do. That kind of love, even if found only once, was worth everything we shared together. Even if only for a short time."

The last thing Alyssa wanted was regrets in her life. And she knew with everything that made her the woman she was that if she didn't take a chance on Shane—on them—she'd regret it for the rest of her life.

"I know you worry about me because I'm always alone," her mother went on, "but I'm okay with the way my life is."

If her mother didn't mind her solitary life, why should Alyssa worry or try to change it? She finally understood that her mother had chosen that life for herself, by not allowing anyone to get too close emotionally—including her own daughter.

Her mother was perfectly content being alone. And Alyssa was not. It was that difference that set them apart. And now Alyssa needed to take the steps to break the destructive pattern that had ruled her life for too long.

"I know I haven't been the best mother," Beth said, cutting into Alyssa's thoughts, "but I've always wanted you to be happy. And I do want you to fall in love, because it's the most precious gift between a man and a woman. When it's right, it's the most wonderful feeling in the whole world."

This was what she'd always wanted from her mother—her affection, her advice, her caring. She'd never doubted her mother's love, but now she *felt* it—though she didn't fool herself into believing this openness and sharing would continue into the future.

Because the moment felt right, because their conversation had evolved into something more emotional than Alyssa had ever expected, she told her mother the truth. "I *am* in love."

"Oh?" Her mother studied her for a moment. "With whom?"

Alyssa felt a telltale heat sweep across her cheeks. She thought about the sweet guy who'd pretended to be her secret admirer, the man who'd transformed his image to be what he believed she wanted in a mate. None of his tactics had been necessary, but they'd definitely caught her attention.

"It's Shane."

A small smile lifted the corner of her mother's mouth, though she didn't appear to be all that surprised by her admission. "Does he know?"

She shook her head. "No. Not yet."

"You know what I think?" her mother asked gently.

"What?" Alyssa whispered.

"I think you need to follow your heart, trust your instincts, and go tell Shane how you feel about him."

Alyssa had to admit that for someone who'd closed her heart off to a second chance at love long ago, her mother was a smart woman when it came to matters of the heart.

Alyssa grinned. "I think you're absolutely right."

Praying that she hadn't completely and totally blown her chance with Shane, Alyssa knocked on his front door, hoping he didn't resent her for sneaking out on him this morning.

He opened the door, and she caught the surprise that flashed across his expression before he quickly masked it behind an air of cool indifference. He stood there, only half dressed, and she had to admit that as good as he had looked last night in his expensive clothes for the party, he looked even better just wearing a pair of his old faded jeans and no shirt, with his hair still mussed from their night together.

"Hey," he said in the way of a casual greeting that gave her no real clue as to how he was truly feeling. "Aren't you supposed to be at your mom's watching the Rose Parade?"

She shifted anxiously on her feet. "I was already there, but you and I have unfinished business to take care of."

"Okay," he said, and opened the door wider for her to enter his house. "Come on in."

She brushed past him, and she could tell he was being cautious with her, not knowing what to expect. Well, they were on even footing, then, because she was feeling the same way about him.

He sprawled on the far end of the couch and rested his arms along the top of it. She, on the other hand, paced across the room from him, trying to shake off the excess energy buzzing through her, trying to calm the rapid beating of her heart and the insecurities doing their damnedest to overwhelm her.

"So, what's up?" he asked in an even, unreadable tone.

She found it ironic that *he* was pretending that last night had never happened. She would have laughed if she hadn't been so nervous about how this conversation would end.

213

"There's a few things I need to say to you."

"All right." His gaze was direct. "I'm listening."

He wasn't going to make any of this easy on her. Not that she blamed him. She had some explaining to do, and some apologizing, too. He deserved both, if not more.

"You are the most stable, dependable person I've ever had in my life," she said, needing him to know exactly what he meant to her. "You're my best friend, and I don't ever want to lose you."

Shane listened to Alyssa's speech. When she'd shown up at his door he'd been cautiously hopeful, but now he recognized yet another spiel about friendship that didn't bode well for him. He didn't care for the path the conversation was about to take, and if she dared to tell him that last night was a *mistake*, he was fully prepared to drag her down to the couch and prove to her just how good a mistake could feel.

"When I went to my mother's this morning, I realized a few things," she said, continuing to pace the length of carpet in front of the TV. "I saw the way she'd lived her life since my father's death, and I knew I didn't want to grow old by myself, never having experienced a close, intimate, loving relationship, even if it meant getting hurt along the way. It was my mother's decision to spend her life alone, and I don't want it to be my choice anymore."

For that statement alone, Shane was very proud of

her. She was standing up for herself, being the strong, gutsy woman he'd always known she could be.

"So, what do you want, Alyssa?"

The smile of longing that appeared on her face made him feel sucker-punched in the stomach. "I want a husband. I want babies. I want the kind of family I grew up without."

And still, no mention of him in that picture she was painting.

"And what about your New Year's resolution?" he asked, needing to know where she was going from here—and where that left him in the scheme of her plans.

"Oh, I plan to stick to it," she said with a self-assured sway to her hips as she approached where he was sitting on the couch. She knelt in front of him, placed her hands on his widespread knees, and met his gaze. "I'm still determined to put myself out there in an intimate and emotional way. With you, Shane. My best friend. My companion. And now, my lover."

He opened his mouth to reply, and she cut him off by placing her fingers over his lips.

"I thought of you being my secret admirer, which I'll admit was exciting at first," she said and touched her fingertips to his jaw in a reverent caress. "I thought of you making so many changes for me. Your clothes. Your hair. And you know what?

Though I'm grateful you care enough to go to such great lengths to prove your feelings for me, *none* of that matters to me. The only thing I care about is that you're the man who knows my heart, my soul, my secrets, and you love me, exactly the way I am. With all my quirks and hang-ups and insecurities."

He gently grasped her wrist, pulled her hand away from his mouth, and settled her palm right over his beating heart. "Yeah, I do."

"You are everything I could ever want or need in my life," she said, a husky catch to her voice. "I think I've always known that, but I was too afraid to take a chance on you. On us."

"And now?"

She looked up at him with huge blue eyes filled with a wealth of emotion. "I need to know if you're willing to take a chance on me, because I'm the one with most of the hang-ups in this relationship."

He laughed at that. "I took a chance on you long ago, Alyssa, hang-ups and all. I'm not about to change my mind about you now." He slid his hands beneath her arms so he could pull her up and into his lap, and she came willingly, settling herself on his thighs and wrapping her arms around his neck. "And when you're ready, I'm going to marry you."

She bit her quivering bottom lip, her eyes shining with moisture. "I love you, Shane Witmer," she whispered.

"I know," he said confidently.

"You do?" She arched a delicate brow. "How?"

It was time for him to 'fess up. "I heard what you said this morning before you left my place, when you thought I was sleeping. About loving me, and how much it hurt." He stroked a hand over her hip and down the side of her thigh, wishing he was caressing her bare flesh instead of soft denim. "Love shouldn't hurt, Alyssa. And I'm going to do everything in my power to make sure that when you think of love, you think of all the good times we've shared, the laughter, and *this*."

He claimed her mouth with his, slow and deep, pouring every ounce of emotion he felt for her into the kiss, until she slumped weakly against his chest. He lifted his head and found Alyssa smiling dreamily at him.

"Oh, I definitely like that part," she murmured.

Oh, yeah, the New Year was full of possibilities. Full of promises for the two of them.

"There's a whole lot more where that came from," he said and gave her bottom an affectionate squeeze. "What do you say we spend the day in bed, so I can show you just how much I love you?"

She sighed happily. "I say lead the way. I'm all yours."

USA Today bestselling author Janelle Denison is known for her sinfully sexy heroes and provocative stories that are packed with sexual tension and emotional conflicts that keep readers turning the pages. She is the recipient of the prestigious National Reader's Choice Award, has been a RITA finalist, and has garnered many other awards and accolades in the romance writing industry. Janelle enjoys hearing from readers, and you can write to her at janelle@janelledenison.com. For information on upcoming releases, visit her Web site at www.janelledenison.com.

MINE AT MIDNIGHT

Jacquie D'Alessandro

This story is dedicated with love and gratitude to Carly Phillips. Thank you so much for inviting me to the party. And also to Janelle Denison and Claire Zion for making this project so much fun. I'd also like to extend my heartfelt thanks to the men and women serving in our Armed Forces for all they do to keep our country safe. You are true heroes in every sense of the word. And, as always, to my wonderful husband, Joe, who makes all my wishes come true, and my terrific son, Christopher, Wishes Come True, Jr.

Chapter One

Merrie Langston quickly zipped up her bright red velvet Santa's elf costume, slapped on the matching white-fur-trimmed hat, then hurried from the back storage room of her store, Perfect Parties. She dared a quick peek at the wall clock and winced. She was going to be late—again.

Snatching up her purse, a Tupperware container, and the tray of cellophane-wrapped cookies on her desk, she hurried toward the front door. The small bells attached to the ends of her curly-toed elf shoes jangled as she stepped onto the sidewalk and struggled with her packages to lock the door. Her red tights offered little protection against the blast of frigid air that whooshed up her short, full skirt, but she grinned even as she shivered. Maybe this year, for the first time in two decades, Lansfare, Georgia, would be gifted with a white Christmas.

After winning her battle with the lock, Merrie

couldn't help but take a second to admire her modest storefront. PERFECT PARTIES was painted on the glass door in bold, festive red and flanked by the columns of poinsettias and holly garland she'd hand-painted down the sides. Boughs dotted with glossy cranberries and wrapped with hundreds of tiny white twinkle lights and a half dozen gold bows surrounded the front window, scenting the air with the delightful aroma of fresh pine. The tree she'd decorated blinked with multicolored Christmas cheer inside the store, framed in the window like a beacon, welcoming one and all to enter. A frisson of pride eased through her. The store looked great. She'd worked really hard, but it was a labor of love.

But enough dallying—she was already late. Good thing she didn't have far to go for her appointment.

She hurried down the sidewalk, elf shoes jingling as she nodded and smiled at the holiday shoppers braving the biting cold. She recognized only Mr. Atkens, to whom she gave a cheery wave. Everyone else was a stranger, not unusual for the Friday before Christmas. The traffic on Main Street was heavy, indicating the holiday shopping rush was in full swing. Thanks to smart advertising and good word of mouth, Lanfare's quaint downtown with its unusual assortment of shops attracted an ever-increasing number of people from neighboring counties and nearby Atlanta.

Another mighty blast of icy air battered Merrie, and she clapped her hand on her head to keep her hat with the tennis-ball-size pom-pom on the end from flying off. She quickened her pace and seconds later arrived at the last storefront door on Main Street. The words TOM FARRELL, CERTIFIED PUBLIC AC-COUNTANT/FINANCIAL PLANNER were printed in somber black block letters on the door. As she struggled to turn the brass knob, the door suddenly swung inward, and she stepped, or rather stumbled, into the warm office, propelled by a blast of cold air.

Her gaze, which was now one-eyed thanks to her suddenly askew hat, fell upon Tom, who was closing the door.

Merrie's one eyeball flicked down the length of Tom's back, and she held in the appreciative sigh that rose to her lips. For an accountant who sat behind his desk all day, the guy had really nice . . . assets. For sure he knew how to fill out a snowy white dress shirt and a pair of charcoal gray trousers. Just then he turned around, giving her eyeball another treat. Since he was taking the opportunity to look over her costume, she allowed her gaze to roam at will.

His thick dark hair, normally neat, currently appeared as if he'd raked his hands through it. She wondered if that had anything to do with the fact that she was ten minutes late for their appointment. Probably, she decided. She'd known Tom for two years now—ever since she'd opened Perfect Parties and hired him as her accountant—and she knew he had a thing about being on time. Not that she didn't—she hated being late, but it just somehow always seemed to happen.

Yet if he was annoyed, it didn't show in his hazel eyes. She'd decided the first time she'd met Tom that even though his features—his strong jaw, straight nose, and high cheekbones—were undeniably attractive, she liked his eyes the best. They were kind, intelligent eyes. Filled with patience. She was especially intrigued that they seemed to change color based on what he wore, sometimes appearing more green, other times more blue, sometimes, like today, almost gray. She'd caught herself staring more than once and now made a conscious effort not to gawk.

For reasons she couldn't explain, she really liked it when he slipped on his black-framed glasses. They surrounded those intriguing eyes, making the gold flecks stand out more. They made him look so . . . serious. So scholarly. Which invariably tempted her to act the class clown to make him smile.

MINE AT MIDNIGHT

Of course, his smile was very attractive as well, but unfortunately she didn't often get to see it. When it came to their meetings regarding her finances, there wasn't much for him to smile about. She'd wondered several times if he was as serious outside the office, but since she'd never seen him out at any of Lansfare's restaurants or nightspots— and there weren't many—she didn't know.

Even though Merrie found Tom attractive and her heart sped up every time she stepped into his office, she'd never acted on those feelings. She was his client, and she didn't want to rock that boat, seeing as how Tom was one of the few financial planners in town. After all, there were lots of fish in the ocean, but how many of them could make sense of your untidy collection of receipts *and* file your taxes?

Besides, handsome and nice though he was, Tom Farrell was soooo not her type. He was, unfortunately, one of those all work, no play sticks-in-the-mud. He was always shaking his head over her bookkeeping methods—like she was the only person in the world who kept receipts in Baggies. And he was always telling her to save, save, save. Sure, a fine theory, but not easy to do when all her time, energy, and, yes, money were needed to keep her business going.

Stomping her elf-shoed feet to get some feeling

back into her chilled extremities, Merrie pushed back her askew hat, then shot Tom a smile. "Thanks for getting the door," she said. "I was about to be blown into the next block. Whew—it sure is frosty out there."

"Freezing," he agreed. "Here, let me help you . . ." He reached out to take the Tupperware from her, but instead she handed him the gaily wrapped tray of cookies.

"For you," she said. "Happy holidays. And also a peace offering for being late. Sorry."

He looked at the gift with unmistakable surprise. "Thank you. What is it?"

"Christmas cookies, silly," she said with a laugh. "Christmas *is* next week, you know." Her gaze panned around his office, and she shook her head. "Or maybe you don't know. Gotta tell ya, Tom, it's lookin' a bit bah-humbug in here." Not so much as a sprig of holly decorated Tom's office. No lights, no holiday tunes, no wreath on the door.

"Scrooge was an accountant, wasn't he?" Tom asked with the hint of a smile. Before she could answer, his gaze flicked over her costume and he added, "Besides, you're decorated enough for both of us. Hosting a party tonight—or are you simply delirious with holiday spirit?"

"Party. For the Baxter twins' sixth birthday. It starts in an hour, so I don't have much time."

"Then let's get started." He gestured toward his desk. She headed across the dark gray industrial carpeting, then slid into the burgundy leather chair across from his cherrywood desk. Once he'd seated himself in his own leather chair, he asked, "Did you bring your receipts?"

"Yup." She grinned. "And not in Baggies this time."

"Excellent. You bought the receipt file I suggested?"

She held out the Tupperware container. "Not exactly." When he simply stared at the square plastic offering, she added, "You have to admit, this is an upgrade from the Baggies." She shook the Tupperware. "Look—it has a lid and everything."

Tom pressed his lips together and fought the urge to rake his hands through his hair—again—and instead just pinched the bridge of his nose. He certainly wasn't surprised that Merrie had stored her receipts in Tupperware. No, his only surprises were that the beige cover wasn't decorated with candy canes, and the amusement he felt. Why he should find it amusing he couldn't fathom, especially since he knew that when he opened that Tupperware the receipts would be crammed inside in no sort of order, but somehow it was just so . . . Merrie.

He blew out the same exaggerated sigh he exhaled every time they had an appointment, and repeated the words that had become something of a mantra between them. "You don't need a financial planner. You need a financial savior."

"Which is why I hired you," she said with the same reply and grin that always curved her lips following his statement—a grin that looked decidedly unrepentant. In fact, it was a grin he'd be more apt to describe as cute. In fact, if he allowed himself to think about it—which he didn't—everything about Merrie Langston was cute, including her elf costume.

Just like with the Tupperware, he hadn't been surprised to see her walking down Main Street in an elf costume. Over the past two years, she'd entered his office dressed as the Easter Bunny, a leprechaun, and the Statue of Liberty—and had somehow managed to look adorable each time. Adorable and bubbly. Her golden brown eyes always seemed to glow with laughter, and her mane of unruly, chin-length honey-blond curls bounced with energy every time she moved. She always seemed to wear that infectious grin of hers that brought out those dimples in her cheeks. He'd never met anyone who smiled and laughed as much as she did, and it had crossed his mind more than once that her parents must have been clairvoyant when they named their baby, because "Merrie" was perfect for her.

He opened the Tupperware container and managed not to grimace when a wad of receipts *boinged* upward like a jack-in-the-box.

"These are all business expenditures, right?" he asked, lifting out a handful.

"Right." She worried her bottom lip between her teeth. "What do you think my chances are of getting my business loan?"

"I'll know more after I go through these expenses and finalize your financial statements. The more financially sound the bank feels you are, the better your chances."

"In other words, since the meeting with the loan officer is next week, this would be a really good time to win the lottery."

"There's no bad time to hit the lottery, but if that's your game plan, we need to have another conversation regarding fiscal responsibility and preparedness."

She made a horrified face. "Oh, no. Not the 'fiscal responsibility and preparedness' conversation again."

He swallowed the laugh that rose in his throat at her comical expression, and forced himself to adopt his sternest air. "I'm going to tape-record that conversation so you can listen to it every day. Twice. Now let's see what's up with these receipts."

He looked at the first one, from an Atlanta department store, and his brows rose. "Can you please explain how Kiss Me 'Til I'm Riled-Up Red lipstick is a *business* expense?"

"I needed it to wear with this costume," she said in a perfectly serious voice. "It's very hard to find just the *right* red lipstick. I'm wearing it now. Doesn't it match perfectly?" She pursed her lips and made a kissy noise, her eyes twinkling with mischief.

He found himself staring at her plump, glossy, red lips, noting with an uncomfortable jolt that her mouth was definitely the sort that could get a man riled up.

He cleared his throat to locate his voice. "Do you wear that lipstick other than with your costume?"

"Not yet—today's the first time I'm trying it out. But I probably will. I like it, and after next week, I won't have much cause to wear my elf costume again until next year." Her Kiss Me 'Til I'm Riled-Up Red lips twitched. "It would be very *fiscally irresponsible* of me to waste a perfectly good twenty-dollar lipstick, don't you think?"

"I suppose." Actually, it would be a crime, given how the rich color complemented her full lips so . . . perfectly. "Since it's part of your costume, I guess that will fly." He set the slip of paper aside and looked at the next dozen receipts, which were from a party supply store, a costume shop, a craft store, and a wholesale club where she bought baking and cooking supplies in bulk for the food she supplied at her parties. So far, so good. Then, another had him raising his brows again.

"Intimate apparel from Victoria's Secret?" he asked, his voice filled with skepticism. "What sort of party is that for? Pajama party?"

"That's not for pajamas. It's for this incredible red lace bra and panty set."

An image instantly materialized in his mind of Merrie, her curves showcased in an incredible red lace bra and panty set, her Kiss Me 'Til I'm Riled-Up Red lips curved into a wicked grin. An unsettling heat rushed through him, and he had a sudden urge to loosen his tie—except he wasn't wearing one.

He blinked to dispel the unwanted image, then adopted his most businesslike tone. "And how is that a business expense?"

"I had to wear *something* under this costume."

Whoosh. Another furnace blast of heat shot through him, this one settling directly in his groin. His gaze skimmed over the top of her red velvet elf dress, and he instantly developed some sort of Superman-like X-ray vision, clearly visualizing her full breasts encased in red lace.

He briefly closed his eyes and gave himself a hard mental slap. What the hell was wrong with him? It wasn't like him to engage in fantasies at the office. Fantasies about clients. Clearly he'd spent too many hours lately burning the midnight oil and not enough time taking care of his admittedly neglected love life. Of course, his libido had been just fine until *she* had walked into his office. Bearing Christmas cookies. And smelling like sugar. Wearing that cute costume. And those darn dimples. Talking about Riled-Up Red lips and sexy lingerie.

"While we have a little leeway with some of these expenses, Merrie, I'm afraid your, um, underwear falls outside any reasonable parameters."

"It can't be considered part of the costume?"

"I think that's too much of a stretch. And not really something you'd want to have to justify to the IRS should the occasion ever arise."

"Okay." She shot him a dimpling grin. "Can't blame an elf for trying."

A mechanical rendition of "Jingle Bells" sounded. "My cell phone," she said, reaching for her purse. She looked at her cell phone, then said, "I need to take this—it's Louis, my Santa."

"No problem."

Tom looked down at the next receipt in the stack, but found his gaze drifting back up when Merrie rose from her chair and paced toward the door, her elf shoes jingling, her phone pressed to her ear.

He found his attention riveted on the way her red velvet costume hugged her feminine curves.

MINE AT MIDNIGHT

How the full, white-fur-trimmed skirt swirled several inches above her knees with her every step. The way her red tights showcased her shapely legs.

The firmly-embedded-in-his-mind image of the lacy red lingerie he now knew she wore underneath all that soft, touchable velvet again rose in his mind's eye.

He blew out a long, careful breath. No way those North Pole elves could look like Merrie—if they did, there would be very little toy making going on, that was for sure.

But these sensual thoughts about her were totally inappropriate, not to mention unwelcome. Merrie Langston was a nice woman, but she was so not his type, it was laughable. He preferred calm, "sedate" women, and God knows "sedate" was not a word he'd ever attach to Merrie. These errant images of her were simply the result of him not spending any time recently with calm, sedate women. Well, that and the fact that he now had a life-size image of Merrie in her red bra and panties planted in his brain. Damn, there was nothing calm or sedate about *that*.

She turned in her pacing at the door and again faced him, and he immediately noticed her stricken expression. *"Vegas?"* she said into the phone, her voice rising an octave above its normal pitch.

Uh-oh. Obviously some sort of crisis. Not that

that surprised him. Merrie definitely struck him as the sort of woman who attracted crises like a bug zapper attracted mosquitoes.

"Not till *after New Year's*?" she said, her eyes widening. "But . . . but . . . well, okay. See you then. It's okay. Congratulations. Bye." She ended the call, then looked at him. The fact that the vivacious Merrie resembled a pale, deflated balloon alarmed him. He rose, then crossed to her, as she seemed frozen in place.

"What's wrong?"

"Louis—my Santa—was calling me from Vegas. *Vegas*," she repeated in a shocked voice. "Called to tell me he eloped with his girlfriend. He would have phoned earlier, but he'd forgotten about the time difference as he'd been, um, busy starting his honeymoon—his honeymoon that will keep him out of town until after New Year's." Her golden brown eyes reflected a distress he'd never witnessed from her before. "I have half a dozen parties booked between now and Christmas Eve, not to mention my charity event at the halfway house Christmas Eve. Also not to mention the Baxter twins' party that's starting in"—she glanced at her watch—"good grief, thirty minutes. I can't host a Christmas party, especially one for kids, without a Santa. I need a Kris Kringle and I need him *now*."

MINE AT MIDNIGHT

"Why don't *you* dress up as Santa?" Tom suggested.

"That won't work. I can't run the party *and* be the entertainment. I need to serve the refreshments, keep the games moving along, take the photos of the kids sitting on Santa's lap—a dozen different things. It's definitely a two-man job." She paced in front of him, her elf shoes jingling. "Who can I get on such short notice to—" She whirled around to face him and fixed him with a look that pinned him to the spot.

"You," she said, pointing at him, as if there were someone else in the room. He glanced behind him, praying another person had magically materialized, but no such luck. "Tom, you could be my Santa."

An uncomfortable sensation that felt like an all-over body cramp gripped him. "No, I couldn't."

"Why not?"

Even if he'd felt so inclined to share with her his personal reasons why the very idea made him so uncomfortable—and he definitely didn't feel so inclined—there was no time to do so. "I'm just not . . . the Santa type."

"I agree that you're not the most jolly guy—"

"Gee, thanks."

"—but you're breathing, and as I'm desperate, that's the only job requirement." She reached out and grasped his hand, and he stilled at the bolt of heat that sizzled up his arm. "Please, Tom. So much of my business is word of mouth, and if Santa is a no-show at this birthday party, it will no doubt cost me future bookings, which is especially bad now that I'm trying to get this loan to expand. I'll work out something for the other parties, find someone else, but there's simply no time for the Baxter party."

He raked his free hand through his hair. "Merrie, look, I—"

"I'll pay you double what I was paying Louis."

"It's not the money."

"I'll grant you a Christmas wish," she said, squeezing his hand, her eyes beseeching his. "I'll wax your car. Clean your house. Pick up your dry cleaning. Anything."

Jeez. If there was a man drawing breath who could resist those distressed, pleading brown eyes, the guy deserved a medal. He was definitely not that guy.

"Don't think I won't make you grant that wish," he said. "I'm thinking along the lines of getting you to curb your spending and use a real receipt file."

"Whatever you want."

"I don't know the first thing about playing Santa," he warned.

Her smile bloomed like a spring flower. "Don't

worry—there's nothing to it. Just 'ho, ho, ho' a lot, and when each child sits on your lap, ask them what they want for Christmas." She bounced on her feet, then stepped forward to plant an enthusiastic kiss on his cheek. "Thank you, Tom. I can't tell you how much I appreciate this. I'll just run out to my van and get the Santa suit. Be right back."

Before he could say a word, she dashed out the door, leaving him with a warm, tingly feeling on his cheek where her lips had touched his skin and the unsettling feeling that he'd just bitten off a lot more than he was prepared to chew.

Chapter Two

Dressed in the Santa costume, Tom gingerly settled himself on the Baxters' dining room chair. Merrie had decorated with festive red and green balloons and ribbons, fearful that any sudden moves would dislodge the pillow stuffing his coat, shift the hat covering his white wig, or cause his fluffy white beard and mustache to slide to the floor. And speaking of that fluffy white beard . . . the damn thing itched like mad. And tickled his nose, giving him a mighty urge to sneeze. He pressed his white-gloved finger under his nostrils to stem the need, suspecting that one sneeze would send his fake hair into his lap.

Good God, how had he allowed himself to get talked into this? All this Christmas stuff . . . it just brought back painful memories he'd prefer remain buried. Every holiday he immersed himself in work, and his plan succeeded—all work, no play, no time for ill-advised, unwanted trips down memory lane. Unfortunately, dressing up like Santa was definitely not the way to keep the memories away.

Besides, he felt ridiculous and uncharacteristically nervous in this costume. What if he screwed this up? The kids would be disappointed, not to mention that he'd be letting Merrie down. He didn't think he could stand to see her eyes filled with disappointment, but damn it, he was waaaay out of his league here. From the moment he'd arrived, he'd been waiting for one of the kids to look at him and accuse, "You're not Santa." None of them had, yet.

Actually, he'd been caught off guard by the rush of pleasure he'd experienced at the kids' excitement when he'd arrived. The way their eyes had widened and lit up. The way his used to when he was a kid. Before it had all been snatched away. . . .

His gaze wandered over to Merrie, who was helping the excited children form an orderly line to wait their turn with Santa. He had to admit that the Baxter party had afforded him the opportunity to observe a side of Merrie he'd never seen before. Her bookkeeping might be an unorganized disaster, but she was a whiz at keeping a party moving. She handled the twelve kids like a pro, moving seamlessly from one game to the next, to opening gifts, to serving snacks, not missing a beat when calmly and good-naturedly taking care of two cups of spilled juice, a cupcake that landed with a splat on the floor, and a bout of tears. She had a natural way with the kids and parents alike, and he had to admire how good she was at her job.

Merrie the elf stepped in front of him. "How ya doin', Santa?" she asked in an undertone.

"The truth? I'm hot, itchy, nervous, and I feel a sneeze the size of Georgia coming on which will knock this entire costume askew, making me the only skinny, dark-haired, clean-shaven Santa ever."

She smiled, flashing her dimples. "Relax. You look great, and believe me, I have that beard clipped on so well, a hurricane wouldn't budge it. Now, all you need to do is follow my lead. Here's Santa's list." She handed him a sheet of paper. "It has each child's name on it, along with a gift they'd told their mom they wanted. The kids are lined up in the order their names appear on your list. Once the child is seated on your lap, ask what they want for Christmas. Consult your 'who's been nice' list, and if they don't mention the toy that's on there, say something like, "Didn't you tell your mom that you wished for a Princess Emily doll, too?" She pointed her chin toward the huge jewel-toned sack resting next to his chair. "The toys are all stacked in the bag in order. All you need to do is reach in and hand them the top one, and I'll take the Polaroid picture. Got it?"

His sense of order had to admire this simple, straightforward plan. "Got it." But did he? Darn it, his palms were sweating inside his gloves. This was so far outside his comfort zone, he must have been insane to agree. But there was no backing out now. Merrie approached him, leading a little girl with dark, curly hair, enormous eyes, and a bow-shaped mouth. The child was dressed in a dark green velvet dress, and her hair was held back from her cherubic face with a silver bow. Tom quickly consulted his list and saw that the little girl's name was Natalie and she wanted a Princess Emily doll. He held out his hand to her. She slipped her small hand in his, then scrambled into his lap, staring up him with an awestruck gaze that immediately rendered him tongue-tied.

"Hey, Santa," Merrie said with an encouraging smile. "What are your three favorite words?"

Wanna go home? Help me, please? Obviously the look he shot Merrie was totally blank, or totally panicked, or both, because she mouthed *Ho, ho, ho*.

Right. Of course. "Ho, ho, ho," he said in his deepest voice, praying he sounded like Santa. "And, um, how are you, Natalie?"

The child's eyes widened to saucers. "How'd you know it was me, Santa?"

"I, ah, know the names of all the children on my nice list. Have you been a good girl this year, Natalie?"

Natalie nodded solemnly. "Yes, Santa."

"What would you like for me to bring you this year?"

The child drew a deep breath, then said in a slightly lisping rush, "A Princess Emily doll, a Princess Emily castle, a Princess Emily car, and a Princess Emily boat."

Tom had no idea who Princess Emily was, but clearly she was in an upper tax bracket. "I see. And you would, um, take good care of Princess Emily?"

"Oh, yes, Santa. The best care ever!"

"Natalie and Santa, look this way," Merrie said. A flash went off, and Merrie sent him a wink and a thumbs-up. Tom reached into his sack and pulled out the top present, which was gaily wrapped in colorful paper covered with nutcrackers and a cheery tag that read: *To Natalie, with Love from Santa.*

"Here you go, Natalie, and don't forget to be a good girl and listen to your parents."

Clutching her present in one arm, Natalie wrapped her other arm around Tom's neck and pulled his head down. "I love you, Santa," she said into his ear. "I'll leave cookies and milk for you." She planted a noisy, damp kiss on his cheek, then hopped down and ran toward a dark-haired woman standing at the back of the room who Tom assumed was her mother based on the resemblance. An odd sensation he couldn't put a name to eased through him, but before he could examine it closely, he had to consult his list again as Merrie was now leading a small boy toward him. Tommy. Who wanted a soccer ball. Then came Joey. Then Alissa. Followed by the Baxter twins, Kevin and Kyle.

On and on they came, and as each child scrambled onto his lap and told him with round eyes filled with wonder what they wanted for Christmas, Tom's apprehension slipped, replaced by a growing genuine enjoyment. The kids were adorable and so excited, and damn, how could it not feel good to have all those little faces shining up at him?

Each time he laughed "Ho, ho, ho," it came a little easier. And so did each conversation with each child. Hey—maybe he wasn't so bad at this Santa thing after all. In fact, by the time Merrie led the last child toward him—a solemn-eyed boy named Andy—Tom was feeling pretty good about this whole Santa gig.

Once Andy was settled on his lap, Tom said, "Ho, ho, ho. I see that you're on my good boy list, Andy. What would you like for Santa to bring you this year?"

"My daddy," Andy said, his face very serious.

Everything in Tom stilled. Uh-oh. According to

Tom's list, Andy was supposed to ask for a remote-control car.

"My daddy moved away," Andy said in a small voice that had Tom bending his head closer to the child to hear. "I want him to come home." His bottom lip trembled. "Mommy doesn't want him to, but I do."

In a heartbeat a plethora of unhappy memories bombarded Tom, and the space around his heart went hollow with sympathy. Damn. He knew exactly how this boy felt, and his heart ached for him. He would have dearly loved to grant Andy's wish, but as he knew from experience, those sorts of wishes didn't come true. And they certainly weren't something that could be pulled out of a sack.

He felt the strong need to say something to the boy, but what? His throat felt tight, and if Andy's bottom lip quivered again, Tom swore his heart would break in two.

"Sometimes moms and dads can't get along with each other," he said quietly, "but that doesn't mean that they both don't love you. No matter what happens, your mom will always be your mom, and your dad will always be your dad."

Andy's lip trembled again. "But I want him to be my dad at *our* house."

"I know, Andy. I know." There was no controlling the flood of sympathy washing through Tom, and he cursed his inability to say something, do something that would help this boy. Shelter him from the further hurts he knew all too well faced him. Not knowing what else to do, he pulled the last gift from his sack and handed it to Andy.

"How will you know where I am on Christmas Eve?" Andy asked, cradling the wrapped box, his eyes filled with distress. "I don't know yet if I'll be at my house or my dad's house, or maybe even Grandma's house—"

"I'll know, Andy," Tom said, giving the boy's thin shoulders what he hoped was a reassuring squeeze. "I'll find you, no matter where you are."

"You *promise*?"

The words were said in a suspicious tone that clearly indicated Andy had already experienced the pain of broken promises. Tom laid his hand over his heart. "I promise. I'll tell you what—how about we take *two* pictures of you and me, so that both your mom and dad can have one. I bet they'd really like that, and you know why?"

Andy shook his head. "Why?"

"Because they both love you. Just as much as you love them."

Andy hesitated, then nodded. "That's good. I won't have to choose who gets my picture." The ghost of a heartbreakingly sad smile trembled on the boy's lips. Then he reached up and hugged Tom tight around his neck. "Thanks, Santa."

"Ready for your picture?" Merrie said, her gaze alternating between Tom and Andy, whose face was buried against Tom's chest.

"We're ready," Tom said, "and we'll need two photos." He ruffled Andy's dark hair. "Hey, let's see who can make a bigger smile at my elf helper, okay? I bet you can smile bigger than me if you really try, but it'll be difficult—I'm a real big smiler."

Andy lifted his head. Still hugging Tom around the neck, he pressed his cheek against Santa's snowy beard and grinned ear to ear.

The flash went off. "That's great," Merrie said, her own grin wide. "One more. Say 'Christmas tree'!"

After the flash, Tom set the boy on his feet, then ruffled his hair. "Merry Christmas, Andy. You remember what I said, all right?"

"I will, Santa. I'll leave cookies and milk for you again. You liked the Oreos I left last year."

Tom rubbed his pillow-stuffed belly and winked. "They were delicious."

His gift clutched in his arms, Andy ran toward an attractive redhead. "Mom, look what I got!"

Merrie approached him and nodded approvingly.

"I couldn't help but overhear. Very nicely done—the entire party, but most especially with Andy. Poor kid. Broken families are always difficult, but especially at this time of year."

The sadness shadowing her eyes and her wistful tone had him wondering if she spoke from experience. Before he could ask, however, she continued. "You were a huge hit." Her grin turned teasing. "You sure you've never done this before?"

"Positive." His gaze flicked toward the departing children and their parents, and he waved. "Now what?"

"Now I clean up. I've asked Mrs. Baxter to take the twins out for a short time so we can get you out of the house without arousing suspicion."

"I can't just walk out?"

She looked horrified. "Of course not." She leaned closer to him, and he breathed in the enticing scent of sugar cookies. Damn, but it was an effort not to pull her onto his lap and nibble on her skin to see if she tasted as delicious as she smelled. "Santa can't just hop into *a car* and drive away."

"Ah. I see. And since there's no miniature sleigh and eight tiny reindeer on the roof . . ."

"Exactly. So just sit tight. As soon as everyone's gone, you can change into your street clothes and escape. Have I mentioned how grateful I am to you for doing this?"

"Yeah—but not in the last ten seconds."

She laughed. "Just wave and 'Ho, ho, ho' for a few more minutes."

With that, she turned and walked toward the departing children. He watched her give the pictures she'd taken of him and Andy to the boy's mom. Heard Andy say, "Santa let me take *two* so Daddy could have one, also."

Andy's mom looked at him, and there was no mistaking the gratitude that flashed in her eyes, and he sent her a wave, which she returned. A few minutes later, after the last of the guests had departed, Mrs. Baxter left with the twins. When the door closed behind them, Merrie handed him a heavy, black plastic garment bag.

"Your clothes are in here," she explained. "If you could hang up the Santa suit, that would be great. There's a bathroom down the hall, second door on the left."

"Yes, ma'am." Tom gave her a jaunty salute, then Ho, ho, hoed his way down the hall to the bathroom. Once he'd closed the door, he looked at himself in the mirror and shook his head in wonder at the white-bearded stranger staring back at him.

Not even his own family would recognize him. He certainly didn't recognize himself—and not just because of the costume. No, the way he was feeling was very . . . unfamiliar. He couldn't put a name

to it, other than to call it surprised. Surprised that
something he'd really dreaded had turned out to be
fun, and equally surprised that he'd enjoyed Merrie's company so much. As recently as this morning,
no one could have convinced him that a woman
and an activity so outside his comfort zone would
be filling him with what suspiciously felt like warm
fuzzies. He'd enjoyed the kids—their innocence and
awe. And Andy . . . well, Andy had touched something deep inside him. Probably because seeing
Andy had been like looking in a mirror.

Tom pulled off his Santa hat, wig, and beard and
for a long moment just stared at his reflection,
allowing the memories he'd buried for so long to
rise to the surface. It had been a long time. Maybe
he was ready to rethink his feelings about the holidays.

He changed his clothes and rejoined Merrie in the
kitchen to find all traces of the party gone, the
counters gleaming, and all her supplies neatly
packed in several large, deep, square plastic
containers.

"I'm all set," she said. She walked toward him,
her elf shoes jingling, stopping when an arm's
length separated them. "Thank you so much for
your help. You were a terrific Santa, and as you
know, you really helped me out of a jam."

"You're welcome. You did an outstanding job

running the party. No matter what happened, you never missed a beat."

"You know what they say—an elf's gotta do what an elf's gotta do."

"And I was really impressed with how well you'd organized everything."

Her dimples flashed. "Your tone indicates you're not only impressed, but shocked."

He raked a hand through his hair and shot her a sheepish grin. "I can't deny I'm surprised. If only you could organize your receipts that well."

"Forget it. I'm *creatively* organized only. Business-wise is an entirely different matter."

"You're telling me."

She planted her hands on her hips. "Ha-ha. So I'm receipt and checkbook challenged. Can you bake a three-layer Black Forest torte?"

"God, no. I can barely boil water."

"I rest my case." She slipped an envelope from a pocket in her dress and held it out to him.

"What's this?"

"Your paycheck."

Tom didn't move. "I can't take that."

"Of course you can." She slipped it into the pocket of his white dress shirt.

He slipped it out, then pressed it into her hand. "Okay, I can. But I won't."

She frowned. "Why not?"

How could he explain something he didn't fully understand himself? "Because I . . . had fun."

Her frown dissolved into a dimpling grin. "So did I. I have fun at every party I host. I still expect to be paid." Her eyes twinkled with mischief. "And besides, unlike my lacy red underwear, paying Santa his wages is a legit business expense."

The image of her he'd bludgeoned back for the past four hours smacked him with the impact of a sucker punch, and he briefly squeezed his eyes shut. *Do not, under any circumstances, think of her lacy red underwear.* He reopened his eyes, only to find himself staring at her Kiss Me 'Til I'm Riled-Up Red lips, which looked so damn . . . kissable. He gave himself a mental slap and shook his head. "Legit expense or not, I won't accept payment. Just consider it a favor from a friend."

She pursed her lips. "As much as I appreciate that, Tom, it places me in a rather awkward position. You see, I want to offer you a proposition."

Proposition? Whoa, baby. Heat whooshed through him, and the word "yes" rushed to his lips. He had to clench his jaw to refrain from shouting it.

"Since you did such a great job today," she said, "I was wondering if you'd consider filling in for the rest of my holiday bookings. I have six more parties between now and Christmas Eve. As much as I appreciate the freebie for today, I'd have to pay you for the other parties. So . . . what do you say?"

Tom drew a deep breath and considered—and the mere fact that he was considering playing Santa really stunned him. Why wasn't he running in the opposite direction? *Because she's standing right in front of you. With those big brown eyes that look like melty caramel. And those delicious red lips.*

Hey, the woman needed help. She was *desperate* for help. She was his client, and as such he certainly wanted her to succeed. They belonged to the same community. They'd known each other for two years—although, as he'd learned today, there was more to Merrie than met the eye. And he couldn't deny he wanted to learn more about her. Besides, he had made a pretty darn good Santa, if he said so himself.

"All right. I'll do it."

Her dazzling smile could have lit a darkened room. "Oh, thank you, Tom, thank you." She launched herself forward, wrapped her arms around his neck, and gave him an enthusiastic hug that had him grasping her waist and taking a step back to retain his balance. Laughing, she planted a noisy, smacking, *mmmmmmwah* kiss on his cheek. Then, still clinging to his neck, she leaned back and beamed at him. "Thank you."

"You're . . . welcome. . . ." His voice trailed off,

and he went totally still, suddenly, acutely aware of her body almost touching his. Of her golden brown eyes shining up at him. Of his hands resting on her trim waist. Of her lush lips so very close.

Her gaze drifted to his cheek, and she made a tsking sound. "Uh-oh. I lipsticked you." She gently rubbed her thumb over his skin to remove the mark, a soothing motion that did absolutely nothing to soothe. In fact, it felt as if she'd lit a bonfire on his face. A scorching flash of desire roared through him, and his hands involuntarily tightened on her waist.

"It's almost gone. . . ." Their eyes met, and this time her voice evaporated, leaving him in no doubt that his desire was written all over his face. Like him, she went perfectly still, and all traces of amusement slowly drained from her face. Her gaze dropped to his mouth, and he barely refrained from groaning.

One taste. One kiss. Just to satisfy this inexplicable, insatiable curiosity. He lowered his head, slowly, giving her the opportunity to stop him, but instead she lifted her face and rose up on her toes.

He brushed his lips over hers, once, twice, experimental touches that enflamed rather than satisfied. He lightly ran the tip of his tongue over her bottom lip, a favor she instantly returned. And in a heartbeat he was lost.

She tasted exactly the way she smelled—sweet, seductive, and delicious. He heard a low groan. Him? Her? He didn't know. Didn't know anything beyond the satiny, luscious warmth of her mouth, the erotic friction of her tongue rubbing against his. The bewitching feel of her pressed against him as he drew her closer and she wrapped her arms more tightly around him.

Heat, want, desire pumped through him, rapidly depleting his control. His hands glided slowly up her back, and he plucked off her hat to sift his hands through her silky soft curls. Everything about her was curvy, feminine, and soft and fit so well against every part of him that was so . . . not soft. She strained closer, shifting against him, and his erection jerked in response.

Some small, barely audible kernel of common sense worked its way through the fog of lust clouding his judgment and reminded him that they stood in the Baxters' kitchen and that this had gone far enough.

He lifted his head and fought to control his ragged breathing. Merrie clung to him, shorts puffs of breath emanating from between her moist, parted lips. A hint of crimson stained her cheeks, and she slowly opened her eyes. A growl of want rose in his throat. She looked glazed, dazed, and thoroughly aroused. Much the way he assumed he must look.

"Holy cow," she said in a breathless whisper.

Personally, he didn't think "holy cow" did that kiss justice, but damn, he was impressed she was capable of speech. He sure as hell wasn't there yet.

She blinked several times, her stunned gaze searching his face as if she'd never seen him before. "I, um, didn't know accountants could kiss like that."

He had to swallow twice to finally locate his voice. "I didn't know elves could kiss like that."

"I'm not sure they normally do. Seems like it would melt the north polar cap."

She could say that again. He felt as if he were roasting from the inside out. And if he didn't step away from her, he was going to kiss her again. Which would definitely be unwise—for some reason he couldn't think of right now, but he was pretty sure there was one.

After slowly releasing her, he took a step back. Her arms slipped from around him, then settled at her sides. He immediately missed the feel of her against him, which was bad. Really bad. But now that she wasn't touching him, his brain was kicking back into action, shouting recriminations at him. Since he felt responsible for starting this . . . whatever it was, it was up to him to cut it off at the pass.

He raked his hands, which weren't completely steady, through his hair. "Look, Merrie, as pleasant as that kiss was, I think we can agree that it wouldn't be a good idea to repeat it." He forced himself not to wince at using a tepid word like "pleasant" to describe a passionate exchange that had steam all but exuding from his pores. "You're my client, and I wouldn't want to start anything that could be construed as a conflict of interest, especially where your loan might be concerned."

As soon as the words passed his lips, however, his inner voice scoffed and shoved the reasoning aside. *Hey, you're her accountant, you prepare her financial statements, but it's not like you're the loan officer.* Now *that* would be a conflict of interest. He could imagine that Merrie's kiss would induce the loan officer to give her not only the money she requested, but also the keys to the freakin' vault.

She nodded, slowly at first, then more vigorously. "You're right, of course." Then her familiar smile flashed. "Besides, it's not as if that kiss could *go* anywhere. Let's face it, personality-wise, we're like oil and water."

"Exactly," he agreed, wondering why he didn't feel quite as relieved as he should. "Like night and day."

"Like wet and dry. So we'll just forget it. Go on, business as usual. Blame the last few minutes of insanity on that common holiday malady, Mistletoe Madness."

MINE AT MIDNIGHT

It took him several seconds to answer because he was still trying to figure out which one of them was "wet" and which one was "dry"—a difficult task because nothing about their kiss could be labeled "dry," and when he thought about *wet* . . . hell, his train of thought completely jumped the track.

"Um, right." Needing to keep his hands busy so he didn't reach for her again, he lifted one of the large plastic containers. "Let's get this stuff loaded into your van."

After they finished and she'd locked the Baxters' front door, she slid behind the wheel of her white van decorated with the Perfect Parties logo while he settled himself in the passenger seat.

On the short drive back to Main Street she said, "I'll make sure you get the details for the rest of the parties, but tomorrow night's is a small holiday gathering at Country Style Furniture for the employees and their families. We'll need to leave Perfect Parties at four thirty." A sheepish half smile pulled up one corner of her mouth. "I might be late for appointments with my accountant, but I'm never late for a party."

He patted the garment bag holding his costume, which lay across his lap. "I'll be ready."

When they arrived back in town, she pulled into the parking lot located at the rear of their strip of stores and braked behind his dark blue Honda.

"Thanks again for stepping up to the plate, Tom. See you tomorrow."

"You bet." He exited the car, closed the door, then waved in response to her cheery smile. She headed toward the exit, and he watched until she turned the corner and disappeared from view. Then he walked slowly to his car, sinking into the driver's seat with a sigh of relief.

It sure felt good to be alone.

Didn't it?

Of course it did. No distracting red lace lingerie-wearing elf to detour his thoughts. No lush Kiss Me 'Til I'm Riled-Up Red lips to bewitch him.

Kiss Me 'Til I'm Riled-Up. Damn. She'd certainly done that.

A frown tugged at his brows, and he recalled her words regarding their kiss: *We'll just forget it.*

Yup, forgetting about it was definitely the smartest strategy. But just as it was a good idea in business, he decided he'd better line up a contingency plan.

Because he had a sinking feeling he was going to need one.

Chapter Three

Merrie took a quick inventory of the snack table while she freshened up the festive Christmas punch with another "snowball" of raspberry sherbet and a bottle of club soda. The guests from Country Style Furniture had deemed her sugar cookies and hors d'oeuvres winners, and both trays needed replenishing. As did the strawberries, marshmallows, and squares of homemade angel food cake at the chocolate fondue station—a huge hit with both the kids and adults. Cups and utensils looked fine, but some more plates and napkins would be needed.

Her critical gaze swept over her colorful and gaily lit wreaths, boughs, mini–Christmas trees, velvet bows, sparkling reindeer, and glittery oversize ornaments, satisfied that they lent the room a merry air. She'd learned long ago that nothing brightened up a space and said "party time" quite like twinkle lights.

Even while her hands remained busy with her tasks, and she smiled and exchanged small talk with the guests, part of her attention was focused across the room where Santa held court amidst some two dozen wide-eyed children who were listening with rapt attention while he read from her much-loved copy of *How the Grinch Stole Christmas*.

She watched him finish a page, then turn the book around so the children could see the illustration of the Grinch getting stuck in the chimney. His gaze wandered across the room and their eyes met. The casual observer would no doubt fail to realize that Tom Farrell was under the white beard and red velvet costume, but to Merrie, there was no mistaking those compelling hazel eyes.

They stared at each other for several seconds, and her heart tripped erratically while the rest of her went utterly still. Was that *desire* in his eyes? It certainly looked like it, but, no, surely not—although that look appeared to contain the same sizzling heat as the one he'd worn after he'd kissed her yesterday.

That darn kiss. Ack. Surely she was merely projecting her own thoughts onto what was clearly a figment of her imagination. Mr. Practical Accountant had no doubt forgotten all about their kiss, as they'd agreed to do. He'd probably wasted no time writing off the incident as a bad investment, or whatever sort of accounting term would apply. Still, there was something in his expression . . . something that had her heart skipping around and the backs of her knees sweating.

With an effort, she recalled herself and mentally scolded herself for gawking. She shot him a smile and an encouraging thumbs-up, then returned her attention to her work. But in spite of that, she remained almost painfully aware of him. Her gaze, which seemed to have developed a mind of its own, constantly strayed in his direction. And when she was facing away from him, she found herself straining to hear his deep voice.

It was all because of that darn kiss. The kiss she was supposed to have forgotten about, should have forgotten about, that she'd tried really hard to forget about. But instead that darn kiss had kept her tossing and turning all last night. There'd been no dreams of sugarplums for her. Nope. Her dreams had been hot, sweaty, sexy fantasies in which a hot, sweaty, sexy Tom had figured prominently. That darn kiss had set her imagination—to say nothing of her libido—on fire. The guy might be an all work, no play stick-in-the-mud, but, damn, he sure knew how to kiss.

Had she really suggested they just forget that kiss? She needed to enter a plea of temporary insanity. Over the last twenty-four hours, she'd managed to shove their kiss from her mind for a total of, oh, about 8.3 seconds. And that was only because she'd dropped the tub of cream cheese on her bare toe this morning and pain had briefly sidelined her thought processes. As soon as she'd determined her toe wasn't broken, *whammo!*—thinking about that darn kiss again.

She'd experienced her fair share of good—even outstanding—kisses, but something about Tom's kiss had simultaneously enflamed her and turned her insides to the consistency of an excellent crème brûlée. The passion between them had flamed so suddenly, with such intensity, it had stolen her every thought. Good Lord, she'd wanted to devour him. Had wanted him to devour her. And she'd clearly sensed he'd wanted the same thing.

Yet somehow sanity had prevailed. And she should be glad. She *was* glad. Pretty much. Sort of. Okay, she wasn't really glad at all. That kiss had reawakened her hibernating hormones, and now they were clamoring for some action. Well, her pesky hormones would just have to go back to sleep. At least until after New Year's. Between now and then she had no time to devote to manhunting.

No need to hunt, her suddenly chatty and helpful hormones informed her. *The guy we want is right over there.*

Feeling as if every cell in her body had morphed

into a laser pointer, Merrie turned and once again found herself staring at Santa Tom, who continued to read from the Grinch book. *Yeah, he's the one,* her hormones stated. *We want to get him alone, then strip that red suit off him. With our teeth. So waddaya say?*

Merrie shook her head to dispel the vivid visual of her peeling red velvet from Tom's body. Tearing her gaze away from Santa, she muttered, "I say no, you stupid hormones. So sit down and shut up."

Much hormone grumbling ensued, but she managed, with a great deal of effort, to ignore it.

On the drive back to Perfect Parties after the Country Style Furniture gathering, Tom forced himself to keep looking straight ahead and not to turn in the passenger seat to look at Merrie.

For cryin' out loud, what was wrong with him? Why couldn't he stop looking at her? Why couldn't he stop thinking about her? Her smile. Her laugh. The way her eyes twinkled with mischief. The silky softness of her hair. The delicious scent of her skin. The seductive taste of her. The sensation of her body pressed against his.

That damn kiss. That was the problem—he couldn't stop thinking about that damn kiss. He'd tried to recall another kiss that had fried his circuits like the one he'd shared with Merrie and had come up totally blank. And he'd had plenty of time to think about it while he'd tossed and turned last night. This woman had his normally smooth-running synapses totally out of whack, and he didn't like it one bit. Everything he'd thought he knew about Merrie that he'd learned over their two-year business association was being shot out of the water. He'd always thought her a bit, well, flighty. Not the sort of person to take anything seriously. But the way she'd handled these last two parties had proved him wrong. She'd surprised him, and he didn't particularly like surprises.

Nor did he like the unsettling fact that he couldn't exorcise their kiss from his thoughts. Nor the fact that Merrie, who'd been her usual smiling, cheerful self all evening, clearly *had* put their kiss out of her mind. Unreasonable or not, that really rankled.

Must be all this Christmasy stuff, he decided. Yeah, that's what had him so uncharacteristically out of sorts. He wasn't accustomed to all this Ho, ho, ho jazz—normally he avoided it like the plague. He was just suffering from an overload of holiday cheer. As soon as he got home, he'd turn on the TV, open a beer, and kick back and relax. And he wouldn't have long to wait, he realized, as Merrie turned the van into the parking lot.

Keeping conversation to a minimum, he helped her unload the supplies. When they finished, he walked her back to her van, making a conscious effort not to get too close to her, to keep his distance from the electromagnetic field that seemed to surround her—and rendered him a piece of metal.

"Did you have a chance to look over the schedule I gave you for the rest of the parties?" she asked as they approached her van.

"Yes. Tomorrow's is at the Little Tot preschool center at three o'clock."

"You'll be a huge hit there, believe me." She shot him a sidelong smile. "Great job tonight. See you tomorrow—I'm off to bake a boatload of Christmas cookies."

Her statement answered the question that had floated around in the back of his mind all evening— did she have a date tonight after the party? He refused to acknowledge the relief that filled him knowing she did not.

"More baking?" he asked.

"*Lots* more baking. Those Little Tot preschoolers will pack away an impressive amount of cookies."

Tom watched her slip into the driver's seat, and a feeling he couldn't explain gripped him. He didn't know the first thing about baking cookies, hadn't had the least desire to involve himself in such a holiday tradition for years, yet suddenly he wanted more than anything to bake Christmas cookies with Merrie.

He dragged his hands down his face. There really was something wrong with him. The awaiting calm and silence of his house should have beckoned him to sanctuary, but for once it failed to entice him. Damn it, he didn't want to be alone. He wanted to be with Merrie. A woman who was all wrong for him. His mind knew it, but unfortunately his heart and his libido were telling him something different. And since she was about to close her car door and leave, he didn't have much time to consider.

"Need some help?" he asked.

"No, thanks. I've got the door." She pulled it closed, then started the engine.

He tapped on the window. "I meant help with the baking," he said after she'd lowered the glass. When she just stared at him, he felt compelled to add, "Of the cookies."

"It's Saturday night," she said slowly. "You don't have other plans?"

It struck him how pathetic that sounded, and he briefly considered claiming some imaginary plans that had been canceled at the last minute, leaving him free for the rest of the evening, but his conscience balked at telling her less than the truth. He also found himself not wanting to say anything that might give her the impression that he had a steady girlfriend—which he currently did not—nor did he want to try and figure out why he wouldn't want her to think that.

"No other plans," he said quietly.

Merrie looked at Tom, illuminated by the glow of the parking lot's security light, his dark hair ruffled by the chilly breeze, and tried to ignore the thrill that zoomed through her at his words. In spite of a Herculean effort for the remainder of tonight's party, she hadn't been able to get Tom out of her mind. His hearty "Ho, ho, ho" had filled the room as he'd sat each child on this lap and listened to what was wanted for Christmas. He'd then given each child a wrapped present from Santa's sack—an adorable stuffed reindeer Merrie had purchased in bulk online.

Each time she'd looked at Tom, each time she'd seen the natural way he interacted with the kids, laughing and coaxing smiles, the ease with which he joked with the adults, she'd wondered if she'd misjudged him. Maybe his sense of fun was just misplaced, rather than surgically removed. An image of him, spending the evening alone, channel surfing and eating cholesterol-laden junk food, burrowed into her mind, and she wondered if perhaps he was *lonely* rather than a stick-in-the-mud.

The thought of Tom being lonely filled her with that fleeting, uncomfortable, hollow sensation she called a "heart ouchie." *We don't want him to be lonely*, her hormones said slyly.

Merrie shot an inward frown at her hormones. No, she didn't want him to be lonely, but getting involved with her financial planner was *not* a good idea—although there weren't any laws against it. Still, their personalities were so opposite. Did she really want to risk her heart by getting involved with someone so stodgy? *We don't think he's stodgy*, chimed in the hormones. *Remember that kiss? Nothing stodgy about* that.

Well, she couldn't disagree there. In fact, maybe her hormones were right. There was no denying Tom was extremely attractive. Maybe it was time to get to know him a little bit better. And baking cookies with him was as good a way as any to do so.

"You know how to bake?" she asked.

"Is that a prerequisite?"

She laughed. "You know what an oven looks like?"

His eyes filled with amusement. "That's the thing you bake in, right?"

"Right."

"Yup. I know what it looks like. It's called a 'dust collector' at my house."

"Hmmm. Exactly how much *do* you know about baking cookies? It's a very serious enterprise."

"I know that they taste hot and delicious when they're fresh from the oven."

"Uh-huh. And do you know how they get into the oven in the first place?"

" 'Fraid not. But what I lack in knowledge, I make up for in the fact that I follow directions well."

The way he was looking at her, his eyes filled with deviltry and warmth, made her knees feel as if she'd imbibed one too many glasses of eggnog. "Follow directions well?" she repeated. "Hmmmm. I guess that works out just fine, because I like giving orders."

"Bossy, are you?"

"Sometimes."

He rested his forearms in the open window and leaned closer to her, totally messing with her breathing process. "I think I can handle it, Merrie."

Probably he could. But based on her breathless reaction to him just being near her, she wasn't sure *she* could. But no way was she going to give up the chance to find out.

"I'd enjoy the company, and the help," she said with a smile, pleased that her voice sounded so light and carefree. "Follow me."

Chapter Four

"And now we just slide the cookie sheet into the preheated oven, and when the timer goes off in twelve minutes, we'll have the most delicious, puffy sugar cookies you've ever tasted," Merrie said, closing the oven door with a flourish. "After they've cooled for about thirty minutes, we can frost and decorate them."

She turned around to face her kitchen helper and had to bite the insides of her cheeks to keep from laughing out loud at the multitude of white smudges marring Tom's dark green Perfect Parties apron. And marking his left cheek. And his nose. And chin. "Looks like you might have gone a little overboard with the flour, big guy."

"You said to use a lot. So I used a lot." Suddenly he looked worried. "Did I use too much?"

She tossed him a clean dish towel and pantomimed that he should wipe his chin. "Nah. It's a soft dough, so you need to be generous with the flour to prevent sticking—and I'd say you were generous." Her lips twitched. "Especially around your jaw area."

"I had an itch." He scrubbed with the towel. "So what do we do while the cookies bake?"

Their eyes met, and heat that had nothing to do with the oven seared Merrie. Good grief, what was wrong with her? He'd asked a perfectly reasonable, innocent question, in a purely nonsuggestive tone— hadn't he? Yes. Surely it was just her fevered imagination that conjured up a half dozen ways to spend the next twelve minutes, all of which started with her backing up Tom against the kitchen counter and leaving floury fingerprints all over his body.

"We, ah, get the next few batches spread out on the cookie sheets." Her gaze flicked to the wall clock. "And I brace myself for the phone call I'm going to receive in about two minutes."

He cocked a brow. "Are you clairvoyant?"

"No. But my mother calls me on this date every year at nine forty-six p.m."

"Family holiday tradition?"

Although he spoke the words lightly enough, she still sensed an underlying tension in his tone that piqued her curiosity. "Birthday tradition. Mom calls every year to wish me a happy birthday and to remind me how going into labor wreaked havoc with her Christmas baking operation. No one received the Langston fruitcake the year I was born, and it was *all* my fault." She grinned. "Mom still likes to tease me about it, and my aunt Delia— Mom's sister who can't stand the Langston fruitcake—still thanks me every year in her Christmas card."

He set the towel down on the counter. "*Today's* your birthday?"

"Yup. Hey, I didn't end up with the name Merrie because I was born on Halloween."

He looked distinctly embarrassed, as if he'd just shown up at a wedding without a gift for the bride and groom. "I had no idea. Happy birthday."

"Thanks."

"How come you're not out celebrating?"

"Because these cookies need baking, and no matter how hard I've tried to train the dough to knead itself and hop into the oven, it won't listen. Besides, I enjoy doing this. Since I opened Perfect Parties, I don't celebrate my birthday until life slows down a bit in January." Just then the phone rang, and Merrie grinned. "Right on time."

He jerked his head toward the family room. "Should I leave to give you some privacy?"

"Don't be silly. Have a seat, and I'll put on a pot of coffee. Besides, I could use the moral support. Since I'm now officially thirty and still not married and providing grandkids, Mom's call this year is going to be a doozy. Wish me luck." She picked up the phone, then said, "Hi, Mom."

Tom made himself comfortable in one of the pale oak kitchen chairs, simultaneously enjoying the incredible scent of baking cookies wafting from the oven and the sight of Merrie measuring grinds into the coffeemaker while she listened to her mother. If anyone had told him as recently as an hour ago that he would be enjoying a homey, domestic holiday scene like this, he would have branded them as certifiable. Yet here he was, basking in the warmth of Merrie's cheery yellow and green kitchen. The jewel-toned glow of the blinking twinkle lights from her enormous Christmas tree, which took up two-thirds of her family room, reflected off her pristine white ceramic-tile floor. Christmasy doodads abounded in the modest apartment, even here in the kitchen in the guises of a Santa paper towel holder, napkins, and dish towels. It came as no surprise when she set two ceramic coffee mugs decorated with grinning snowmen on the counter.

While she was engrossed in counting out coffee scoops, he took the opportunity to admire her profile. Her nose was really cute—small and straight—and he liked the way it sort of wrinkled when she laughed. She smiled at something her mother said, creating that beguiling dimple in her cheek. She'd pulled her shiny, tawny curls back into a haphazard knot from which a half dozen unruly tendrils had sprung free. The style left her neck bare, filling him with the desire to touch his lips to her pale skin to discover if she tasted as luscious as she looked. And damn, she did indeed look luscious. His gaze drifted over her red T-shirt, which read *Ho, Ho, Ho. Can't Wait to Bake Some Mo'*, down over her faded jeans that hugged curves he could sum up in one word: sinful. Or two words: extremely sinful.

She opened the fridge, then bent over to look for something on a lower shelf, and Tom had to draw several careful, deep breaths at the myriad of fantasies the sight inspired. She straightened, and he jerked his gaze upward—only to collide with hers. She stilled, a container of half-and-half in her hand, and her expression left no doubt that she was aware she'd just been on the receiving end of an extended ogle.

Her gaze steady on his, she slowly approached the table, and his heart performed some sort of acrobatic movement that surely would have garnered a "ten" from the Olympic judges.

After setting the half-and-half on the table, she slid onto the chair opposite him and said into the phone, "As a matter of fact, there's a handsome man with me right now, Mom." She listened for several seconds, then a blush bloomed on her cheeks. She briefly looked up at the ceiling, and when their gazes met again, her eyes sparkled with mischief.

"No, Mom, the handsome man and I are not having sex. He's helping me bake cookies. What? No, he's not gay. He's an accountant. His name is Tom." She covered the mouthpiece and whispered to him, "My mother says 'hi.' "

Tom waved. "Hi."

"Tom says 'hi.' Tom's also a financial planner. Yes, he's very smart. Yes, I know Uncle Morty was an accountant, but Tom's not like Uncle Morty." She blew out an exaggerated sigh. "Okay, I'll ask him." Shifting the mouthpiece away from her lips, she asked him, "You're not wanted for embezzlement or anything, are you?"

Tom nearly choked on the laugh that caught in his throat. "No."

"No, Mom, he's not. Yes, he does have a nice voice, although how you can tell since he said only one word is a mystery to me." She listened for several seconds. An odd expression flashed in her eyes, then she said, "I don't know," rousing his curiosity about what her mom had asked.

Just then the stove timer chimed. "Oops, my cookies need to come out of the oven, Mom, so I've gotta go. Thanks for calling. . . . I'll see you around four o'clock Christmas Day. Miss you and love you. Bye."

She hung up, then huffed out a prolonged, "Whew! Talk about saved by the bell! The inquisition was about to shift into high gear." Slipping on an oven mitt that looked like a reindeer, she opened the oven and slid out the cookie sheets, the delicious scent of warm cookies filling the air. Tom's mouth watered, and he rose to get a better whiff.

"When do we get to eat some of those?" he asked.

"Not until they're cooled. And frosted. And decorated." She shot him what he suspected was supposed to be a stern look, but the effect was ruined by the honey-gold corkscrew curl obscuring her left eye. "And not a minute before that. Cookie baking is serious business around here, buster. No fooling around in the kitchen." She pointed an imperious reindeer-mitted hand at the rolled dough on the wooden cutting board. "Get busy with that cookie cutter." She winked at him. "Told you I could be bossy. You still sure you can handle it?"

"I'm sure." But even as he said the words, doubts snuck in because making cookies suddenly wasn't topping his list of things he most wanted. No, hitting the top of that list was yanking Merrie into his arms and satisfying this ever-growing, gnawing need to taste her again. To know if he'd imagined the heat that had sizzled between them the first time they'd kissed. But since he was supposed to have forgotten all about that kiss—yeah, right—he picked up the star-shaped cookie cutter and got busy.

While she arranged the stars he cut out on the cookie sheets, she said, "Sorry about the 'gay' and 'embezzler' stuff with my mother. She's something of a character."

"Actually, I thought it was funny. It sounds like you two have a nice relationship."

"We do—now. We had our share of rough patches, though, when my folks divorced."

A familiar pang hit Tom, followed by a wave of sympathy. "How old were you?"

"Fourteen."

He passed her another star. "I was nine when my parents split up."

They shared a commiserating glance. Then she said, "I can look back on the divorce now and realize it was for the best, but at the time—really until after my first year away at college—it was the worst thing I'd ever experienced. How about you?"

"Yeah, it was pretty bad."

She filled in the last few empty spaces on the cookie sheets. After sliding the shallow pans into the oven, she set the timer, then poured two cups of the freshly brewed coffee. Once they were seated across from each other at the round oak kitchen table, she continued. "The thing I hated the most was being shuffled back and forth between my parents. And the holidays, especially Christmas, were the worst. After the divorce, Christmas changed from a joyous, magical time into a bone of contention between my parents, who continued to feud even after the ink on the divorce papers was long dry."

Tom sipped his coffee and nodded. "Sounds like my family. The Christmas the year before my parents split was the best one of my life. My dad had a business trip to New York the week before Christmas, and me and my mom went with him. We saw all the store windows along Fifth Avenue, skated at Rockefeller Center, ate lunch at the Carnegie Deli, and saw the Christmas show at Radio City. They took me to see Santa at Macy's, Herald Square, and I'd never been so excited in my life because I knew that *that* was the *real* Santa. I asked him for a G.I. Joe and a new bike—and not just any bike. A Trailblazer XP 5000, at that time the Lamborghini of bicycles."

She smiled at him over the rim of her coffee mug. "And did you get it?"

"I sure did. Was the first kid on my block to have one." Poignant nostalgia filled him at the memory.

"That was the last Christmas we spent together as a family."

"You got shuttled back and forth?"

"Oh, yeah. My mom deeply resented having to share me on Christmas, especially with my dad's new wife, Cindy, whom Mom didn't like at all. Although she never came right out and said so, Cindy made it abundantly clear that she only tolerated my presence for my dad's sake. My dad was caught in the middle, trying to please everyone, unable to please anyone, and the whole holiday season just turned into a yearly stress-filled ordeal that couldn't be over fast enough as far as I was concerned."

She reached across the table and touched his hand that gripped his coffee mug. "How sad for you. It was hard enough without feeling unwanted on top of it all."

The compassion in her eyes, for a kid who'd had the rug jerked out from under his holiday illusions, could only come from someone who'd experienced that same thing. And he couldn't deny he found that commiseration somehow comforting—oddly so, as he rarely ever dragged those memories out of the vault.

He looked down at her slim fingers resting on the back of his hand, and a frisson of warmth raced up his arm. He liked the way her skin looked next to his. Liked the soft brush of her fingertips against him. Releasing his mug, he gently entwined their fingers.

"You still see the holidays as an ordeal," she said softly.

He shrugged. "Christmas holds very few happy memories for me. I do my best to ignore it by throwing myself into work this time of year even more than usual. It's not difficult, what with the high volume of year-end transactions and deal closings."

"Where do you spend Christmas?"

"Usually with friends. My dad and Cindy are cruising the Mediterranean this year. My mom died five years ago. Cancer."

Her eyes filled with sympathy, and she squeezed his hand. "I'm so sorry. And I understand. I lost my dad three years ago. How's your relationship with Cindy now?"

"Fine—now that I'm no longer a child in need of my dad's attention. I don't see them very often as they're quite the intrepid world travelers. Cindy's actually a nice woman, just not one who's fond of kids. She and my dad are very happy together. Is your mom remarried?"

"Oh, yes." She laughed and shook her head. "My stepdad is a total character, just like my mom. The two of them are like a comedy routine. I call them the Marilyn and Ed Show. They're semiretired, live in a condo in South Carolina in a golf course community. Neither one knows the first thing about the sport, but they *love* driving their new golf cart. If mom operates the golf cart the same way she does a car, I can only imagine that the groundskeepers aren't too happy."

Her expression grew thoughtful, and she slowly stroked her fingers along his, in an almost absent way. Her touch inspired a wealth of heated lust and awakened a plethora of nerve endings that ached to be stroked in a similar fashion. He shifted in his seat and wondered if she had any idea what she was doing to him.

Finally she said, "I find it intriguing that we come from such similar family backgrounds, yet we've responded so differently to like circumstances. Now I understand why your office looks so bah-humbug. I bet your home does, too. Do you have a Christmas tree?"

"No."

"You responded to your situation by basically blowing off Christmas, and I responded by completely embracing it."

He pointedly looked around the gaily decorated room. "Really? I hadn't noticed."

Her lips twitched. "Ha-ha. But my folks' divorce made me determined not to lose the Christmas spirit and magic I'd loved as a kid." Her expression turned serious. "I think every child deserves a special Christmas. No child should have that innocence and magic taken away."

"I agree. But life isn't always all candy canes and gumdrops."

"Maybe not. But I want to make Christmas as special as I can, especially for kids who already know that the other three hundred and sixty-four days of the year aren't magical."

Tom nodded slowly, understanding dawning. "That's why you host the kids' party at the halfway house on Christmas Eve. That's why you dedicate such a large chunk of your time and personal funds to that project—funds I'm always advising you to save."

A blush stained her cheeks. "Well, that *is* your job."

"You never told me the reasons behind what you do."

"It didn't matter. I wouldn't stop hosting that party no matter how dire a financial picture you painted for me. The kids love it, and it . . . fulfills me."

The timer chimed. She slipped her hand from his and rose. He immediately missed the feel of her skin. "Back to work," she said. "One more batch to go in the oven. The first ones we baked have cooled off. You ready to frost and decorate?"

"You bet. I love frosting."

She shot him an arch look over her shoulder as she slid the pans from the oven and replaced them with the next batch. "The frosting is for decorating. *Not* for eating."

"Aw, c'mon. I don't get even one little taste?" He dipped his chin and looked up at her with his best *please, oh, please* expression.

"Listen, that pleading look won't get you anywhere with me." She looked at him again, then heaved a sigh. "Okay, maybe it will. Sheesh. How long did it take you to perfect *that* look?"

"Years."

"I believe it. It's potent. All right. You may have *one* little taste—but not until after all the cookies are decorated."

"Wow. You're a hard woman, Merrie Langston. Setting out cookies and frosting in front of a man and expecting him to resist? What do you think I'm made of—steel?"

She leaned her hips against the counter and flicked her gaze over him in a way that raised his temperature a good ten degrees. Reaching out, she lifted from the counter a glass bowl filled with fluffy white frosting and cradled the container against her stomach. With deviltry dancing in her eyes, she slowly dragged her index finger through the frosting, then lifted it to eye level. "Baking cookies is all about willpower, Tom."

"Yeah?" He walked slowly toward her, drawn to her and that frosting-laden finger like Ulysses to the Sirens. He knew what willpower was. Usually. In fact, his was normally pretty damn good. But something about this woman boded very poorly for his control. And he'd known it when he'd offered to help her bake. Had known in his gut that he'd wanted more than baking to happen here. Hell, he'd known it since they'd kissed. Had known it well enough to make sure he had a condom on him—just in case. Well, just in case was bearing down on him like an avalanche. He'd fought this attraction all evening, but one fingerful of frosting and he was ready to throw in the towel. "And here I thought baking was all about mixing up the right ingredients."

"That, too. But you need willpower not to eat all the frosting before it's spread on the cookies." She moved her finger toward her mouth, but he closed the distance between them with a final step and reached out to gently snag her wrist. With his gaze steady on hers, he slowly drew her finger into his mouth.

He liked the heat that flared in her eyes, the way her irises darkened from golden brown to a color that resembled caramel smoke. And the way her breath caught in her throat. After he'd finished his treat, he slipped her finger free, then pressed her palm against his chest, right above the spot where his heart rapped hard and fast. The warmth of her hand heated him through the cotton of his polo shirt, and his muscles jerked in response.

"Delicious," he said softly. "But not enough." Taking the bowl from her, he slipped his own finger into the creamy fluff. After setting the bowl on the counter, he slowly touched his frosting-covered finger to her bottom lip. Her tongue peeped out and his treat disappeared.

"No fair," he said. "That was mine." He rubbed another thin layer of frosting over her bottom lip, then stepped closer, until their bodies touched. Then he leaned down and lightly brushed his tongue over the sweet spot.

A long sigh of pleasure escaped Merrie, and she braced her less-than-steady knees to keep from slithering to the floor. Of course, with the counter pressing against her hips, and his hard body fitted so delightfully snug against hers, chances were slim she'd actually be able to slither, but since her knees were threatening to take an extended vacation, she wrapped her arms around his neck—just in case.

"Hey, if you do that again," she whispered against his lips, "you'll be in big trouble. I mean it."

"Thanks for the warning." He glided his finger over her lips again, then licked away the frosting with teasing strokes of his tongue.

"Oh, you're in big trouble now," she said in a breathless voice, her heart pounding in anticipation as he dipped into the bowl again. But two could play this game. This time she grabbed his hand and slowly sucked his finger into her mouth. Fire ignited in his gaze. He shifted against her, his erection pressing against her belly, and she inwardly cursed the layers of clothing that separated their skin. Her tongue circled his fingertip, and a growl sounded in his throat.

"Yeah, I'm definitely in trouble," he agreed in a hoarse rasp. He wrapped his free arm around her and drew her more tightly against him. "I thought you said no fooling around in the kitchen."

She dragged his finger from her mouth and uttered the simple truth. "I'm not fooling around. Are you?"

"Hell, no." He leaned in and lightly grazed his teeth over her earlobe. "I'm dead serious. And I can think of a lot more interesting things to spread that frosting on than cookies."

She actually felt her eyes glaze over. "God, it's hot in here." Tingles of pleasure tripped down her spine, and she tilted her head to give his wandering lips better access to her neck. "Must be the oven."

"No, it's not. But you know that saying: if you can't stand the heat, get out of the kitchen."

"I can stand it," she said, but instantly wondered

if she could. The months since she'd last had sex suddenly felt like a decade drought—and she was dying to end the dry spell.

He lifted his head, and his gaze settled on her with such intensity that it felt as if he'd burned her. Releasing her, he flattened his hands on the counter on either side of her, bracketing her in, and she knew that nothing short of sweaty sex with this man would put out the fire consuming her.

"You sure you can stand it, Merrie? Because something about you and the aroma of cookies and . . . *you* are having a really bad effect on my self-control."

Oh, my. "Bad in what way?" she asked, impressed that he could still lay claim to any self-control since hers had been thoroughly kidnapped by her unruly hormones.

"As in you wreak havoc with it."

"Funny. That doesn't sound bad to me at all. I, um, have condoms in the bedroom."

"I have one in my wallet."

"Gotta admire a guy who thinks ahead."

His eyes flashed. "You like hard and fast? 'Cause I don't think there's much chance of slow and easy happening this time."

Wrapping her arms around his neck, she rose up on her toes and arched against him, pressing breasts that ached for his touch against his chest. "Slow and easy can wait. Right now, hard and fast sounds . . . delicious."

In a heartbeat his mouth covered hers in a hot, deep kiss that drenched her in sensation. His tongue rubbed against hers with an erotic friction, radiating heat that made her feel as if she'd turned her oven to "broil" and hopped inside. He tasted like warm sugar, and his hands . . . hmmm, his hands were magic. And everywhere. Gliding down her back. Coming forward to palm her breasts. Teasing her nipples through her shirt and bra into aroused, aching peaks.

A feeling that bordered on desperation overwhelmed her. Wanting, needing, to touch him, she yanked his shirt from the waistband of his jeans and ran her hands up his smooth back. Not enough. She grabbed the ends of his shirt and lifted. He helped, raising his arms so she could pull the soft cotton over his head. The shirt hit the floor.

His nicely muscled torso and abs clearly indicated he crunched a lot more than just numbers, and she planned to admire all those lovely muscles. Later. Once this fierce hunger consuming her was satisfied. Right now, way too many clothes still stood between them, and she wanted them off. And clearly so did he. He grabbed the ends of her T-shirt, and seconds later it joined his shirt on the floor.

Teasing her with nipping kisses, interspersed with ragged breaths, he unfastened her jeans. She kicked off her shoes, he toed off his loafers. She fumbled with his belt, damn stubborn thing, while she wriggled to help him slide her snug denim over her hips. A sigh of relief escaped her when she stepped out of the constricting material and kicked it aside, leaving her dressed only in her lacy red bra and panties.

But her sigh of relief turned into a gasp of pleasure when he grasped her buttocks and lifted her onto the counter. He stepped into the V of her splayed thighs, and his mouth once again descended on hers, obliterating all thoughts except those of him. His hands skimming over her skin, awakening every pore. His clever fingers unfastening her bra, then teasing her nipples into aching points. His lips blazing a heated trail down her throat, across her chest. His tongue circling, tormenting her beaded nipple before he drew the aroused bud into the hot, wet silk of his mouth, then lavishing the same attention on her other breast.

Slapping her palms on the counter, Merrie let her head fall limply back. She arched toward him, offering more of herself, and simply gave herself over to the intoxicating sensations bombarding her.

Her body responded to each exquisite tug on her

breast with a deep answering pull in her womb. He ran his hands along her inner thighs, spreading her legs wider. Then his fingers slipped beneath her panties to stroke her aroused feminine folds. A long moan blew past her parted lips, and she moved sinuously against his hand. He slipped one, then two fingers inside her, relentlessly stroking until the tight coil of need exploded. A ragged cry of pleasure ripped from her throat as an intense orgasm throbbed through her.

Aftershocks were still rippling along her nerve endings, her breath still coming in gasps, when she vaguely heard the sound of a zipper. Then what she assumed was the condom wrapper tearing. Deciding this required further investigation, she forced her head upward, dragged her eyes open, and watched him roll the protection over his erection. If she'd been capable of speech, she surely would have uttered something *very* appreciative, but somewhere along the line she'd forgotten how to speak English.

Before she could catch her breath, he pushed aside the damp wisp of lace that composed her panties, and thrust deep. Merrie's eyes slid shut, and locking her ankles behind him, she ground against him, wanting more. He obliged, grasping her hips, thrusting hard and fast. Pleasure ripped through her again, dragging a long "ooohhhh" from her lips. Tom groaned, thrust a final time, and she wrapped her arms around his neck, holding him tight. He buried his face against her neck, and she absorbed the racking shudders of his release.

She wasn't certain how many seconds passed before Tom lifted his head. With their ragged breaths intermingling, their eyes met. He looked as bamboozled and disoriented as she felt.

It took her two tries before she found her voice. "Wow. I have to admit, I would have pegged an accountant as the type to make love in a bed. I'll never fall victim to stereotyping again."

A quick grin flashed across his features. "I'd be happy to make love to you in a bed—if we can manage to get to one. Although I have to say that this counter is the perfect height."

"No complaints here."

"If this is what cooking is all about, no wonder so many men become chefs."

"I gotta tell ya, you're pretty handy in the kitchen." Merrie suddenly became aware of an insistent beeping. "Sounds like the cookies are done."

"That timer's been making noise for at least five minutes."

"You're kidding. I didn't hear it."

He waggled his brows. "You were . . . busy."

She laughed. "Yeah, well, you know, an elf's gotta do what an elf's gotta do. But those cookies are officially burnt to a crisp."

"I know exactly how they feel. But I have a great idea. Let's shut off the oven, take a nice, warm shower, then grab that bowl of frosting. And I'll show you that accountants are just as handy in the bedroom as they are in the kitchen. How does that sound?"

"Like the best damn birthday present I've had in years."

Chapter Five

Five days after their kitchen counter encounter, Tom entered his Main Street office and flicked on the lights with an air of determination. This morning he would be productive and catch up on the work stacked in his in-box—work he normally would have already accomplished, but playing Santa at Merrie's parties was eating up a big chunk of his time.

To say nothing of the time he'd spent with her *after* the parties.

Heat flashed through him, and he tried to push aside the four nights' worth of sensual images blinking through his mind like a slide show. Merrie in the shower, his wet, soapy hands skimming over her, then making love while the warm water sluiced over them. Lying amongst the tangled sheets with her, licking swirls of strategically placed sweet frosting from each other's body. Sharing a bathtub picnic of grapes, apple slices, and wine.

The bewitching feel of her, the luscious taste of her, were so firmly embedded in his senses, even blindfolded he could have picked her out of a crowd. And it wasn't just in bed that he enjoyed her. He liked talking to her. Listening to her. Decorating cookies with her. Liked her infectious smile, warm laughter, and teasing sense of fun.

Drawing a deep breath, he sank into his leather chair and thoughtfully sipped his usual morning take-out coffee from Lansfare Java Hut and tried to put his finger on why he felt so discombobulated.

He'd enjoyed the sexual fun and games over the past few days, but his feelings were a jumbled mass of contradictions. There was no denying he was drawn to Merrie, in a way he'd never experienced with any other woman. Not even Eileen, and he'd actually considered popping the question with her. While he'd always liked Merrie, had found her attractive ever since he'd met her two years ago, he'd never anticipated their friendship and business relationship taking this unexpected turn. She was so different from what he'd always thought was his "type." Yet none of the women he'd dated over the past few years, all of whom had been his "type," had affected him the way Merrie could with a mere smile. He wanted her, desired her, with an intensity that stunned him, and he couldn't say he was too happy about it.

The woman was all wrong for him. He was a planner; she flew by the seat of her pants. He was a realist; she was a dreamer. He led with his head; she led with her heart. They were just too different for this to last.

So just enjoy it for now, his inner voice advised. *Quit overanalyzing everything. She's hot, you want her, she wants you, 'nuf said. When the flame burns out, you'll both move on.*

Right. He took another sip of coffee, then nodded. "Right," he said out loud.

But, he realized, even saying the word aloud didn't make it feel any more right. It was one thing to indulge in a temporary fling. The problem was that his heart was balking at the word "temporary" in a way that alarmed him.

His gaze shifted to the vivid red poinsettia sitting on the windowsill. Merrie had brought it to his office the morning after their first night together, saying that his digs needed a bit of Christmas cheer. He had to admit that the fiery red leaves added some color to his normally austere office. And brought an image of Merrie to his mind. And—

Damn, was he *humming*? Yup. The vibration in

his throat comfirmed it. Not only humming, but humming "Have Yourself a Merry Little Christmas."

Great. Now he had Christmas carols—and one with her name in the title, no less—stuck in his head. And his stomach rumbled with a craving for Christmas cookies. He hadn't felt like this about Christmas since he was a kid, and it was all her doing. She just seemed to spread magic wherever she went. Part of him liked it, but another part of him found it . . . unsettling. He didn't like having his routine disrupted. He had his own groove, and it worked for him. *You're not in a groove*, his inner voice scoffed. *You're in a rut. Big difference.*

Was he? He looked around his office and realized that except for the poinsettia, it looked . . . bare. Lonely. And lately, hadn't he been feeling just that way?

Maybe. Maybe that's why Merrie was affecting him in this unprecedented way. He was lonely. *Anyone's* company would have been a welcome diversion. Wouldn't it? Yeah. That's all this was. People didn't fall in . . . *like* at the drop of a hat.

But as soon as the thought entered his mind, he thought of Rick. He'd served as best man at his friend's wedding three years ago, an event that had come as a surprise to everyone. He and Rick had roomed together for four years during college, and never had Tom met a more confirmed bachelor. But then Rick had met Sue and *whammo*—bachelor-boy fell like a two-ton water balloon tossed from the roof—sidewalk splat and all. He could still hear Rick saying in that bemused voice, *I don't know what happened, man. I took one look at her and I knew. Tried like hell to talk myself out of it, but there was no way. She was the one.* Three years later, they were going strong and expecting their first child. Just proved that when it came to matters of the heart, there was no predicting what might happen. Still, if love was going to hit him over the head, wouldn't it hit him with a woman who was more . . . sedate? More his type?

Another image of Merrie popped into his mind, and he forcibly pushed it aside. He had to get some work done. Had to stop thinking about her. Tonight—he'd think about her tonight, after his work was finished. When they were naked in bed—

He blew out a long breath. Damn. This was going to be one hell of a long day.

That night, after a successful party for the Lansfare Chamber of Commerce, Merrie parked her van in the spot closest to the Perfect Parties door, then turned to Tom, who sat in the passenger seat. He still wore his Santa suit, although he'd removed his hat, wig, beard, and the pillow that made him

Santa-chubby. He'd been unusually quiet during the fifteen-minute ride, and she'd wondered what he was thinking. One look at the hunger in his heated expression answered *that* question. Her pulse quickened in anticipation—and relief that she wasn't alone in entertaining carnal thoughts. Before she could say a word, he leaned over, unclicked her seatbelt, then hauled her onto his lap, an impressively smooth maneuver considering the console between them.

"How'd you know I was just thinking that I wanted to sit on Santa's lap?" she asked with a smile, sifting her fingers through his thick, dark hair, her legs dangling over his seat's armrest.

"Great minds."

"Are you going to ask me if I've been naughty or nice?"

"Sweetheart, I already know."

"Hmmm. Well, you know, an elf's gotta do what an elf's gotta do. So, what's the verdict—naughty or nice?"

"You're a delicious, bewitching combination of both."

Before she could even think of a reply, he pulled her closer and proceeded to reduce her to slush with a toe-curling, window-fogging, open-mouthed, lush kiss. His hand settled on her knee, then slowly prowled up her leg, under her elf dress.

"Are you wearing those red lace panties you tried to deduct as a business expense?" he asked, punctuating each word with a nipping kiss along her jaw.

"No."

"Damn."

"Just call me 'commando elf.'"

His head jerked up and he stared at her, while his hand skimmed the rest of the way up her leg . . . and cupped her bare bottom. Fire flared in his eyes.

"I wore panties at the party—wouldn't want to shock the Chamber of Commerce," she said, teasing his bottom lip with a fingertip, "but I slipped them off before we drove back here. I wanted to be prepared just in case Santa felt like making out in the parking lot."

Beneath her skirt, his hand urged her legs apart, then teased her sex with a light, circular motion that dragged a groan from her throat. "We could get arrested for what I want to do to you in this parking lot, Merrie."

Any reply she might have made evaporated into a sigh of pleasure when he slipped first one, then two fingers inside her. "You feel so good," he said, his voice a ragged groan against her lips. "So wet. So hot. So tight."

She spread her legs wider, and he kissed her deeply, his tongue imitating the rhythmic, seductive strokes of his fingers. His erection pressed against her hip, and although she was desperate to touch him, her sprawled position across his lap and his bulky costume hindered her.

Breaking off their kiss, she panted, "Want you . . . inside me."

"Next time. I want to watch you come. Come for me, Merrie."

His words—uttered in that deep, seductive, aroused tone—his intense expression, and his talented, relentless fingers all conspired to propel her over the edge. An intense orgasm gushed through her, and she cried out, drowning in glorious, exquisite sensation. When her spasms subsided, she weakly dragged her eyes open and met Tom's avid gaze.

"Beautiful," he whispered, easing his fingers from her, then brushing his lips over her forehead. "You're . . ." He shook his head, as if at a loss for words.

"One satisfied elf," she supplied with a sated sigh.

A corner of his mouth lifted. "I was thinking more along the lines of 'incomparable.' "

The runaway feelings for this man she'd been unsuccessfully trying to corral for the past week ambushed her once again at the lovely compliment. And every ambush prodded her closer to the precipice yawning before her. How much longer could she cling to the edge before she took the plunge and fell, utterly and completely? Her self-preservation gene—the one that kept trying to tell her this was happening too fast—was being effectively stomped into the ground by the unstoppable yearnings of her heart. And where Tom was concerned, she very much feared her heart was in charge. He'd proven himself so much more than the stodgy stick-in-the-mud she'd thought him to be. He was sweet and kind. Funny. Generous and smart. And in bed—well, there was nothing stodgy or boring about him there.

"Incomparable," she whispered. "I was just thinking the same thing about you."

"There's that whole great minds thing again." He clasped her hand, bringing it to his lips to place a warm kiss on her palm. "Could I interest you in an invite to my place—or do we need to bake more cookies tonight?"

"I'll need a few more batches for the Christmas Eve party at the halfway house, but I'll have tomorrow and all day Christmas Eve to make more. It's tradition that I bake them the day of the party. Wouldn't be Christmas Eve without cookies in the oven."

He frowned. "Tomorrow morning is our meeting with the loan officer at the bank. You sure you'll have enough time?"

"Plenty. Especially since there's no party on the schedule for tomorrow." She grinned. "Certainly more time than if *you* helped me bake, Mr. Let's Get Naked and Try Out This Frosting While the Cookies Burn."

He tickled his hand up her bare thigh. "Didn't hear any complaints at the time."

"And you won't hear any now. You are a *lot* of fun to bake with—"

"Same goes."

"—but a time-saver, you are not." A frown pulled down her brows. "Tom, about the bank loan—what do you think my chances are?"

He blew out a long, thoughtful sigh. "I wish I could tell you I thought it was a lock, but I can't. Based on your financial statements and income projections for next year, there's definitely some risk involved. This is a serious undertaking, for both you and the bank. But we'll show them how serious you are, how important this is to you, okay?"

"Okay."

He brushed another kiss against the inside of her wrist, shooting a tingle up her arm. "So . . . what about that invite to my place? You've never been— and I even cleaned up in case you'd say yes. Vacuumed and everything."

"A man who knows how to operate a vacuum cleaner? Be still, my heart. How can I refuse that?

But unless I stop by my apartment first, except for my elf costume, I'll have nothing to wear."

"Nothing to wear—yeah, that's a shame. Really."

She giggled. "Okay, no need to stop at my place. How far away do you live?"

"About ten minutes."

"I'll follow you."

A quarter of an hour later, Merrie parked her van behind Tom's in the driveway of a brick ranch located in an established neighborhood on a tree-lined street on the opposite end of town from her apartment. "Nice area," she said, exiting her car. "I didn't know you lived in a house."

"Better investment than paying rent." He held her hand as they walked up the cement walkway to the front door. "Property values in Lansfare are increasing sharply because of its proximity to Atlanta—close enough to commute to the city, but enough distance to offer the advantages of suburban living. This particular area is booming because of the easy access to the interstate."

"Guess I should have listened to you two years ago when you told me to start saving up to buy a house."

"Setting aside savings is always—"

"A wise investment in the future," she finished, citing the advice he'd given her dozens of times. "Unfortunately, saving isn't my strong suit."

"As the man who sorted through your Baggies and Tupperware container of receipts to prepare your financial statements, I pretty much knew that."

He unlocked the door, and Merrie stepped over the threshold into a modest foyer with cream-colored walls and an oak hardwood floor.

"Do I get a tour?" she asked, craning her neck around.

"Sure." He shot her a smile. "It won't take long since most of the rooms are empty. Saving isn't your forte—decorating isn't mine." Exiting the foyer, he pointed left and right as he led her toward the back of the house. "Empty living room, empty dining room."

"Where's the prerequisite bachelor workout equipment?"

"Spare bedroom. I use the other spare as a home office."

They entered the family room, which contained a comfortable-looking, oversize tan leather sofa, a matching chair and ottoman, and an oak coffee table with magazines neatly stacked in the corner. Except for two framed photos on the mantel, there were no personal touches in the room.

"Nice," she murmured. "But I can see you're not a big one for decorative doodads."

"It's not that I don't like them. I just don't know

what to get, what goes with what. I'm happy if I can keep the place more or less straightened up. I probably shouldn't admit this, but this is the neatest it's been in weeks."

"How hard can it be to keep a house with hardly any furniture in it clean?"

"Beats me, but it is."

She wandered toward the photographs. One depicted a smiling couple she judged to be in their fifties, dressed in matching tropical print shirts. They stood on a ship's gangway behind a white life ring that proclaimed WELCOME TO ST. THOMAS in bold, red letters. "Your father and Cindy?"

He crossed the room and stood behind her, gently massaging her shoulders. "Yeah. From their cruise last summer."

She looked at the other photo. A younger, smiling Tom, dressed in a black graduation cap and gown, held a diploma folder in one hand and had his arm slung around the shoulder of a woman who could only be his mother. She had the same kind, hazel eyes and dark hair. The same winning smile.

"College graduation," he said. "I attended Yale, my mom's alma mater. We had a terrific time that weekend in New Haven, completely oblivious to what was waiting right around the corner. Two months later she was diagnosed with an inoperable brain tumor."

Merrie's reached up and squeezed his hand that rested on her shoulder. "I'm so sorry."

"Me, too. But glad we had that memory. It's my favorite picture of her."

His words called to mind her favorite photo of her and her father, sitting in lime-green inner tubes, floating down the Chattahoochee River the summer before he died. They'd laughed and splashed like kids, and, like Tom, she was glad they'd shared that memory.

Looking over her shoulder, she said, "Not that I'm not pleased that you opened up shop here in Lansfare, but why, with a degree from Yale under your belt, didn't you go to work for some hotshot accounting firm?"

"I did. For three years—until I'd saved up enough money to strike out on my own. I didn't like fighting traffic every day, and I had no desire to live in the city. I always knew I wanted to be my own boss. My dad was a corporate executive, and he was never around—a fact that greatly contributed to the breakup of my parents' marriage. Hard to be a good husband and father when you're married to your job. I don't intend to let that happen to me. I want to be able to spend time with my wife, be a hands-on dad. Not be a slave to some big company that will dictate my life and my schedule."

An image of Tom with a toddler perched on his

shoulders, while the shadowy figure of a woman watched them, flashed in Merrie's mind. A yearning so strong it bordered on pain suffused her, and she realized with undeniable clarity that she was hideously jealous of that nameless, faceless woman. That she wanted to *be* that nameless, faceless woman. Which meant—

"Obviously wanting to be your own boss is something you can relate to," he said, yanking her from her thoughts.

She blinked, one foot now dangling over the emotional precipice—her other foot precariously balanced on a banana peel. "Uh, yes."

"I have something for you," he said, taking her hand and leading her into the kitchen. Like the family room, the kitchen was neat but devoid of any extra adornments. Pale yellow walls, white cabinets, terra cotta ceramic tile floor. The dark green countertop was bare except for two plates and a glass stacked on the drain board, a yellow cookie jar that looked like a ceramic tennis ball, and a shoe-box-size package wrapped with Christmas paper. Looking at the package, she realized it was the only thing in his home that acknowledged Christmas. No tree, no wreaths, no twinkle lights. The realization made her heart hurt for him.

He picked up the package and handed it to her. "For you. Happy birthday."

Pleased and surprised, Merrie held the weighty package, alternating her stare between him and the gift. "Should I open it now?"

"Sure—unless you don't want to know what it is."

Truth was, she was dying to know. She held up the box to her ear and gently shook. "Hmmm. No ticking, so it's probably not a clock." She sniffed the paper. "Doesn't smell like perfume, and it's too small for a Mercedes."

He laughed. "Do you always shake and smell your presents?"

"Always. Just to up the suspense. Then I lose all control, and it's a free-for-all." In proof of her words, she ripped off the wrapping paper with the enthusiasm of a kid plunked down in a sweetshop.

The box was from Agatha's Antiques and Curios, Merrie's favorite store in historic Lansfare. Agatha's carried an eclectic assortment of unusual items. "I love this shop."

"I figured as much after you mentioned it the other night."

"I did? I don't remember."

"Maybe you were distracted. We were in the bathtub at the time."

"In that case, I was *definitely* distracted."

Setting the box on the counter, she carefully lifted the lid, then separated several layers of gold tissue paper. A gorgeous snow globe lay nestled amongst the tissue, and she gently lifted it from its gilded nest. Holding the holly- and candy-cane-decorated base, she shook the globe and watched sparkling snow swirl around a grinning Santa. With a sack filled with toys slung over his shoulder, and more gaily wrapped gifts stacked at his feet, Santa stood in front of his sleigh, surrounded by his eight tiny reindeer and—

A smiling female elf. Who was handing Santa a star-shaped cookie, presumably a "one for the road" treat before he began his Christmas Eve rounds.

"It plays music," Tom said, reaching out to twist a silver knob. The tinkling melody of "Have Yourself a Merry Little Christmas" filled the room. "It reminded me of you. Of . . . us. Of the fun we've shared this past week."

She had to swallow twice before she could manage to speak around the lump of emotion swelling in her throat. "It's beautiful, Tom. Perfect. I don't think I've ever received a more thoughtful present."

After carefully setting her gift on the counter, she reached up and cradled his handsome face between her palms. Looking into his eyes, her heart seemed to swell. She felt herself teeter for a second, but there was no stopping the inevitable. After drawing a deep mental breath, she stepped over the edge of the cliff. She hadn't meant to for this to happen, wasn't convinced it was the smartest thing she'd ever done, but there was no denying her feelings. She'd tried to ignore them, tell herself she and Tom were too different, but he and his snow globe had her leaping over the edge into the unknown and accepting the irrefutable truth: she was head over elf shoes in love with Tom.

Everything in her wanted to instantly blurt out the truth, but a tiny voice cautioned her to remain silent. To wait. To let him mention the L word first. She'd learned the hard way that some men equated "I love you" with "life sentence with no chance of parole." She'd give it some time. After all, their relationship had only taken a romantic turn a week ago. Still—they'd known each other for two years. And he cared for her—she could see it, feel it, in the way he treated her. Touched her. Looked at her—just like he was looking at her now. With all that "I want to smear frosting on you and gobble you up" heat that made her knees disappear.

Okay, she'd give it some time. A week. That's definitely all her patience could stand. If he hadn't tossed the L word into the ring by New Year's, she'd just have to take her chances and do the tossing herself.

Rising onto her toes, she wrapped her arms around his neck and pressed herself against him.

"Thank you for my gift, Tom. I love . . . it." Not precisely the words she longed to say, but close enough. For now. And best of all, he showed no signs of masculine panic at the casual mention of the L word. Very encouraging.

"I'm glad. You ready to continue the grand tour?"

"Absolutely. What's the next stop?"

"The fridge, where there's a bottle of wine chilling. Then the pantry, where I've stocked up on several cans of chocolate frosting. Then onto the master bath, where there's a jet tub waiting. Then our final stop, my bedroom."

She waggled her brows at him. "What awaits me there?"

He leaned down and whispered in her ear. She felt her eyes widen. Heat seared her as if the earth had just moved closer to the sun.

He straightened and shot her a scorching look. "How does that sound?"

"Very naughty . . . but, oh, so very nice."

Chapter Six

Tom awoke to the sounds of "Santa Claus Is Coming to Town" pouring cheerfully from his alarm clock radio. After slapping the OFF button, he sleepily rolled over and reached out for Merrie but encountered nothing but comforter. He opened his eyes and saw a sheet of paper propped on her pillow. Snatching the note, he quickly scanned the words.

> *Good morning, Sleepyhead,*
> *Happy Day-Before Christmas Eve! I didn't want to wake you. Had to go home to shower and prepare for this morning's loan meeting. I brought your Santa costume home so I could get out the chocolate frosting stain from last night. I was thinking— since I've seduced my accountant with my red lace lingerie, could it now be considered a business expense? Definitely something we need to discuss.*

MINE AT MIDNIGHT

He chuckled at the big smiley face she'd drawn after that sentence, then continued reading:

I'll see you at the bank at ten a.m. Smooches, Merrie. P.S. I have a surprise planned!

A surprise? He couldn't help but grin. If it was anything like the one she'd sprung on him by going commando under her elf costume, he couldn't wait.

Next to her name on the note she'd left a vivid lip imprint in a color he instantly recognized as Kiss Me 'Til I'm Riled-Up Red. He slowly traced his fingertip over the crimson mark, as if he could capture the seductive feel of her lips from the paper.

The seductive feel of her lips . . . Heat zapped him like he'd just backed up into an electric fence. A vivid memory of those seductive lips prowling all over his body rushed blood to his groin, and he groaned. Last night, like every night they'd shared, had been . . . incredible. And not just because of the sex, although there was no denying the sex had been scorching. No, he and Merrie had shared more than their bodies. They'd laughed. Exchanged stories about their lives. Their friends and family. Their most embarrassing moments. Their greatest triumphs. He couldn't recall ever feeling more . . .

alive. Being with her somehow made everything that came before her seem . . . empty.

Empty? He sat up and tunneled his hands through his hair. Damn it, this was insane. His life wasn't empty. He had friends, a good job, a nice house—all very fulfilling. *Yeah, but there's no one to share it all with*, piped up his inner voice. Turning his head, he looked over his shoulder at the vacant space where she'd lain next to him, and realized he didn't like the look of that barren spot. Didn't like that he'd woken up alone. Didn't like being solo in his bed, which only last week had seemed the perfect size, but now appeared waaaay too big. And empty. And lonely. Because Merrie wasn't in the spot where she . . . belonged.

"*Augh.*" He rose and headed toward the bathroom. How was it possible that in the mere course of a week's time this woman had turned him and his entire life upside down? She'd infiltrated his every thought. Occupied every corner of his mind. Every time he saw the color red—which was, like, every two seconds at Christmas—he thought of her lips. Which in turn led to thoughts of her mouth. Her mouth on him. His mouth on her. Her smile. Her laugh. Her—

"See?" he muttered, turning on the shower spray. "It's happening again." And it—whatever the hell "it" was—was happening way too fast. He needed to take some time to determine where—if anywhere—this madness was going. Decide what— if anything—he intended to do about these unsettling yet undeniable feelings Merrie inspired. And as soon as this morning's meeting at the bank was finished, he'd take some time to do just that. But right now he needed to focus all his attention on getting Merrie her loan.

An hour later, wearing a conservative navy pinstriped suit and armed with his briefcase and best professional demeanor, Tom entered the lobby of the Lansfare Savings and Loan. And halted as if he'd walked into a wall of glass.

He'd stopped by the bank yesterday to make a deposit, and the only holiday decoration had been a six-foot artificial tree adorned with jewel-toned ornaments in the far corner of the lobby. Not so now.

Now the room was illuminated with enough white twinkle lights to cast a glow over a small city. Painted, life-size papier-mâché figures of Santa and Mrs. Claus stood grinning guard at the ends of the white marble teller counter. He instantly recognized the figures as belonging to Perfect Parties.

His gaze panned around the room, jolting to a halt when he spied Merrie. Merrie, standing next to a rectangular serving table festooned with glittery garland, holly berries, and a dramatic Christmas tree centerpiece made from glossy, round green ornaments. Trays filled with her oversize cookies flanked the tree, along with a punch bowl and a silver coffee urn. Bank employees lined up around the food, picking up red, green, and gold tableware, which was laid out on an adjoining table decorated with two animated Victorian dolls garbed in holiday apparel. And speaking of holiday apparel . . . Tom could only stare in disbelief. Merrie was wearing her elf costume.

Tom briefly closed his eyes, but when he opened them again, yup, she was still wearing the costume. At that moment she looked his way. Their eyes met, and she smiled and waved. He merely stared at her. After saying something to the man she'd been speaking to, she crossed the lobby toward Tom, her elf shoes jingling with her every step.

"Good morning . . . and surprise!" she said with a dimpling smile as she joined him. Lowering her voice to a conspiratorial whisper, she said, "Since I guess a big kiss wouldn't be appropriate, how about some fresh-brewed coffee?"

His gaze raked over her costume. "*This* is your surprise?"

"Yup." Clearly she read something of his displeasure in his tone or expression because she frowned and peered at him. "What's wrong?"

Shaking his head with disbelief, Tom grasped her

arm and led her into the corner. With each jingle of her elf shoes, his annoyance grew. When they had as much privacy as they could get, he said in an undertone that didn't quite hide his anger, "Speaking of 'wouldn't be appropriate,' what on earth are you doing?"

She blinked. "I'm throwing a little party for the bank employees. Nothing fancy, just—"

"This is *not* a party, Merrie. This is serious business. What the hell were you thinking to show up at a *business* meeting dressed like an elf?" He glanced at his watch. "We still have a few minutes. Hurry up and change your clothes. I'll stall the loan officer if necessary, but don't dawdle. I'm sure he won't take kindly to being kept waiting."

For several seconds she stared at him in a way that made him wonder if he'd just sprouted another head. Then an expression he'd never seen from her before flared in her eyes. Her narrowed eyes.

"There's no need to stall anyone," she said in an uncharacteristically chilly voice. "Mr. Bingham, the loan officer, is already here."

"So he's already seen you in that getup. Not good." Frustrated, he raked a hand through his hair. "Why on earth couldn't you have just worn a suit like a normal person?"

Her eyes narrowed further, and he realized she was angry. Fine. Why should he be the only one?

"I have no intention of changing my clothes. In case you haven't noticed, I'm not the suit type."

A humorless sound passed his lips. "Not the suit type? Well, clearly that statement will go down in the annals of history under the title 'truer words have never been spoken.'"

Something that looked like hurt flashed in her narrowed eyes. "Are you *trying* to be insulting, or just merely ridiculous?"

"You, who dressed in jingly shoes and an elf costume for the most important business meeting thus far in your career, think *I'm* being ridiculous? *I* want you to get this business loan, and I'd expected you to act in a proper, businesslike manner."

"There is nothing improper about this," she said, her voice low and tight. "I'm serving cookies and punch—not condoms and porn. As for a businesslike manner, that's precisely what I'm doing. I want a business loan, and throwing parties is my business. I wanted to give the loan officer a good feel for the sort of business I run."

"You could have accomplished that with a portfolio of photographs. Did the loan officer know you'd planned this?"

"No. It was a surprise. As for a portfolio of photos, well, clearly that's how *you* would have chosen to go about it, but I wanted to give a hands-on demonstration. I've given the bankers a good sense of the sort of person I am."

"You certainly have. They now know without a doubt that you possess two traits that make bankers very nervous about parting with their money—you're unpredictable and don't take things seriously."

They glared at each other for several seconds, and he could almost feel the tension bouncing between them. Finally she said, "What you call unpredictable, I call spontaneous. And for your information, I take plenty of things seriously. But I actually think the problem here is that *you* take way too many things way too seriously."

"Certainly when it comes to business matters, yes, I do," he shot back.

"Miss Langston?" asked a deep voice behind them. Tom turned and saw an unsmiling Dave Bingham, the bank's chief loan officer, approaching. After exchanging greetings, Dave asked, "Shall we go into my office?"

They fell into line, with Tom bringing up the rear behind Merrie, and he forced himself to refrain from wincing with every jingle of her damn elf shoes.

Once they were all seated in the glass-walled office and pleasantries had been exchanged, Dave said, "I've gone over the financial statements Tom prepared, Miss Langston, and quite frankly, I was concerned with some of the numbers. But I've watched you this morning, and I noted how efficiently you turned our lobby into a veritable winter wonderland in only an hour's time. And supplied our employees with the tastiest cookies and punch I've ever sampled.

"However," he continued, his tone and expression grave, "your financial standing is not as strong as I'd like. Still, I cannot ignore your talent, ingenuity, and drive, all of which have tipped the scales in your favor. I'm going to approve your loan, Miss Langston, but because your financial statements clearly indicate Lansfare Savings and Loan would be taking on more risk, the bank will need to charge you a higher interest rate than if your numbers were more favorable."

Relief washed through Tom, and he looked at Merrie, whose attention remained firmly fixed on Dave.

"These are the terms the bank is offering," Dave said, handing a sheet of paper to Merrie. "If they're acceptable to you—"

"They are," Merrie said, her relief all but illuminating the room.

"Excellent. There are some documents to sign.

Then you'll be all set." He held out his hand. "Congratulations, Miss Langston."

Merrie jumped to her feet and shook Dave's hand with such enthusiasm, her elf shoes jingled. "Thank you, Mr. Bingham."

"You're welcome." He smiled. "Now let's get your signature on those papers so I can help myself to another one of those delicious cookies before the tellers eat them all."

Tom cleared his throat. "Congratulations, Merrie."

She turned to him, and when their gazes met, his stomach performed an uncomfortable, jittery dance at her expression. Traces of anger still lingered in her eyes. But it was the other emotion he clearly read that cramped his insides: disillusionment.

"Thank you," she said in the flattest tone he'd ever heard pass her lips.

He watched in silence as Merrie scrawled her signature with a flourish on the loan papers.

"The funds will be at your disposal by the start of business on the twenty-eighth," Dave said. He escorted them to the lobby, shook their hands in parting, then made a beeline for the cookie table, leaving Tom and Merrie alone. Before Tom could speak, Merrie said, "If you'll excuse me, I need to start cleaning up my supplies."

"I'll help you—"

"No, thank you." She looked up at him, and an unpleasant sensation he couldn't name filled him at her cool, impersonal stare. She'd never looked at him like that before. Actually, he'd never seen her look at *anyone* like that before. He didn't like it one bit. "I don't need your help."

"Look, Merrie, I'm sorry that we argued earlier—"

"I'm not. In fact, I think it's good that we cleared the air."

"Cleared the air? What does that mean?"

"It means that the laughs we've shared over the past week clouded the fact that we're very different. It's good we were reminded before I . . . we became any more . . . involved."

A frisson of annoyance, and damn it, hurt, pricked Tom, and a frown pulled down his brows. "We've shared a lot more than just laughs, Merrie."

She shrugged. "Maybe. But what we don't share is the same outlook on life, and until this morning, I'd unfortunately forgotten that. You obviously don't understand me or approve of me. I can't force you to do so, nor can I change the way I am. I've tried that in the past—it doesn't work, and it's not the sort of relationship I want to be involved in. I've also mistakenly stayed in relationships well beyond their expiration date, and I won't do it again. You and I . . . we've clearly reached our expiration date."

For several seconds Tom simply stared at her resolute expression, her words reverberating with an unpleasant echo in his mind. Then he pulled in a deep breath and told himself that the empty feeling in the pit of his stomach was relief.

He cleared his throat to dislodge the dry lump that seemed stuck there, and forced himself to say, "You're right, of course. We're very different." He'd known that all along. He was facts and numbers, she was fairy dust and magic. He was sturdy boots, she was elf shoes. Their . . . attraction, or fling, or whatever label he slapped on it, would have fizzled out soon anyway. So ending their personal relationship, making a clean break here and now, was good. Yup, it sure was.

"What about your party tomorrow tonight at the halfway house?" he asked.

"You're off the hook. I have the Santa costume, and I'll make other arrangements. No problem. I'll send you a check for the other parties."

He was off the hook. Perfect. She'd make other arrangements. Terrific. She'd send a check. Great. So that meant all that was left was to say—

"Good-bye, Tom."

There was no missing the finality in her tone. His inner voice yelled at him, demanding he do something, say something, but what else was there to say? Except, "Bye, Merrie."

She didn't hesitate another second. Turning on her heel, she walked across the green marble floor toward the table where she'd set up her snacks. After casting one final look in her direction, Tom walked swiftly from the bank.

Chapter Seven

By four o'clock on Christmas Eve afternoon, Merrie would have thought she'd be all cried out, but darn it, it seemed like her stupid tears sprang from an endless well.

Since arriving home from the bank yesterday, she'd wrapped presents and baked cookies for tonight's halfway house party—crying all the while. By midnight, bone-tired and baked out, she'd listlessly entered her bedroom—and stared at her bed, where she'd made love with Tom. Knowing a sleep-hopeless situation when she saw one, she remade the bed with a brand-new set of sheets, hoping that would erase the memories of Tom that permeated her bedroom, but it proved such a useless effort, she had to wonder if she'd need to get rid of the bed altogether and repaint the room as well.

Wrapped in a red chenille blanket, she'd spent the looooong, lonely night huddled in her recliner chair—the sofa was out, as she'd made love with Tom there—blowing her nose, wiping her eyes, and thinking. Hey, no one could accuse her of not being able to multitask.

Just as no one could accuse her of not being a fool—because, man, she was some kind of first-class fool.

She'd barely managed to drag herself through today, and now, with her halfway house party scheduled to begin in only a few hours, she needed to get a grip. Instead, a sniffling groan escaped her as she wrapped another teddy bear in bright red paper.

How could she have let herself fall in love with a man so totally wrong for her? Just recalling the way he'd looked at her yesterday at the bank, as if she were flakier than piecrust, dribbled a fresh onslaught of tears down her cheeks, which really annoyed her because she *hated* to cry. She didn't cry "pretty" like some women did, with dainty tears leaving glistening silver tracks down their porcelain cheeks, and their eyes looking dewy and vulnerable. No, she cried big, sloppy, slurpy tears that turned her nose runny, her skin blotchy, and her eyes swollen and bloodshot. She hiccupped out noisy sobs that twisted up her face like a wrung-out sponge and made her head hurt, and boy, right now she was nursing the mother of all headaches.

Well, hell, she might as well have a headache. It went along just fine with her heartache. And might as well toss in her hurt and anger, too. *Lots* of anger. Who the heck did Tom Farrell think he was, anyway?

" 'Why couldn't you have just worn a suit like a *normal* person?' " she mimicked in a deep voice. "Humph. Like I'm *ab*normal because I like to draw outside the lines." She slapped a bow on the wrapped bear and started on the next one. "Thinking outside the box got me my loan, didn't it, Mr. Serious? Your financial statements wouldn't have gotten the job done."

Her conscience slapped her, and she grudgingly muttered, "Okay, okay, the financial statements only reflected the truth, and if I'd watched my finances better, that truth would have been more attractive."

Still, hearing Tom utter that "normal person" crack had hurt. A lot. But not nearly as much as his *Not the suit type? Well, clearly that statement will go down in the annals of history under the title 'truer words have never been spoken'* statement. Obviously he preferred the "suit" type. She'd known it, yet foolishly she'd allowed herself to believe, to hope, that he'd decide that even though she wasn't the suit type, he still preferred her.

Well, that ship had clearly sailed. And she was

not happy that it had left the port with her heart tied to the propeller, getting shredded to bits. She'd never felt for any man the way she felt about Tom, which could lead her to only one conclusion: love sucked. Big time. And it *hurt*. Well, she was through. Never again.

"That's my New Year's resolution, a week early," she said, sticking on another bow. "I'd be better off with a dog."

Good plan. Right after Christmas she'd get herself a dog and forget all about Tom Farrell. After all, how long could exorcising him from her thoughts take? *Oh, probably only a decade or two*, her inner voice sneered.

As they had countless times since yesterday, a barrage of images blinked through her mind, stilling her busy hands. Tom, smiling at her. Laughing with her. Kissing her. Holding her. Baking with her. Looking at her in that dark, hot, hungry way that liquefied her knees. Showering with her. Making love to her. Over her. Under her.

Yeah, probably a decade or two would be needed.

Especially since memories of him haunted her *everywhere* she looked. Her bedroom. Her bathroom. Her sofa. Her van. Her kitchen. All of her usual happy places were officially unhappy. In spite of what the Christmas song proclaimed, all was not calm, all was not bright.

MINE AT MIDNIGHT

A tear plopped onto her wrist, and she impatiently swiped the back of her hand across her wet eyes.

Damn it, he could have stayed at the bank.

You told him to go.

Insisted they talk.

You told him it was over.

Or called her.

You gave him his walking papers.

Yes, she had, and he'd offered no resistance at all. None. Zippo. Nada. Obviously he was fine with her decision—which just proved that she'd done the right thing. If he didn't care for her the way she cared for him, she was better off without him.

Unfortunately, that didn't make it hurt any less.

Her watery gaze involuntarily shifted to the coffee table, and she stared at the snow globe Tom had given her. A fresh batch of hot tears pushed behind her eyes. Had it been less than forty-eight hours ago that she'd contemplated telling him she loved him? Her insides cringed. Thank heavens for once she'd kept her feelings to herself. He probably would have screamed and jumped out the window in total panic. Or worse, have mumbled something like, "Oh, um, thanks."

Reaching out, she wound the music box. The bell-like sounds of "Have Yourself a Merry Little Christmas" brought a hard lump to her throat.

Jacquie D'Alessandro

A merry Christmas?

No, not this year.

On Christmas Eve morning, Tom sat at his kitchen table, his head cradled in his hands, a cold cup of untouched coffee at his elbow. A dull headache throbbed insistently behind his gritty eyes, but the pain was barely noticeable since the rest of him felt so . . . gutted. Except for the numb spot in his chest where he surmised his heart must still be beating since he hadn't dropped to the floor—not that it actually *felt* like it was still beating. Most likely he should be grateful for that one numb spot, seeing as how the rest of him hurt like a raw wound—and had since she'd walked away from him yesterday.

When he'd arrived home from the bank, Tom had entered his house, locked the door, plopped his briefcase onto the floor, then walked slowly toward his bedroom. When he reached the doorway, he'd halted and stared at his unmade bed. At the rumpled sheets where only hours before he and Merrie had made love. Made love, he suddenly realized with a painful jolt, for the last time.

The rest of the day had passed in a foggy blur of trying to convince himself that everything was good. He was free. Unencumbered. No more playing Santa. He should be turning cartwheels. He hadn't had a chance to think or breathe for the past week, not since she'd shown up in his office with her Tupperware container filled with receipts and shanghaied him—yes, damn it, *shanghaied* him, with her big caramel-colored eyes, Riled-Up Red lips, and talk of lacy red underwear—into being her Santa.

And he'd almost succeeded in convincing himself everything was good—but then the night had come. He'd thought his bed had seemed lonely and empty that morning? Ha! That was nothing compared with how empty and lonely that bed had been last night. He'd stared at the ceiling, reliving every moment he'd spent with her. Every touch. Every smile. And as dawn had crept through the windows, he'd been forced to admit that everything was most definitely not good.

With a groan, he now lifted his head and scrubbed his hands down his stubbled cheeks. After his sleepless, miserable night, today wasn't shaping up to look much better. *Why* couldn't he just write the entire affair off? Accept last week for what it had been? Insanity. That's what the last week had been. He hadn't just stepped outside the box. He'd axed the box into kindling and set it on fire.

Pushing to his feet, he poured his cold coffee down the drain, then served himself a fresh cup. He sipped the strong brew, the caffeine seeping into his system, and thought about the women he'd dated over the past few years, and realized they'd all pretty much been the same. Conservative, executive types. Few of them had particularly challenged him. And few of them had particularly interested him. They'd been safe. And essentially boring. If there was one word that he'd *never* use to describe Merrie, it was "boring."

He stared into his steaming mug. No other woman had ever made him laugh the way Merrie had. Made him feel as if he were caught up in a vortex filled with life and color and happiness. A place where loneliness didn't exist. No, Merrie didn't fit into the mold of what he'd always assumed, always believed was the type of woman he wanted to be with, spend his life with, but he could now only conclude that he'd always been *wrong*. He'd never felt like this about anyone because he'd been dating the *wrong* women.

If he'd asked Merrie for a date the first time he'd met her two years ago, when he'd taken one look at her and practically been knocked flat, then he would have figured this all out two years ago. Would have realized that she was the woman he wanted. Yes, she was quirky—but so what? He'd come to the irrefutable conclusion that he liked quirky. Needed quirky. In fact, he . . . *loved* quirky.

He blew out a long breath and tunneled his hand

through his hair. Great. Perfect time to realize he loved her—*after* she'd told him to get lost.

He frowned, then shook his head. The hell with that. He knew what he wanted under his Christmas tree, and it wasn't the heave-ho from the woman he'd fallen ass over backwards for. No, he wanted Merrie, elf costume, jingly shoes, and all, under his tree. And by damn, he was going to find a way to make that happen.

He set his coffee on the counter, experiencing the first stirrings of hope since he'd walked out of the bank. Of course, before he could maneuver Merrie under his Christmas tree, he'd have to actually *get* himself a Christmas tree. Filled with purpose, he strode toward his bathroom. First up, a shower and shave. Then, he had a lot to do. Plans to make.

And an elf to win.

Chapter Eight

Her arms laden with stacked trays of cookies, Merrie staggered up the steps of the halfway house, her elf shoes jingling. The door was opened by a grinning Lauren Porter, one of the full-time workers at the organization that offered shelter to mothers and their children in need of temporary housing. Most of the women had left abusive partners behind and were waiting, hoping to start new lives. Merrie thought them the bravest people she'd ever met.

"I'll send a few teenagers out to unload your van," Lauren said. "What else needs to be brought in?"

"Everything in the back. While they unload, I'll set up the food and games." After the children were finished eating, she'd get Lauren to lead them in a game so she could duck into the bathroom and change into the Santa costume.

"As always, your Santa's a huge hit with the

younger kids," Lauren said, grabbing the top two trays from her stack, then leading the way toward the kitchen. "We weren't expecting him so early, but hey, for Santa you adjust."

"*My* Santa?" Merrie repeated, bewildered.

Lauren paused in the doorway to the rec room and nodded. "Check it out," she whispered with a smile. "They're enthralled."

Merry stepped into the doorway and stared. Santa sat on a folding chair, showing his audience a picture from the book he held, a print she instantly recognized as being from *How the Grinch Stole Christmas*. More than two dozen kids sat on the floor gazing up at the picture with rapt attention. A few tired-looking mothers sat amongst the group, most holding babies or toddlers. As if sensing the weight of her regard, Santa turned in her direction, and she found herself looking directly into Tom's eyes.

A bolt of confused joy ripped through Merrie, and she pressed her lips together to keep them from trembling. She didn't know exactly why he was here or what it meant, but surely he wouldn't have come if he didn't care for her—at least a *little* bit. And for now, until they had a chance to talk, that was enough to lift the heaviness weighing upon her heart.

The next few hours flew by in a whirlwind of

excited children playing games, eating snacks, and receiving not one, but *two* gifts from Santa, as Tom had brought his own sack filled with presents. It was after eleven p.m. when all remnants of the celebration were finally cleared away.

"Thanks, Merrie and Santa," Lauren said with a tired smile. "The party was terrific. You gave all those kids, and their moms, something special to remember." She tried, unsuccessfully, to stifle a yawn. "Do you need any more help?"

"No, thanks," Merrie said. "We'll leave through the kitchen door. I'll turn off the lights on our way out."

"Okay. Since that door will lock automatically behind you, I'm heading up to bed. G'night. And merry Christmas."

After Lauren left, Merrie turned toward Tom, who'd removed his snowy wig and beard and was regarding her through solemn eyes.

"Alone, at last," he said.

She swallowed to locate her voice in a throat gone dust dry. "It was nice of you to come here tonight. I . . . wasn't expecting you."

"I know." He approached her, and her heart pounded with anticipation. When only an arm's length separated them, he reached out and captured her hands. Warmth skittered up her arm. "There's something I'd like to show you, Merrie. At my house. I know it's late, but would you be willing to drive over?"

She studied his serious hazel eyes and could clearly see that he wanted to talk to her, and obviously he didn't want to do so here. Since she couldn't deny she wanted to hear what he had to say, or that she had a few things of her own to tell him, she nodded. "All right. I'll follow you."

Twenty minutes later, she stood on Tom's porch, waiting for him to unlock his front door. The cold, still air seeped through her elf costume, eliciting a shiver. All the homes surrounding his on the quiet street were aglow with holiday lights, but Tom's remained dark—which not only ignored the holiday spirit, but also wasn't helping him to locate his door key. Finally the door swung inward.

The foyer was cast in total darkness. "It would be much easier to see whatever you want to show me if some lights were on," she said in a teasing voice.

"You want lights—I'll give you lights." He stepped behind her and rested his hands lightly on her shoulders. "But first, close your eyes. And no peeking."

"All right."

He gently nudged her, and she walked slowly forward while he steered her by the shoulders. Although she was mightily tempted to peek, she kept her promise not to. After he drew her to a stop, she felt him step up close behind her, eliciting another shiver that had nothing to do with the cold. "You can open your eyes," he said softly, the words brushing across her ear.

Merrie opened her eyes and saw . . . darkness. Then, in a blink, she heard the click of a switch being flipped, and gasped as suddenly the room was illuminated by the glow of hundreds of white twinkle lights. Tom's formerly empty living room—or was this the formerly empty dining room?—now resembled a winter wonderland, complete with a fully decorated and lit Christmas tree that filled the room with the redolent scent of fresh pine.

Clasping her hands to her chest, she said, "Tom . . . it's beautiful." Tearing her gaze away from the tree, she turned to face him. "*You* did all this?"

His expression turned sheepish. "Yeah. You're the only elf I know, and since you weren't here, it was all up to me." Uncertainty flashed in his eyes. "Does it look okay?"

She hoped her smile didn't look as shaky as it felt. "It's beautiful."

There was no mistaking his relief. Taking her hand, he pulled her gently toward the tree. "I saved one ornament—for you to hang." He reached down and slid out a single ornament hidden under the tree, then held up the ceramic piece. Merrie's chin trembled as she looked at the smiling Santa holding up a sign that read: "Have Yourself a Merry Little Christmas."

"You did all this for me?"

"Yes. But as I was doing it, I realized that it was also for me—to make up for the holiday spirit that I'd been missing. That you'd made me want again." He handed her the ornament. "Will you do the honors?"

Not trusting her voice, she merely nodded, then reached up to hang the ornament on a high branch.

"Perfect," he said. "*Now* it's done."

A quick laugh escaped her. "You did all the work."

"But it wasn't complete until now. 'Christmas' isn't complete without 'Merrie.'" He moved to stand in front of her, and his gaze searched hers. "Seems like we're a good team."

Merrie's heart flipped over. Before she could reply, he took her hands and entwined their fingers. "Merrie, I'm sorry." He blew out a long breath. "Sorry we argued, sorry I hurt your feelings. Yesterday and today were the two most miserable days of my entire life—and I mean that literally. I did the math. I've been alive for 11,289 days, and out of those 11,289 days, the last two win the prize, hands down, as *the* Most Miserable. I never want another day like them."

Well, she didn't know the exact numbers of days she'd been alive, but the last two held that same dubious honor for her. "That's a lot of math."

"I did a lot of thinking. Mostly about what you'd said yesterday. You said I should know what sort of person you are, and man, did I give the wrong answer. I *do* know what kind of person you are. You're sweet and kind. Unselfish and funny. Full of life and spontaneity. Vibrant and generous. A bit too generous sometimes, as your credit card receipts prove, but we can work on that." One corner of his mouth lifted. "Hey, if everyone were capable of keeping their finances straight, I'd be out of a job."

Stepping closer to her, he drew her into his arms. "You make me laugh," he said softly, "and feel good in ways I've never felt before. I shouldn't have criticized your think-outside-the-box surprise at the bank. You knocked the socks off that loan officer— the same way you knocked mine off the first time we met. *And* you bake the best cookies I've ever tasted. *And* you've brought meaning and joy back into Christmas for me. *And* do you have any idea how difficult it was for me to get a Santa suit on *Christmas Eve*? It cost a freakin' fortune! *And* I had to scour every store in Lansfare to find all these white twinkle lights. *And* look at this—"

He released her and held up his hands, rotating them in front of her. "I got, like, two dozen paper cuts from wrapping all those toys I bought."

Suppressing a smile, she clasped his hands and brought them to her lips to bestow gentle kisses on his abused fingers. "It was for a good cause."

He immediately sobered. "I know. I looked at those kids and moms tonight, and I was so proud of you for giving this night to them. I realized that I don't count my blessings nearly as often as I should. And you . . . you're the greatest blessing of all."

He once again drew her into his arms, then cupped her cheek in his palm. "I enjoyed the toy store today, and I even liked wrapping the gifts, except for the whole paper cut thing. Only one thing was missing—and that was you. I missed you. All the color was gone without you. Everything felt empty and hollow. Especially me. I don't want to miss you anymore. I love you, Merrie."

Merrie tightened her hold on his shoulders and prayed her knees didn't deteriorate completely. Darn it, there was a Christmas tree and a gazillion lights in here, but where was a chair when a girl needed one? "You love me?"

"God, yes. I'm so crazy in love with you, I can barely think straight."

Okay, she *really* needed that chair. "I love you, too."

He squeezed his eyes shut for several seconds and muttered something that sounded distinctly like, "Thank God." Then he crushed her to him and kissed her in that bone-destroying way of his. When he lifted his head, she took a few seconds to catch her breath, then said, "I did a lot of thinking as well, Tom. I know I need to take a firmer grasp on my finances if I want Perfect Parties to succeed in expanding. The loan worked out this time, but next time I want to get that lower interest rate." She reached up, standing on her toes, and looped her arms more securely around his neck. "I definitely need a financial man in my life, and I think I know just the guy."

A slow smile lit his face, a beautiful smile that had her grinning in return. "Wanna know what I want for Christmas, Santa?" she asked.

"Absolutely."

"Tom Farrell."

"Well, that works out very nicely because it just so happens that Tom Farrell wants you, too."

He lowered his head, and their lips met again in a lush, deep kiss filled with passion and promise. When they finally surfaced for air, he said, "You know, you still owe me that Christmas wish you promised me."

"I didn't forget. You said you wanted me to organize my receipts."

"I do. But that's not my wish. Tell me, what are you doing every day for the rest of this year?"

She laughed. "The whole week of it that's left? Nothing special."

"And every day next year?"

Everything in her stilled—except her heart, which sped up to double time. "Some party commitments, but nothing else that's carved in stone."

"And the year after that? And the year after that?" He brushed his lips lightly over hers. "And the year after that?"

"I . . . I guess that depends on what you're doing."

He rested his forehead against hers. "Perfect answer, since my Christmas wish is that we spend those years together. I want this holiday to be the first of many, many more we spend making magical memories."

"That sounds . . . perfect. But now it's my turn. What are you doing in April? I need an Easter Bunny."

He jerked upright and stared at her. "Huh?"

"And I'm thinking you'd make a really cute— although a sort of tall—leprechaun."

She had to press her lips together to keep from bursting out laughing his at horrified expression. Just then she heard clock chimes coming from the family room.

"It's midnight," she said. "Christmas Eve is over."

"I still have a few more seconds." He framed her face in his hands. "I want you to be mine, Merrie. I want to be yours. What do you say to us making memories together for the next fifty Christmases?"

She cocked a single brow. "Only the next fifty?"

He made a great pretense of pondering the question. "I *suppose* I could be convinced to up the offer to the next sixty."

"Yeah? How?"

"Someone who wears Kiss Me 'Til I'm Riled-Up Red lipstick could probably figure it out."

"Ah. Then I'd say I'm your gal."

"Exactly what I've been trying to say. So . . . will you marry me?"

Merrie smiled into his beautiful eyes, then leaned back in the circle of his arms. When she saw his expression, she said, "Good grief, you actually look *worried*."

"I am. This proposing business is very nerve-racking. Especially when the askee hasn't answered."

"Crazy man," she said, shaking her head. "Yes!"

She strained upward, planting enthusiastic kisses all over his face.

"Right answer." He dipped his knees and swung her up into his arms. "For my next proposal, I say we head for the bedroom and start making some more Christmas wishes come true."

Merrie held onto his neck and pressed her cheek against his. "Going to be difficult, seeing as how you've already made all mine come true, but lead on. After all, an elf's gotta do what an elf's gotta do."

USA Today bestselling author Jacquie D'Alessandro grew up on Long Island, where she fell in love with romance at an early age and dreamed of being swept away by a dashing rogue riding a spirited stallion. When her hero finally showed up, he was dressed in jeans and drove a Volkswagen, but she recognized him anyway. They married after both graduated from Hofstra University and are now living their happily-ever-afters in Atlanta, Georgia, along with their very bright and active son, who is a dashing rogue in the making. Jacquie writes both contemporary and Regency–era historical romances filled with two of her favorite things—love and laughter. She loves to hear from readers and can be contacted through her Web site at www.JacquieD.com.